BREAKING MATT

REGAN URE

Cover Design: © L.J. Anderson, Mayhem Cover Creations

Formatting by Mayhem Cover Creations

ISBN: 978-1-911213-20-8

I dedicate this to my stepfather, Jeff.

Table of Contents

Chapter One

I was sitting in the college cafeteria eating a sandwich while paging through a book. I finished the book and closed it. Checking my watch, I figured I still had a few minutes before Courtney would be meeting me so we could head together to our next class. I packed my book away and discarded the rest of my lunch in the bin nearby before sitting down again. Feeling tired, I rubbed my forehead as I surveyed the cafeteria. It was after lunchtime so it was fairly empty.

There were a few tables with some students grabbing a late lunch. My eyes drifted to the lone guy sitting and leaning back, openly watching me.

When my dark-brown eyes met his striking green ones, I felt a connection cross the distance between us like a shock of electricity vibrating through the cells in my body. Despite feeling a little unsettled by the immediate reaction to the way he looked at me, I refused to look away or show how much one look from him had affected me. I met his gaze with open interest. Most guys would look away, feeling intimidated, but this stranger didn't.

Instead he held my gaze. I didn't have a preference for looks when it came to the guys I got involved with; it was more a confidence, a way about them, that attracted me rather than them having blue or green eyes, or light or dark hair. I liked my guys strong enough to handle me.

I was honest enough to admit I knew I was high maintenance. It was probably why I was drawn to guys with a strong personality, because I needed someone to stand up to me. If I could walk all over the guy I tended to get bored quickly.

My body trembled slightly as I held his gaze and his smile deepened, showing off his sexy dimples. My stomach dipped at the open appreciation in the sweep of his eyes over me. He was gorgeous, and for a moment I was momentarily stunned at the physical reaction I felt with just a look from him in my direction.

He had brown hair with streaks of blond that reached just past his ears. But his most striking features were his eyes and dimples.

"Sarah." A familiar deep, annoying voice pulled me away from the sexy stranger.

"Ryan," I greeted stiffly, turning to the person who had interrupted me, leaving only a hint of friendliness.

His brown eyes were boring in comparison to the sexy stranger who had held my attention only moments before. Ryan smiled confidently. It only increased my irritation with him. I stiffly returned it, trying not to be blunt and rude but it was hard. It wasn't wise to encourage him with falseness. I had made it clear we were over. Most guys got the message and moved on swiftly with someone else—but not him. He was holding on to the hope we would get back together, but it wasn't going to happen. No matter how many times I told him, he still had trouble understanding. It had been a month already. How much longer would it take before he realized I was never going to get involved with him again?

"I didn't see you at the party on Saturday," he said, leaning forward with both hands on the table. He was used to girls falling at his feet. I was an anomaly. We'd hooked up for a couple of weeks before he'd become too needy, which had sent me running in the opposite direction. Ever since, he had been showing up all the time, trying to get me to go out with him again.

His closeness was making me uncomfortable. Sitting down with him looming above me made me feel intimidated and I didn't like the feeling. I collected my stuff and stood, evening the playing field.

"I had plans with someone else," I told him vaguely. The truth was I had been out with Courtney, but I wanted him to believe I had been with another guy. I hoped it helped drive the point home I was no longer interested.

My mind was pulled back to the stranger I had been looking at before Ryan had interrupted.

"I miss you," Ryan said, his voice softer. I shook my head as I hitched my bag over my shoulder.

"Don't." I didn't want to cause a scene.

Usually I was pretty good at choosing guys, but I had made a mistake with Ryan. He was too sensitive to have gotten involved with me. He had developed feelings I hadn't returned and it hadn't taken me long to grow tired of his clinginess.

"Sarah...we were so good together," he argued softly, straightening up to his full height. I had to look up at him for our eyes to hold.

"I don't know how many times I need to say this," I said. "We're done. It didn't work out and you need to move on."

His jaw tightened as he silently watched me.

"I'm sorry," I said. The truth was that I wasn't, but I needed to handle him with care. I didn't want this situation blowing up in my face. This wasn't the first time I had made a mistake with choosing the wrong type of guy, one who developed emotions even though I was upfront and clear about what I wanted out of the relationship. "But don't waste your time on me. Go and find some nice girl."

He was handsome in a preppy kind of a way. He had neatly cut brown hair that emphasized his toffee-brown eyes, making him nice to look at. I knew there were few girls who wouldn't jump at the chance to be his girlfriend. That fact only irritated me more. Why was he bothering me when he had his pick of girls?

"You're special," he said. I fought the urge to roll my eyes and I had to stop myself from saying something bitchy.

I gritted my teeth briefly, trying to find the right words to deliver my next message.

"I'm sorry, Ryan. I'm not interested."

I left before he could stop me or say anything else. I walked quickly, trying to get out of the cafeteria and put space between us. For a moment I remembered the sexy guy with the striking green eyes. He was exactly what I needed. I was on the prowl for my next guy and he would do nicely. Besides, it would help ensure Ryan realized I wasn't interested in him.

I got my phone out and called Courtney.

"Where are you?" I asked, walking hurriedly to my next class with a quick look over my shoulder to make sure Ryan hadn't followed me. Thankfully there was no sign of him.

"I'm on my way," she said, sounding a little out of breath.

"I had to move," I said, pressing the phone closer to my ear as I weaved through the students toward my next class.

I had already decided to wait outside there for her.

"Why?" she asked.

"Ryan."

There was no need to elaborate.

"Ugh! It's been a month already. Surely by now he would have realized it's not going to happen."

"Apparently not," I mumbled, feeling more annoyed that I had to make a point of avoiding him.

"I think you may have to be careful with this one. He is definitely stalker material." I didn't want to hear that. It was the last thing I needed. There was a hesitant pause. "Maybe you should mention it to your parents?"

"No way!" I shook my head. "You know what my parents are like."

I had spent half an hour on the phone with my mom reassuring her everything was going well and that I did not need a bodyguard. To a normal person it would be overkill; but in my family, having a bodyguard was like owning a pet.

My mother came from a very wealthy family and it was considered a reasonable precaution to ensure our safety. It didn't help that my father worked as a district attorney. He dealt with some unsavory characters and made enemies, which only increased my mom's insistence that I needed someone to watch over me.

"What if it gets worse?" she asked.

I frowned slightly. It wasn't something I had considered. Ryan was persistent—but dangerous? No, I didn't believe it.

"He's annoying, but harmless."

"Okay, fine. Where are you headed?"

"Our next class," I said, the door already in sight as I walked closer.

"I'll be there in five." She ended the call.

Despite saying to Courtney that Ryan was harmless, I wasn't really convinced he was going to leave me alone. I needed to move on to my next guy to ensure any hope Ryan still harbored would end with the realization that I had someone new in my life.

That would work.

What is he doing here? I thought when I noticed the sexy stranger from the cafeteria in my class fifteen minutes later.

I didn't remember seeing him in this class before. Maybe he was new. I allowed myself to watch him silently while he sat a couple of rows in front of me. He wrote something down before he leaned back, keeping his focus on the lecturer.

He was just my type. Hot and confident. It was a lethal combination I had a weakness for. I didn't want a nice guy— I wanted someone who would set me alight and keep me wanting more.

I was already daydreaming about having his strong hands with long slender fingers tightening their hold on my body. My body warmed with want. A few girls gave him a brief smile or a look over their shoulder, making it clear they were interested. He smiled back.

My forehead creased when I felt a moment of jealousy. They were treading on a guy I had already marked for myself.

Courtney gently poked me in the ribs and gave me a questioning look. I smiled and looked to the sexy guy. Her eyes followed mine.

"Nice," she whispered under her breath at me. I nodded slightly in agreement.

I was already coming up with a way to approach him and what I would say. I wasn't really nervous; I was more excited. I enjoyed the chase of getting the guy I wanted.

The rest of the class dragged on, and when it finally came to an end, I felt a jolt of excitement. My eyes were fixed on my target as he put his book away and hitched his backpack over his shoulder. Broad shoulders: another thing I liked.

"Go get him," Courtney said softly from behind me as I walked up to him, not giving any of the other girls who had shown interest in him the chance to make their move.

He turned and stopped when I walked up to him.

"Hi," I said, giving him a wide smile.

"Hi." His voice was strong and calm. Everything about this guy fit in with what I was looking for.

"Are you new?" I asked as we started to walk out of the class side by side.

"Kind of," he said. "I started a month ago."

"I'm Sarah."

"Matthew Weiss." The fleeting look he gave me was enough to make my stomach dip.

There was no way I wouldn't have noticed him if he'd been in my class for the last month. But I let it go.

"You free on Friday?" I asked as I gave him a sideways look.

"Sure," he said. "What do you have in mind?"

There was a thrill of attraction as his eyes briefly met mine. Oh man, this guy was hot. I didn't want to come on too strong because some guys were intimidated by that, so I decided to make a play but keep it light.

"There's a party on campus on Friday," I said. I told him where it was going to be. He nodded.

"Are you going to be there?" he asked, coming to a stop to give me his full attention.

I faced him. "Probably." The directness of his eyes made me swallow.

He got his phone out of the back pocket of his faded jeans and looked expectantly at me. I gave him my number. His fingers brushed over the keys as he programmed my number in.

"I'll see you there," he said before he walked away, leaving me slightly surprised at his sudden departure. I watched with growing interest as he disappeared down the passageway.

Usually guys gave me their number, not the other way around. This one wasn't needy like Ryan. He was just what I wanted, and he would be enough to drive home to Ryan that I wasn't available anymore. It was a sure thing to get him to back off.

"And?" The voice of my friend brought me back from my thoughts.

"I really like him," I said.

"You and every other girl with a pulse," she remarked.

I shrugged. What I wanted I got—and I wanted Matthew. There wasn't any other option.

"I think he's interested," I said, still remembering the way he had looked at me. It was enough to make me combust on the spot.

"He took your number," she said with a one-armed shrug, like she considered it to be a good sign.

Leaving it at that, we walked out the front entrance.

"Ryan alert," Courtney whispered beside me. It only took me a few moments to find his familiar form on the pathway I usually walked to go home.

"Crap," I mumbled, looking around quickly to find another way home.

"I'll distract him," Courtney said with determination. "You can sneak around to the side."

"I'll call you later," I told her before I slinked away quickly. I wasn't in the mood for another run-in with my ex.

I caught a brief glimpse of Courtney strolling up to him confidently. She flicked her honey-blond hair effortlessly as she focused her hazel eyes on my ex. She had his full attention while I hurried around the side of the building.

By the time I got home I was more than annoyed. Ryan was backing me into a corner and I didn't like it one bit. I couldn't continue like this. Something needed to happen for him to back away.

I rubbed the back of my neck as I kicked off my shoes and sat down on the sofa. I closed my eyes for a moment as I relaxed, putting my feet up on the small coffee table.

My phone started to ring and I opened an eye to glare at my bag. It continued to ring and I got up to fish my phone out of it.

"Hi, Mom," I answered, trying to keep the irritation out of my voice. I adored my mother. She wasn't just a parent to me—she was also my best friend.

"Hi, sweetheart," she said, and the sound of her voice washed over me like a protective blanket easing all my worries.

"What's up?" I asked. We usually spoke first thing in the morning. She rarely phoned me in the afternoon.

"Nothing. Why? Can't your mom call you in the afternoon?"

There was something up. I could tell by the faintest sharpness to the tone of her voice. We shared everything. Why was she keeping something from me?

My mind ran wild with possible reasons.

"You know I love talking to you anytime," I told her cautiously. There were so many times I was grateful she was my mother. It made up for the lack of closeness I had with my father. He was the head of the family and issued orders like a drill sergeant.

My mother always explained his shortcomings on the fact he'd been raised in a family where there hadn't been a lot of affection or emotion. It wasn't something I could imagine and I felt sorry it had stunted my father emotionally.

"I just wanted to find out how your day went," she said.

She was lying—I could hear it in her voice. There was an edge of worry that most people wouldn't pick up on but I knew my mom too well to fall for it.

Was she calling to make sure I was okay? Was there a reason I wouldn't be? There was a part of me that wanted to know, but there was also the part that didn't. Ignorance was bliss.

There had been so many times there had been a threat that had never actually materialized. So many times I had been worried and scared of something that had never happened. I wasn't going to allow that to happen again.

So I let it go and didn't directly ask her what was going on. Instead, I walked around the room talking to my mom about what she'd been up to and what color she had decided to repaint the house.

I didn't tell her too much about my day other than the college work I was busy with. It was the ideal opportunity to mention Ryan, but I stopped myself. It would just stress her out more and I didn't want her to worry. Besides, I wasn't convinced he was anything other than an annoying ex-boyfriend who was struggling to get the message that I wasn't interested in him anymore. I didn't believe for one moment he would harm me.

Chapter Two

Friday Night

Ugh! I thought to myself as I ducked into a nearby room, closing the door quietly behind me. I was hiding from my ex. He was looking for me and I couldn't stand to be around him. Not for one more second. I had reached the end of my patience. If he found me now there was no telling what I would do and say to him.

Enough is enough! There would be no diplomacy or tact in what I would unleash on him. I leaned against the door as I briefly closed my eyes. This was beyond frustrating.

Even setting him up with a beautiful girl from one of my classes hadn't worked. Vicky had been interested when I had suggested Ryan. I was convinced she would be enough to capture his attention, but he hadn't even given her a second look. I crossed my arms as my feelings of frustration gave way to anger.

I didn't like that someone could impact my life the way

he was. I was used to making my own decisions and doing what I wanted when I wanted.

Taking the fact I was hiding out in a stranger's room while I could hear music playing through the house notched my anger up. I should have been downstairs with Matthew, who had been talking to another girl when Ryan had found me.

It didn't help that I was feeling out my depth with Matthew. Things hadn't gone according to plan. If I was honest, my plan had completely failed. The first day he hadn't called I reasoned he didn't want to seem too interested. By the next day I was feeling nervous. By the third I was questioning whether I had imagined his interest.

I wasn't used to waiting around for a guy. They usually fell all over me. I was attractive and was used to guys hitting on me.

I had long dark hair with dark-brown eyes framed by thick dark eyelashes that brought out my eyes. I was a younger version of my mother.

There had been a moment of realization earlier that I was in a situation I had never experienced before—and I didn't like it one bit. He had caught me off guard and I struggled with what to do next. It would have been easier to walk away and admit defeat, but I was too stubborn for that.

I kept the distance between us, refusing to look in his direction. But nothing I did seemed to follow the path that others had walked before. He was an anomaly.

The girl in me wanted me to go up to him and find out why, but the determined part refused to give in to it. It would be showing a weakness for him. I understood guys well. If I came on too strong it would send him scattering in the opposite direction.

Playing harder to get was the way to go. So for the last week I had controlled every slight look in his direction, making sure not to meet his eyes. It wasn't like I would have ignored him if he'd made the move to talk to me, but he hadn't.

When the night of the party had arrived, I had felt nervous about the night that lay ahead. Usually I was confident and sure of myself—but for once I wasn't. I only had doubts. I had no way of knowing whether my tactics had worked or if I might have pushed him in the opposite direction.

How long did I need to stay here? I checked my watch. I'd been hiding for five minutes. I paced in the small room, trying to figure out what to do about my annoying ex and the sexy stranger who didn't seem to be interested in me.

A few minutes later there was a slight knock on the door.

I froze as I stared at the door. Had he found me? If it was him, I wouldn't be responsible for my actions. I had never gotten physical before but I was very tempted to slap some sense into Ryan.

When I didn't immediately reply, there was another knock. More insistent.

Should I answer or not?

"Sarah?"

It didn't sound like Ryan. Then I realized who it was.

"Matthew?" I stood by the door with my hand reaching for the handle.

This couldn't get any worse. The guy I had been trying to attract had discovered me hiding out in one of the spare rooms upstairs.

"Are you okay?" he asked. How had he known where I was?

"Yeah." I opened the door. His eyes met mine and I felt the familiar pull of my attraction to him. I wondered if he felt the same.

"What are you doing?" he asked, searching the room

behind me.

"Hiding." I don't know why I admitted it. I knew it would only lead to more questions.

My eyes scanned the hallway to make sure there was no sign of Ryan.

"From who?" he asked, following my gaze.

"The ex."

"Was that the guy I saw you talking to earlier?"

He'd noticed? I thought he'd been too busy chatting up the girl I'd seen him with to notice. I smothered the sharp pang of jealously I felt—instead of talking to me, he'd been too interested in the bimbo who had hung on his every word.

I nodded, leaving the room and walking back to the stairs. Matthew followed beside me.

It was then it dawned on me. I stopped to face him.

"Why did you come looking for me?" I asked.

He shrugged. "The bathroom downstairs was busy so I came upstairs. I saw you duck into one of these rooms alone. I thought it was strange."

I continued to hold his gaze as I debated his answer. With a slight inclination of my head, I walked away.

"Is he harassing you?" he asked, putting a hand to my wrist to stop me at the top of the stairs. His touch sent a thrill of awareness through me. It was hard to think coherently with him so close. My pulse quickened.

It took me a few seconds to recover from the unfamiliar reaction. His eyebrows knitted together with concern.

"'Annoying me' would be a better description." It didn't seem to ease the concern on his features.

"Do you need me to have a talk with him?" he asked as his frown deepened.

"No. I can handle it." I wasn't a damsel in distress who needed a knight to swoop in to save me.

"Yeah, it looked like you were handling it well back there

hiding in the room."

I pinned him with a glare as I tugged my wrist free from his grasp.

"So I don't have it all figured out. It's not like I have experience with stalkers," I muttered, turning away from him and intent on walking away.

"Stalking sounds pretty serious."

His words stopped me. I looked back at him over my shoulder. Despite his obvious concern, all I could think about was the moment he had shown interest in a girl who hadn't been me. It had put a dent in my ego—one which hurt more than I wanted to admit.

"Why don't you go and find the girl you were chatting up earlier. I'm sure she is much more interested in your company than I am."

And with that I left him at the top of the stairs without a look back in his direction. Telling him off had been a rash thing to do but it had been hard to control my anger. I was upset. He unsettled me and I didn't like it one bit. I went to find Courtney.

"Where have you been?" she asked. "I've been looking for you for the past ten minutes."

"I was hiding," I answered, surveying the crowd for my stalker.

Ryan's actions had gone past those of a boyfriend who couldn't come to terms with the ending of our short coupling. His actions were becoming more serious, which put me in a difficult situation. I had to figure out a way to deal with him or I would have to tell my mom about it—even when I knew what that would lead to.

"Ryan?" she questioned, and I nodded.

"You're going to have to do something about it before he becomes a real problem."

She was right but I had no idea what to do.

"Here," she said, giving me a plastic cup. "You need it more than I do."

I downed the liquid, feeling it burn down my throat. My eyes watered and I handed her the empty cup as I began to splutter.

And at that moment I caught Matthew watching me across the room. No girl in sight. I averted my gaze from his, refusing to acknowledge him. He'd had his chance. I didn't pine for any guy. I had put his initial actions down to someone who was playing his own game of hard to get, but I had to admit I had probably been more interested than he had been.

"The sexy stranger is watching you like a hawk," my friend whispered under her breath.

"He had his chance." I gave my shoulder a lift and dropped it. "It's time to find someone else to help me give Ryan the message that I'm not interested."

I scanned the crowd, looking for a suitable replacement for Matthew.

"I need another drink," Courtney said before she headed in the direction of the kitchen.

I swung my hips slightly in rhythm with the music as I tried to shake off the anger I was still feeling. It was a useless emotion that wouldn't get me any closer to my goal of finding a nice guy to flirt with. And I had to find one quickly before Ryan found me.

There was a cute blond guy in the corner, but I dismissed him. I liked tall guys, and he wasn't tall enough. It wasn't just his physical attributes that failed to keep my interest. There was no connection.

My gaze slid to my next potential guy. He had dark, tousled, come-to-bed hair. His eyes caught mine and he gave me an appreciative smile. He was dressed in a pale-blue shirt and faded jeans. While he checked me out I did the same to him. The thing was, even though he was hot—there was nothing wrong with him—I just didn't want him. Despite his looks I didn't feel any attraction.

I frowned. What was wrong with me? Maybe I needed to try someone else. My next candidate I found in a group of four guys to the left. He was tall and lean but it was hard to make out his features because he had his back to me. He turned slightly and I got a closer look at his profile. Nice. But when he angled himself differently so I could see his features better, I didn't like the shape of his eyes or the fact that he had freckles.

Matthew had smooth skin and not a freckle in sight. I caught myself. Why on earth was I comparing guys to Matthew?

With him on my mind I found myself scanning the crowd, but he was nowhere in sight. No doubt he'd gone to find the blonde he'd been talking to before.

Distracted, I never spotted Ryan until it was too late and he had stepped in my line of vision. I had spent valuable time thinking of Matthew when I should have been flirting with his replacement. And now I didn't have anyone to use to get rid of Ryan.

"Sarah," he said in that seductive voice that I found irritating. He reached out to touch his hand to my arm but I swayed slightly out of his reach. I didn't want him to touch me.

"Ryan," I greeted, unable to hide my annoyance.

I tried my best to look at the crowd, which was getting a little rowdy, so I wouldn't get pulled into a conversation I didn't want to be a part of.

"Did you come alone?" he asked, sliding close beside me —too close. I pulled away slowly, trying to put some space between us.

"It doesn't matter if I have or not," I said, feeling bitchier by the minute. My patience had been pushed too far and I was done trying to be nice.

"I think what you say and what you feel are two different things," he said arrogantly. "You're too headstrong to admit you made a mistake by breaking up with me."

My mouth dropped open. I was stunned. He was so oblivious, living in his little bubble where his thoughts tied everything up neatly in a bow.

Had he never been dumped before? Was that it? Did he not know how to graciously handle a brushing off? He did remind me of the type who was so used to getting what they wanted that they struggled to process the unexpected.

"Ryan," I started, feeling my temper rise. My hands curled into fists as I tried to maintain control of my rising anger. I was over this. We were finally going to have the conversation I had been trying to avoid the past weeks. Being nice hadn't helped. It was time to be direct and to the point, and if needed, I would be mean.

"There you are!" a voice interrupted behind me as a hand touched the small of my back. The touch took me by surprise.

I didn't have time to figure out what was happening. Matthew stood beside me, leaning closer, and then he was kissing me. It turned out to be only a brief touch of his lips against mine but the effect was instant shock and it vibrated through me. He smiled as he straightened beside me, showing off his dimples before he turned his attention to Ryan.

I touched my fingers to my lips, still unsure of what had happened. I was still seconds behind as I tried to figure out why the sexy stranger had kissed me. I began to frown. Matthew's hand rested on my waist and I was about to pull him off me.

"And you are?" Matthew asked Ryan. His eyes were intense with an unspoken threat.

Ryan swallowed as he looked from Matthew to me. I

18

dropped my hand as the realization reflected in his features. Then it finally dawned on me what Matthew was doing. He was helping me make a point to Ryan.

I put my arm around Matthew's waist, making a point of leaning into him slightly as I watched Ryan take in the affectionate action.

"You and him?" he asked slowly.

"Yes." There was no hesitation. Even though I was still angry with Matthew, I went along with it. I needed this. To emphasize my words, I looked up at Matthew and at that point he looked down at me.

The way he looked at me pulled the air from my lungs. I was glad I had the support of my arm around him to keep me up. He looked like he couldn't wait to get me into the nearest room—and naked. I swallowed.

"I...didn't...realize," Ryan stuttered. Even though I didn't want to pull my attention from Matthew, I caught Ryan turning and leaving.

Thank goodness. He had finally gotten the message.

"Thanks," I muttered under my breath to Matthew as I dropped my arm from his waist.

"I think you should stay close," Matthew whispered with his eyes still fixed on the back of Ryan, who was making his way through the crowd. His hand was still on me.

"Surely that isn't necessary. It's not like he thinks we would lie about it," I argued. I didn't want to spend any more time than I had to in Matthew's company.

He let out a deep breath before he turned to face me.

"Do you really want to take the chance?" His eyes were as hard as emeralds.

The direct impact of his eyes on me made me swallow again. I hated how he affected me. I became a stuttering idiot every time he set his sexy eyes on me.

He had a point. If I ran the risk of Ryan discovering we

were a lie, then he would never take me seriously again, even if I did move on for good. I pressed my lips together, not liking that I would have to spend the rest of the night in Matthew's company.

"Fine. Just no chatting up any other girls," I said, making it clear I wouldn't be made a fool of.

His forehead creased slightly.

"I was just talking to her, nothing more." He clearly felt the need to explain.

"I don't care." I looked away, scared he would see the truth in my eyes. "I just need you for tonight. After that, you can do as you please."

He studied me for a moment with a pensive look.

"I don't want to screw every girl I talk to."

Why did he feel the need to explain that to me? Was I making something out of nothing? I shrugged my shoulders, acting like I didn't care—but the truth was, I did.

I cared way too much.

Chapter Three

"Stop looking for him," Matthew said, pulling me closer. "If you give him more attention he'll keep hounding you."

We were standing together. I resented the warmth of his hand that seeped through the thin layer of my top.

His logic made sense but I didn't want to look at him. It wasn't that he wasn't nice to look at—he was so good-looking it was hard to concentrate when he set those dark-green eyes on me. It muddled my brain and made it harder to think logically.

"Fine," I muttered, making of point of looking at him.

"That's not going to work," he said, studying me for a moment.

Then he lowered his head and kissed me before I knew what was happening. My hand went to his chest as I savored the feel of his lips moving against mine. It lasted only a few seconds before he stopped and looked back at me confidently. I struggled to remain standing, my knees unsteady.

"That's better."

"Why?" I managed to get out breathlessly.

"You need to look like you at least like me." I didn't like him. I was attracted to him but I didn't like him very much at all.

I glared at him. "Don't do that again."

Instead of looking apologetic, he smirked at me. "The next time I kiss you it will be because you ask me to."

This guy's ego was astounding.

"As if," I muttered under my breath.

His hand went to the small of my back and touched it gently.

"Is that really necessary?" I asked, looking up at him, but his gaze was fixed across the room.

"Your stalker is watching. It's time to play the part," he said, looking back down at me.

The way he looked at me made me want to pull him close and cover his lips with mine. I'd been attracted to guys before but what sizzled between us was nothing I'd ever experienced before.

"I'm not going to ask you to kiss me." I was determined to resist him, there being a stalker or not.

He pulled me closer and my hands went to his hard chest. I swallowed hard, fighting my hardest to act immune while he held me.

"That's your choice. I don't have to worry about an ex-boyfriend who won't take no for an answer."

He had me backed into a corner. If I didn't kiss him and play the part, Ryan would continue to make my life impossible. This was the only way to ensure he left me alone.

"I hate you," I whispered before I pulled him down, but he resisted. I was only a breath away from his lips. My eyes flickered to his lips before they returned to gaze up at him.

"Ask."

I wanted to tell him to go to hell. Instead I reluctantly did as he said.

"Please kiss me."

His smile widened to show off his sexy dimples before he kissed me. I swear everything around us ceased to exist. My hands crept up his body to link around his neck. I opened my mouth, needing to taste him. There was no reasoning, just instinct that led me. His tongue caressed mine. I pressed myself up against him and his arms tightened around me. His every movement was in sync with my needs.

I don't know who pulled away first, but I was left standing and trying to catch my breath. Matthew, despite his confidence, didn't look unaffected by what had just taken place.

It made me feel good that he wanted me as much as I wanted him. This wasn't one-sided.

"It didn't take you long." Courtney broke our reflective mood. "Here," she said, shoving a drink into my hand.

"Thanks." I took a big gulp to bring me back to reality.

"And you are?" Courtney eyed Matthew.

"I'm Matthew. The new boyfriend."

"That was quick," my friend said, elbowing me in the ribs. "I'm Courtney, the best friend."

"It's nice to meet you, Courtney," Matthew said, giving her a smile that seemed to make her putty in his hands.

"He's not really the boyfriend," I said. "He's just helping me get rid of Ryan."

Courtney raised her eyebrow. "Where is that idiot?"

"Around." Matthew was already scanning the party, looking for him.

The crowd beside me got a little rowdy and someone bumped me. Matthew caught me before I fell.

He moved me to the other side of him. "You okay?

"Yeah." My drink had spilled over my hand so I wiped it

on my jeans.

Matthew glared at the guy who had stumbled into me. "Watch it!"

The change was so sudden. The easygoing guy I had first met disappeared, and in his place was someone with an air of danger. It made him all the more irresistible. Girls didn't want boring good boys. No, we all wanted the ruthless bad boy who only we could tame. I shook myself mentally. I was starting to sound like a romance novel.

"Sorry...it was an accident," the guy said before he turned back to his group of friends.

Another guy joined our group. I didn't recognize him. He had darker hair than Matthew but they had the same color of green eyes. They could have passed for brothers.

"This is my friend Mark," Matthew said, introducing him to Courtney and me.

"Sarah," he said, inclining his head in my direction.

"Nice to meet you." Despite my frostiness toward Matthew, I greeted his friend with a genuine smile. It wasn't his fault his friend was an ass.

"Hi, Sarah." I studied Mark as Matthew introduced him to Courtney. There was no way to miss the interest my friend showed as she looked him up and down.

The two men were the same height and both were lean and muscular. But Mark didn't make me all warm and fuzzy inside with one look.

My mind was feeling chaotic with thoughts of what I wanted to do to him even though I was still annoyed he had been chatting up another girl. But it was more than that. This was the first guy who hadn't behaved like I expected guys to and it had taken me by surprise.

For the next half an hour, Courtney flirted shamelessly with Mark. It was hard to read whether he was interested or not. I had to admit that if I weren't pretending to be with

Matthew, I probably would have tried my luck too. But the chemistry I shared with Matthew made it impossible to replace him with someone else. It was inconvenient, to say the least.

What didn't help was the fact he seemed to know how much I was attracted to him, which made him even more annoying. He was so sure of himself.

I had just finished my fourth drink. He was helping me out but I couldn't allow myself to obediently follow along. No. I was determined to get a bit drunk and become a handful. I didn't have a great threshold for alcohol, which would help my plan along.

"I need another one," I said, handing my empty cup to Matthew. He took it from me and then studied me. I was already feeling a little wobbly.

"You sure you're up for another one?" Matthew asked with his hand on my hip. He could feel I was already a little unsteady. Could he see the glazed-over eyes that would be a sure sign I had drunk enough?

I pouted. "Please."

I gave him that girly look that was hard for guys to say no to as I leaned closer, putting both my hands up against his chest as I gazed up at him.

"I'll get the next round of drinks," Mark offered. I turned to face him and put a hand on Matthew to steady my legs.

"You're not going to put anything that you shouldn't in it?" I asked, trying to gauge if I could trust him enough.

Taking drinks from strangers was a no-no, but technically I knew Mark. He was Matthew's friend. But I had only known Matthew for a week.

"No," he said, trying to suppress a smile. I surveyed him before I looked up at Matthew, my hand clutching his shirt.

"Can I trust him?"

"Yes."

And that was all I needed. There was something about Matthew that made me trust him.

"I'll go with," Courtney added. That was even better.

"You're going to regret this in the morning," Matthew said softly beside me.

I gazed up at him. For a moment my annoyance with him was forgotten. He had the most beautiful eyes. They were hypnotic as he looked down at me. I was trying to figure out if it was the color that made them so pretty—or was it his long eyelashes that framed his eyes, bringing out their color?

"That's the fun part. At the moment I don't care." I was feeling reckless and it wasn't often I felt free to do what I liked when I wanted to.

Being brought up in a wealthy family, I had been taught to behave in a certain way. Having too much to drink would be frowned upon. In a way it was my way of rebelling against what I had been taught was acceptable and what was not.

My mom had been pretty lenient but my father was a stickler for rules. He would probably have a heart attack if he knew what I got up to. It was another reason I didn't want a bodyguard. My antics would surely be reported back to him and he would put a stop to it. Sleeping around like I did with guys would also be something that I would be lectured for. And it wasn't like I was irresponsible—I used protection and I got checked regularly to make sure I was clean.

"You have pretty eyes," I said to him. He smiled as he shook his head slightly. I reached up and touched his one dimple.

"I don't think you should drink anymore."

"Don't lecture me," I said, putting my body up against his. His smile waned and I saw the intensity of his eyes darken.

"I'm an adult and I can make my own decisions. Even if I regret them in the morning." Our eyes were locked together and for a moment it became harder to draw breath.

His lips were so close to mine. I wanted to kiss him but I hesitated. He was so unlike any other guy I had ever met and it scared me. Getting too close to this one would be dangerous.

"Do you want to kiss me?" I asked. I needed to feel like I was in control of what was happening between us.

In my mind if I at least got that confirmation, taking it further would come more naturally and I would be more sure of the end result.

There was a moment of silence.

"You know I do," he answered. His voice was hoarse as his gaze dropped to my lips.

It was the first time I had seen a vulnerability in him. He had given me exactly what I had needed. I felt like I was back in control.

"Good." I pulled away from him, taking him by surprise. I turned slightly away from him but I stayed close enough to feel him standing slightly beside me.

Mark and Courtney arrived with our drinks. Feeling happier, I took my drink and swayed to the music, content on watching everyone dance.

"I can't believe he is still hanging around," Courtney muttered from beside me.

"Who?" I asked, leaning closer to her.

"Ryan." And across the room, he was there, watching me.

"I think it's time to leave," Matthew suggested from beside me.

"But I'm having fun." My voice had come out as a slight whine.

"The fact he is still watching you means he isn't convinced that we're really together. He needs to see us leave together."

I frowned. His logic was sound. I put my glass down on a table nearby.

"I was going to get a taxi home," I said, trying to think through my alcohol-muddled mind.

"I'll take you home myself," Matthew said, his hand gripping my arm. I leaned closer and he put an arm around me. I burrowed in closer, sliding my arm around his waist. I breathed him in. He smelled so good.

"Mmm."

"Will you make sure Courtney gets home okay?" Matthew asked Mark.

"Yeah. I will."

With that, Matthew guided me through the throng of people. When we left through the front door and the fresh air hit me, I swear I felt drunker than before.

I missed a step and Matthew grasped me closer to him as he led me to his car.

"You know what?" I began to babble. "You could be a murderer."

"You think so?"

I nodded, my head feeling heavier than before.

"Yeah. Are you going to kill me?" I arched an eyebrow at him.

His chest vibrated with a low laugh. "No."

"Good."

I leaned my head against him, feeling tired.

It didn't take long before I was safely tucked in the passenger side of his car. He secured my seatbelt. The car was much nicer than what most guys drove and it still held the new smell of leather.

I watched him dreamily when he slid into the car and started it up.

"You okay?" he asked.

I nodded slowly. My body was angled toward his and my

face was resting against the seat.

"If you need to throw up, just shout," he said before he backed out and started to drive.

He was so handsome. I watched him with fascination as he drove. I took in every motion—when his eyes lifted to look at the rearview mirror, when his eyes scanned the cars around us when we stopped at a traffic light.

"You didn't have to," I said, breaking the silence.

"Do what?" he asked. His concentration was still on the road in front of us.

"Take me home."

"It's nothing."

But it wasn't. There weren't many guys who would do what he had.

He pulled up in front of my apartment block.

"How did you know where I live?" I asked, feeling confused as I shifted in the seat to look out the window.

"You told me earlier."

I didn't remember telling him, but maybe I had forgotten.

He got out as I struggled with my seatbelt, but as much as I tried I couldn't open it. A few moments later the door opened and he unbuckled my seatbelt for me. He helped me out. He closed the door before he put an arm around me and led me to my building.

"Which floor?" he asked when we got to the elevator.

"Four."

I liked the way his arm tucked me into his side. I was already deciding what to do when we got to my apartment. Despite my earlier anger at him, I was attracted to him. The attraction hummed between us with every brief touch.

Outside the door of my apartment I gave him the keys and he opened the door. I walked in and put my hand against the wall to keep myself upright as I kicked off one shoe and then the other.

Matthew closed the door. He led me to my bedroom and he surveyed it before helping me sit down.

"You going to be okay?" he asked, scanning my features. Did he think I was going to throw up?

"No," I said, shaking my head.

He bent and brought his eyes level with mine. "What do you need?"

I reached out and grabbed his shirt. "You."

I tried to pull him closer but he resisted. I frowned. Most guys would have jumped at the chance to sleep with me. Was I not attractive enough? Why did he have a way of taking my confidence away and making me feel inept?

"Don't you want me?" I asked, my voice filled with the hurt I was feeling.

"I want you," he said, holding my gaze. He reached out and caressed my cheek. "Trust me, I want you. But not like this."

"Like what?" I asked.

"I don't want you to regret it in the morning."

What guy gave up the chance at sex because he didn't want me to regret it in the morning? Was this guy for real?

"I won't. It doesn't matter if I'm drunk or sober. I want you."

Even if when I was sober I didn't want to.

He smiled at me. "I'm glad to hear that."

In the morning I would probably rue the fact I had revealed so much to him, but at that moment I didn't care.

"Will you at least kiss me again?" I asked, needing a closeness with him.

He moved closer. On his knees, he cradled my face and brought his lips to mine. I slid my hands around his neck as his mouth moved against mine.

I didn't want the kiss to end—and when he broke his

mouth from mine I felt disappointed.

"I'll call you tomorrow." Our eyes held for a few more seconds before he stood up. I lay down and he covered me with a blanket.

He left with a soft click of my bedroom door as he closed it behind him. I stared after him. I felt unsettled.

Chapter Four

My mouth was like sandpaper when I woke up. It took one eye open to survey my surroundings to confirm I was in my bed. Thank goodness. My hand went to my throbbing head.

I had drunk too much last night. When memories from the night began to flood back I covered my face with my pillow, feeling mortified. I'd practically thrown myself at Matthew and he had turned me down. My already fragile ego was even more dented now. With Matthew, I was always on the back foot, unsure of how things would unfold.

The easiest route would have been to hide out in my bed, ignoring what happened. But I couldn't allow it to eat at me. I dragged myself out of bed and to the kitchen to find some painkillers. A quick look at the clock that hung on the wall told me it was after eleven already.

I poured myself some water to drink with the tablets and gulped them down, emptying the glass of water.

My phone started to ring. I followed the sound to my bedroom and found my cell on my side table. It was a number I didn't recognize, maybe it was Matthew. Last night he had told me he would call. I ignored it, holding my phone in my hand as it continued to ring. Eventually it stopped. I wasn't ready to face him yet. I put my phone down by the sofa and went to take a shower.

Afterward I pulled on sweats and a shirt. My phone rang for a second time, but this time it was my mom.

"Hi, Mom," I said as I tucked the phone between my ear and shoulder while I rummaged through my kitchen cupboards looking for something to eat.

"Hi, baby," she said in a voice that was far too cheerful for my current state.

"Not so loud, Mom," I mumbled, trying to ease the sudden pounding in my head that had been caused by her high-pitched voice.

"Did you go out last night?" she asked, probably already knowing just from the sound of my voice that I was struggling with a hangover.

"Yeah," I breathed quietly.

I couldn't find anything to eat. My cupboards were nearly empty. I wasn't good at keeping my kitchen stocked, I was usually too busy with everything else to worry about grocery shopping. I closed the cupboard door and sighed. All I had was some cereal and coffee. A quick look in the fridge confirmed I was out of milk.

"What are you doing?" my mom asked.

"Looking for food." I waited for the lecture.

"I keep telling you to stock up when you do your grocery shopping. Then at least you don't have to grocery shop often and you'd still have food in your kitchen."

I rolled my eyes as I listened to the same lecture I'd received countless times. I knew it all by heart, but I didn't interrupt my mom. She was doing it because she loved and cared about me.

"I know, Mom," I agreed. "I'll try to do that next time."

We didn't talk for too much longer. At least by the time I said goodbye my head was feeling better. The painkillers I had taken were starting to kick in.

Tired and still feeling a little delicate I sat down on the sofa. I put my feet up on the coffee table and leaned back into the conformable sofa as I switched on the TV. Mindlessly watching the TV, I tried to decide what type of takeout I was going to order. There was no way I wanted to go out and get something.

There was a knock at the door. I got up and walked to see who it was. I wasn't expecting anyone. I racked my memory, trying to figure out if I had forgotten something.

I looked through the peephole and saw Matthew standing outside my front door. My hand went to the door handle. What was he doing here?

It took me a few moments to work through the initial embarrassment I felt from the events of the last night before I opened the door. Unlike me, he didn't look like he was struggling with the aftereffects of the night before. His eyes were clear and bright. I bet mine were still slightly red.

"What are you doing here?" I said to him as I leaned against the doorframe.

"I called earlier but you didn't answer," he said.

"Why did you call?" I crossed my arms as I waited for his answer.

"How much of last night do you remember?" he asked, studying me.

"All of it." Even if some parts were a little mortifying. I dropped my gaze momentarily.

"Can we have this conversation inside your apartment?" he asked when a nearby neighbor left their apartment, but not before giving us a look of interest.

I stepped back and allowed him inside. Once the door was closed, I followed him into my living room, and he turned to face me.

"How are you feeling?" he asked. The sound of his voice with a trace of concern made me feel warm and fuzzy inside.

"I've definitely felt better." My headache was gone but I was still dehydrated and in need of some food.

"I'm not surprised. You had quite a bit to drink last night."

"Isn't being young and irrational all part of the college experience?" I countered, not liking the lecturing tone of his voice.

"How long has Ryan been giving you trouble?" he asked, moving on to the next subject.

"I'm not sure that's any of your business." I crossed my arms as I faced him.

He ran a hand through his hair. "Don't be difficult."

"I'm not. Pretending to be my boyfriend doesn't give you the right to meddle in my affairs."

He smirked at me. "What if I don't want to pretend anymore?"

"I'm not sure I know what you're trying to say." I arched an eyebrow at him.

"We have already established we have a mutual attraction."

Despite my resistance, I couldn't stop the tinge of heat that traveled up my cheeks. There was nothing I could say that would take back what I had said last night.

"So what?" I gave him a dismissive shrug.

"I like you."

"Your actions this past week gave me a different impression," I said, finding it hard to believe. He hadn't called me the entire week. Those weren't the actions of a guy who was interested.

He sighed. "I know your type."

I frowned. I was a type?

"You like to be in control, but you like a guy you can't walk all over."

My frown deepened. Was I that easy to read?

"You were playing me?" I asked, not liking the fact the tables had been turned.

"No more than you played me."

He was right. I couldn't complain when I had done the same thing.

"So what changed suddenly?" I asked, still not trusting what he was saying.

"I don't like the fact Ryan is becoming a nuisance."

"He is annoying," I agreed. I ignored the warm feeling in my chest when I heard the protectiveness in his voice. Ryan would have pestered me more had Matthew not played the part of the new guy in my life. "But I'm sure after last night he got the message loud and clear."

"I'm not so sure of that," he admitted. "I don't think he's going to be so easily deterred."

He paused for a moment. "We can get to know each other better, and it'll keep Ryan off your back."

I considered his proposal. This was the perfect time to brush him off, to stop anything from developing between us. But I couldn't. He was an enigma I couldn't read, and even though I didn't like that I didn't know what he was going to do next, it was exciting.

For once I was willing to relinquish some control to see what happened. Besides, I remembered the kiss we had shared last night. The chemistry between us was too addictive for me to walk away.

"What do you say?" he prompted. Suddenly he was closer and it became harder to think.

My eyes flickered to his lips. I remembered our kiss and how it had lit me up. The space between us became magnetic, pulling me closer, but he didn't touch me, making it clear if this was what I wanted I would have to make the first move.

Slowly I lifted a hand and slid it behind his neck, pulling him closer. I pressed my lips to his. The moment our mouths connected I felt a thrill of excitement spread through me.

Our mouths fused as his tongue swept against mine. I locked my hands around his neck as his hands went to my hips. Our tongues danced together. With one kiss I felt swept away, unable to form a thought.

"I take that as a yes," he said when he ended the kiss, still with his hands on my hips. My skin tingled beneath his touch. It took me a few seconds to come back down to earth, and I nodded. He was irresistible.

"You hungry?" he asked.

"Yeah, I haven't eaten today."

Feeling a little embarrassed at the effect he had on me, I stepped back, needing space between us.

"Do you want to go out or would you like me to make something?" he offered.

"You cook?" I asked, and he nodded.

I didn't think I had ever dated a guy who had offered to make me a meal. They usually took me out. It made his suggestion all that more special. I didn't feel like going out but I didn't have any food. "I haven't got anything. I've been meaning to do some grocery shopping."

"I can go and get some stuff. I'll be back in about half an hour," he offered.

"Okay," I said.

He pressed a quick kiss to my mouth, taking me by surprise, before he left. I stood there feeling fazed for a while before I decided to go and put some jeans and a less comfy shirt.

For the first time I felt nervous, and a weird feeling in the pit of my stomach kept me anxious until he came back. He walked in with two full grocery bags.

"I thought you were just getting enough for lunch, not the whole week," I said, peering into the bags. There was milk and bread among other things.

"I wanted to make sure you had at least the basics." He began to unpack the bags and I leaned against the counter as he packed the stuff away.

It was like he was completely at home. I wasn't sure how I felt about that.

"What are you going to make?" I asked, allowing him to take over. It wasn't something I did often but I was tired and hungry.

"I can make steak or pasta," he said, giving me the choice.

"Pasta," I picked. Steak would be too much on my delicate stomach.

"Then pasta it is."

I sat down on the counter and watched as he got the ingredients and began to make our food.

"Where did you learn to cook?"

"At home. My mom was big on the equality thing. Whatever she taught my sisters, she taught me."

I liked his mother already. I had always wanted a sibling, despite my friends assuring me that having one was a pain in the butt and nothing to be envious of.

"How many sisters do you have?"

"Two younger ones."

So he was the older brother? Was that what had made him want to protect me from Ryan or was it just because he liked me? It was probably a bit of both. Not that it really mattered.

"Any brothers?"

"Nope."

We talked while he cooked. He was nineteen, a year older than me. He came from a traditional family, with two younger siblings and parents who had just celebrated their twenty-fifth wedding anniversary. His mother worked as a teacher and his father was a lawyer.

"So what made you decide to study business management?" I asked. He was in the same subjects as I was.

"It seemed to be the most versatile thing for me. I couldn't quite decide what I wanted to do." He mixed the sauce and pasta together. "It's done."

It smelled so good that my stomach grumbled, reminding me how hungry I was. He helped me off the counter and to my feet.

We dished up and sat down on the sofa.

"Wow, this is amazing," I said after trying the first mouthful.

He shrugged. "I like cooking. I find it relaxing."

I hated cooking. To me it was a chore I tried to avoid as much as I could. It was an added bonus, not that he needed it. He was good looking, nice and easy to talk to. And he could cook.

So what was wrong with him? No guy was this perfect. The only avenue we had yet to test was the bedroom. Would all of this lead to disappointment in the sack? He was an amazing kisser but it didn't necessarily mean it would equate to him being a good lover.

Those thoughts plagued my mind while we ate. I put my plate on the table when I was done. Matthew finished not long after me.

"Thank you," I said. "That was great."

"You're welcome."

"So I've told you about me. Do you have any siblings?" he asked.

I didn't like to reveal too much too soon. I didn't know him well enough to reveal the workings of my complicated family.

"I don't really like to talk about my family. I have a mom and dad. No siblings." I shrugged. He didn't really need to know more.

"Tell me something about yourself then?" he suggested, trying another avenue of conversation.

Usually when I dated a guy we were too busy making out and stuff like that to do too much talking; I liked it that way. And the only way to shut him up would be to put his mouth to better use.

I smiled to myself, knowing exactly what I needed to do as I shifted closer to him. Like before, the closeness pulled us together like a magnet. It was impossible to fight.

I leaned over to him and his hand cupped my neck, guiding me closer to him. His kissed me, shutting out the outside world. I needed more. I touched my tongue against his and he caressed mine with his.

Something ignited inside me and it burned for him. A need I had never experienced before took hold of me, making me grip his shirt to pull him closer. His free hand slipped under my shirt and his thumb caressed my side while he deepened the kiss. The slight touch of his hand against my skin was like an electrical shock going through me.

I groaned as I allowed the want of him to sweep over me like a tidal wave I had no power to withstand. I was usually the aggressor, but Matthew took control and I found myself on my back with him above me. But now it didn't matter. All that did was finishing what I had started.

I wanted him.

"Bedroom," I mumbled against his mouth and I felt the momentary coolness when he moved off me but moments later he picked me up.

I wrapped my legs around him while tightening my arms around his neck, covering his mouth with mine. I grinned against him as he carried me into my bedroom. It was only when he slid me down to my feet that he hesitated. "Are you sure—"

I pulled him down to kiss me. This was what I wanted.

After a flurry of activity of shirts being pulled off and jeans being unbuttoned, we found ourselves on my bed. He undid my bra and I let it fall free. His hand reached out and cupped one of my breasts, brushing his thumb over the nipple. Hot need pooled between my thighs. I pushed him down and straddled him, wanting to take control and ease the ache he had created. He had a hard, defined six-pack. I ran my hands over it lightly. He closed his eyes briefly, savoring the touch.

"I want you now," I said, making sure he had explicit confirmation I wanted this to happen. There was no indecision from me.

"Condom," he murmured before I kissed him briefly.

I reached out a hand and fished a foil packet from my bedside table. Next I was flat on my back and he was sliding my underwear down my legs. He discarded his boxers.

He took the foil packet and opened it, sliding the protection on.

I lay back, allowing him to part my legs with his knee. I reached for him as he lay over me. My legs held his hips securely as he lined himself up with me.

"Are you sure?" he asked. It was my last out but I had no need for it.

In response I pushed up and felt him enter me. With that he lost control and joined us together in one swift motion.

I gasped at the fullness and began to pant as our bodies moved together toward the release we both needed. His mouth was hot against my skin as his powerful body rocked into mine. I wrapped my arms around him, needing him as close as we could be.

His pace quickened and I could feel the buildup. I was hanging on by a thread, my hands gripping his shoulders when he pushed into me. I felt myself shatter. The climax throbbed through me and I closed my eyes as I rode the release.

Matthew followed soon after as he tensed above me before he slumped over me. I wrapped my arms around him.

Chapter Five

One month later

I gazed at his sleeping form beside me. Watching his chest rise and fall with each breath was hypnotic and comforting.

The last four weeks had been a whirlwind. When I thought back to our first night together, I smiled. It had been amazing. And the sex had only gotten better.

I lay on my side with my head propped up by my hand as I reached out and trailed my fingers down the side of his face. He smiled in his sleep, which gave me a warm feeling that started in my chest and spread outward. I retracted my hand from Matthew slowly so I wouldn't wake him.

He had fit into my life like the missing piece of a puzzle. I was in unchartered territory with him. It had started off with an attraction that was stronger than anything I had ever experienced, but now I had to admit whatever we had going on between us had become more than just a physical thing.

There was a moment of unsettled nervousness in my stomach at that thought. I didn't like feeling vulnerable to someone else. Logic and reasoning dictated I walk away. It was too late to escape unscathed, but it would hurt a lot more if I stayed.

Matthew had made his presence in my life known to Ryan, who after a week had stopped trying to talk to me altogether. I was relieved he had finally moved on and started dating a girl named Summer.

Matthew also knew exactly what to do to set me alight with one kiss. In the bedroom we were so good together—none of my previous lovers compared. He was perfect. I knew it wasn't possible. There had to be something wrong with him and I kept waiting to discover what it was.

I had been with enough guys to know it was only a matter of time before you discovered something wrong with them. There was that part of me waiting for Matthew to fuck it up. It was a pessimistic approach, but I couldn't help it. I wanted to enjoy all the time I had with him before it came to an end, which was inevitable.

Feeling restless because of my thoughts, I slipped from the bed, reaching for Matthew's shirt and pulling it on. I gave Matthew, who was sleeping on his stomach with the sheets covering him up to his waist, one last glance. Just the sight of him was enough to make me want him again. He was like a drug—I couldn't get enough of him. I pushed myself to leave before I got back in bed and woke him up with the softness of my mouth trailing against his body. I couldn't solve everything with this physical closeness. It made it impossible to form a rational thought.

In the kitchen I made some coffee. While I drank it I looked out the window, trying to make sense of how I felt about Matthew. It had only been a month but it had felt so much longer. I sipped my drink.

I heard soft footsteps. Warm hands settled on my

shoulders and he pressed a kiss to the side of my cheek. My chest felt like it had been shaken about when he slid his hands down my arms and enfolded me in a soft embrace. He had that way of tilting my world with just his presence.

"Why didn't you wake me?" he said softly. I leaned back into him, savoring him and how he made me feel.

"You were sleeping so peacefully." I didn't reveal I'd been watching like some besotted teenage girl. It was bad enough I was wrestling with the fact I cared more about him than I ever had for any other guy. There was no way I was going to reveal to him how I felt. I didn't like the fact that he held so much power over me.

Admitting my feelings would be giving him insight to the vulnerability he held in his hands. Somehow, without my even being aware of it, the power in the relationship had shifted to him.

He gave me one more peck on the cheek before he walked over to the kettle and switched it on. He was bare-chested and wearing only jeans. The sight of his cut six-pack was enough for me to feel heat in my veins. I watched him lean against the counter with his eyes fixed on me.

"You okay?" he asked, obviously picking up something in my gaze.

I made myself smile. "Yeah, of course I am."

He didn't seem to be convinced because he continued to silently study me.

The start of a phone ringing pulled his attention away from me.

"I've got to get that." He disappeared out of the kitchen.

I slid off the chair and followed quietly behind him. At the door I stopped, listening as he answered the call.

"Yeah," I heard him say.

He was always so secretive when he was on his phone. It made me uncomfortable; it was like he was hiding something from me. Was he cheating on me with someone else? It had crossed my mind more times than I liked to admit. I hadn't confronted him about it. I didn't want to come across as some insecure girl. Besides, I had no proof.

Despite my attempt to eavesdrop further, I couldn't make out the rest of the conversation. Feeling frustrated, I went to finish my coffee. He returned a few minutes later.

"Who was that?" I asked conversationally as he made his coffee.

"My mom," he said without hesitation. "She wanted to check up on me."

I bit my lip as I considered his answer. Had it just been an innocent phone call from his mother like he said? Was it my fear of my own feelings that was making me blow all this out of proportion? But my gut instinct disagreed. He always went into another room to talk on the phone. People who had nothing to hide didn't do that.

He sat down across from me before he reached out and took my hand into his. My skin tingled as the warmth of his hand enclosed mine. Just with a touch I felt the flutter of excitement despite my suspicions. It was as if the way I felt superseded any thoughts of betrayal.

He lifted my hand to press a kiss to it. My heart did a weird jump in my chest and it took every ounce of control I had not to reveal how he was affecting me.

"So what are you doing today?" he asked.

I shrugged. "Not much. Courtney needs to get some new clothes so I thought I would tag along." I swallowed. "What are you going to do?"

I watched him closely to try to see if I could tell if he was lying.

"I've got some assignments to do and I'll probably go to the gym. Nothing exciting."

There was no doubt he worked out. Just this morning I

had trailed my hands over those hard, defined muscles, loving the feel of them. I felt myself swoon at the memory.

While we finished our coffee I tried to evaluate every look and every word he spoke. I was driving myself crazy, wrestling with the feeling he wasn't being honest but having no way of knowing what he was hiding.

"I'm going to take a shower," he said, getting up. "You want to join me?"

Smiling, I shook my head. "Next time."

The thoughts of betrayal were enough to dampen the thought of having unbelievable sex with him in the shower. He left and I finished my coffee.

When I entered my room I saw his phone on the side table. I hesitated as I wrestled with my need to know if he was being deceptive. The sound of a message on his phone was enough to tip my decision and I walked over to it and picked it up.

I miss you. When are you going to come and visit again? Taylor.

Anger and shock vibrated through me as I clutched his phone in my hand. Although I had been suspicious, being faced with the confirmation he had been cheating on me was enough for me to see red.

"What are you doing?" a voice behind me asked.

I turned to face Matthew. He stood with a towel wrapped around his waist. His hair was wet and water droplets were sliding down his chest. His eyes appeared guarded as they took in his phone, still in my hand.

"How could you?" I asked, feeling the hurt spread through me, making it impossible not to taint every memory I had of us together—our first night together up to this moment of betrayal.

"What are you talking about?" he said angrily as he stepped forward and yanked his phone from my grasp.

47

I watched while he read the message before he shook his head at me. His action made me angrier than before.

"Is that her name? Taylor?" I said, fighting to save some dignity.

"Who do you think Taylor is?" he asked, his voice calm, which only intensified my growing despair.

"Don't treat me like I'm stupid!" I yelled, tightening my fists.

My chest hurt and I could feel the sting of tears, but I held them off.

"Sarah," he said in that soothing voice he used to deal with me when I was feeling emotional.

I glared at him. "Don't you dare 'Sarah' me."

"This isn't what you think it is," he started, but it did nothing to ease the ache in my chest. "You think I'm cheating on you?"

I pressed my lips together as I continued to glare at him.

"Why?" he asked, stepping closer. He scanned my features as if he was trying to decipher something. "Have I given you any reason to believe I would?"

"You always take phone calls in another room," I stated, feeling the need to bring it out in the open. I didn't for one second believe I was some needy girl who was making a mountain out of nothing. "It feels like you're keeping something from me."

"So you assumed it was because I was calling another girl?"

I nodded.

"Why didn't you just ask?" His eyes held mine.

"I was scared of the answer," I got out.

He looked down at his phone and tapped the screen a few times. What was he doing?

"Here is Taylor," he said, giving me the phone.

I took it from him and looked down at the picture. The

girl was beautiful, with shoulder-length platinum hair. She had striking blue eyes. She stood beside a guy with a tattoo sleeve who had one arm around her. He had midnight-black hair, and his blue eyes were looking at the girl in the photo with adoration.

"The guy with her is her boyfriend, Sin Carter."

I had jumped to conclusions and now I felt like an idiot. I handed the phone back.

"Taylor is my friend."

There was nothing I could say that would take back the accusation, but I mumbled, "I'm sorry."

He approached me and I dropped my eyes to the floor. He lifted my chin with a finger.

"She's been dying to meet you," he said.

"Really?" I looked at him with surprise. "You've told her about me?"

He nodded. He took my hand into his and pulled me closer.

"Would you like to meet her?"

I nodded. "Yes, I'd like that."

He hugged me and pressed a kiss to my forehead. His lips lingered like he didn't want to let go of me, and I wrapped my arms around him.

"We can go through to visit them next weekend."

The only friend of his that I had met was Mark and I was excited to meet his other friends. But still, none of this had explained away his need for privacy with phone calls. I ignored the thought.

A week later we were on our way to meet his friends and I was happy but I couldn't stop the feeling of nervousness at the thought his friends might not like me.

"Do you think they'll like me?" I asked, feeling apprehensive about the meeting. Matthew meant a lot to me.

"Don't worry, they'll love you," he assured me. He took my hand in his and gave it a reassuring squeeze.

Despite his words I was still feeling nervous as I stood outside the door, waiting as Matthew knocked. He hadn't told me a lot about them but I was so excited to meet his friends that I hadn't cared. The door opened and a beautiful angelic-looking girl greeted me with the biggest smile. Her long platinum hair framed her small face and her bright blue eyes sparkled as she continued to smile with excitement. I remembered her from the photo. Taylor was even more beautiful in person.

"Hi," I greeted her. Matthew was standing just behind me.

"Come in," she gushed, giving me an unexpected hug. Even though the hug had taken me by surprise, I hugged her back.

My eyes took in the guy who was standing behind her. He was the total opposite to Taylor. He had a tattoo sleeve on one arm and a lip piercing. I wasn't one for tattoos, but they were beautiful. He was the boyfriend I recognized from the photo.

"Hi," he greeted me as I stepped into the apartment. They looked like complete opposites. Taylor looked like an angel. Sin Carter, with his black hair, piercings and tattoos, looked like a rebel who lived his life the way he wanted to whether it was against the rules or not.

As I greeted him it was hard to believe that people who were so different in appearance could look so happy together —and there was no doubt by the way that Sin looked at her that he was head over heels for her.

I didn't believe in love but it was hard to dispute when I took in the couple in front of me. The way they looked at each other, it was like no one else existed.

Taylor hugged Matthew.

"It's so good to see you," she said. "I liked it better when I saw you nearly every day."

Taylor and Sin were in college. Apparently that was how they met. Matthew had told me they had met in college and had become fast friends.

Matthew and Sin shook hands before we were ushered inside.

All had been going well and despite only meeting Taylor for the first time, I kept having the feeling that I knew her from somewhere. For most of the lunch I was trying to figure out why her name sounded so familiar. It was only later when we were finished eating when I had finally placed where I knew her from.

"Weren't you the girl who was kidnapped?" I blurted out. Matthew straightened up beside me and touched my hand with his. Taylor looked at me, a little shocked by my sudden question. Sin wrapped a protective arm around her.

They all looked at one another for a moment. The look on her face confirmed I was right.

"I thought I recognized you from somewhere," I added. It had been all over the news and at the time it had made my father even more nervous about my safety. I don't know if he had been scared more by the fact that we were the same age or by the fact that it had been local.

"My father is the district attorney and he'd been looking at the case before the guy had confessed," I explained further. He'd just gotten promoted when it had happened. My father wasn't allowed to discuss ongoing cases with me, but after the guy had confessed, he had told me about it.

There was an awkward silence.

"I'm sorry. I didn't mean to upset you," I said apologetically. I tended to say things without thinking.

"It's okay," she said, trying to give me a warm smile. This time it never reached her eyes.

Sin and Matthew shared a look and I had a feeling something more was going on that I didn't know about as I looked around the table.

"It must have been awful," I said, trying to remember all the details of it. I'd read she'd been taken from the scene of an accident.

"It was," she said softly. "But all that matters is that he's locked up."

"I don't think this is something Taylor wants to talk about," Matthew said, making me feel bad I'd brought it up.

So I let it go and Matthew steered the conversation to safer subjects.

Later, when we got back to my place, my inability to remember all the details of what had happened to Taylor had left me curious. I checked the story out on my laptop after Matthew had left. I googled her name and I found the article I was looking for. I read it and the missing parts began to fall into place.

There had been someone in the car with her at the time of the accident. Her bodyguard had been knocked unconscious when she'd been taken. The moment my eyes read over the name of person, it felt like I couldn't breathe. It felt like my heart had splattered onto the floor.

Matthew Weiss. He was a bodyguard.

Chapter Six

Later that day

"Is it true?" I asked, pinning him with a glare. I crossed my arms as I waited for his answer.

His eyes held mine. I saw the truth in his eyes; I didn't need words to confirm it.

"Yes."

Shocked and hurt, I spun around, unable to look at him while I dealt with the betrayal.

I could feel his eyes on me as I stood with my back to him. The feelings I'd had for him had been ripped from my chest, and now all that was left was the hollow pain. Most girls would cry and mope around eating junk food while trying to mend their broken hearts. I wasn't like that—none of that was going to ease the hurt I was experiencing. The only thing that was going to make me feel better was to make him experience the same pain. Glancing over my shoulder, I saw his eyes fixed on me.

Revenge was the only way. I needed payback.

"Sarah."

His voice reached inside me somewhere I kept my hurt, and the pain intensified. I turned and looked back to face the scenery outside of my window, and then closed my eyes for a moment as I tried to keep the pain from bubbling over to the outside for him to see. It took me a few moments to push it down again. No words were going to heal the crack in my heart. It was like trying to close up a wound down to the bone with a Band-Aid. It wouldn't heal. It would fester.

The only way to heal the wound was to keep it fully protected from being injured again. Building a wall around my broken heart was the only way to protect it from further damage.

I had to hold on to the anger that flared up inside of me at the thought of his betrayal. Anger simmered below the surface, and I hid my broken heart as I turned to face him. I surveyed him, trying to pretend my damaged heart didn't race at the sight of him or experience that weird feeling inside my stomach that felt like a flutter.

Our eyes met and I felt my heart break a little more. Before, the sight of him would have lifted me to the clouds where I'd float around, intoxicated with him, but now the sight of him turned my stomach and I felt physically ill. His deep green eyes pierced mine and I was reminded of his lies. I lifted my chin in determination as I walked to him.

"I can explain," he argued. His eyes pleaded with me but I kept the wall around my heart up to keep him from getting to the most vulnerable part of me. He'd lied to me. It didn't matter why. The pain wouldn't allow me to listen to any explanation he had.

I remained silent until I was so close I had to look up at him. His eyes darkened as his eyes dropped to my lips. It was a visible confirmation of the effect I had on him. The chemistry between us had been explosive. I leaned closer and he swallowed hard. My lips were so close to his as I raised myself up on my tiptoes so our eyes were level. It would have been so easy to ignore the pain and press my lips to his. I wanted to glide my hands through his silky light brown hair.

He would put his arms around me and pull me close. I'd be able to lean into him and breathe him in. Before the lies it would have felt like heaven, but now I felt like I was burning in hell. The agony of my feelings were suffocating me from inside. Every time I saw him I was reminded of his deception.

"You really think there is an excuse for the way you lied to me?" I asked calmly. I had to show him I was indifferent to him and everything we'd shared meant nothing now.

He reached out a hand to pull me closer but I stepped back, putting myself out of reach. If he touched me there was a chance I would falter, and I had to be strong.

"No, Matthew," I said in a steady voice as I shook my head. I looked at him without any visible emotion. Keeping a handle on the emotions inside of me was hard but somehow I managed to keep him from seeing them.

"I'm sorry," he said, dropping his hands to his sides. His eyes still held mine.

"That's it? You expect to say sorry and everything will be forgiven?" I said, struggling to contain my anger. I was hurt and he thought two simple words were good enough to erase all the lies? Every kiss, every touch between us, had been marred by his deceit.

"I never meant to hurt you," he said softly. Did it make it better to deal with? Did it soften the impact of the lie? It didn't.

"But you did," I said, crossing my arms.

I wanted to kick myself for admitting it. I wasn't supposed to show how upset I really was.

"When I took this job, I knew there would be some

deceit. Your father explained your reluctance to have a bodyguard and I was told to watch over you from a distance," he said softly. "It was only when Ryan started to become an issue that things changed."

"Why would my father use you when you failed to protect Taylor?" I asked, feeling a little satisfied I could remind of him of his failure.

"I came highly recommended from one of his friends." He pressed his lips together.

"So was taking me to bed part of your job description?" I asked, feeling my hurt rise up. I bit my lip as I waited for his answer.

"I was told to do whatever it took to protect you. I wasn't completely comfortable with it."

"Then why did you do it?"

Our eyes met.

"It was too late for me to walk away. I cared already. I told myself I could keep things from getting out of hand but clearly I was wrong."

So he hadn't just been playing hard to get in the beginning. He'd been trying to keep his distance. It wasn't enough to ease the grip on my chest that physically hurt.

"I'm so glad to hear that," I said sarcastically.

I had gone after him, not the other way around, but I ignored that fact. Betrayal blinded any logical thinking. I didn't believe him. Everyone had a choice and he'd made the wrong one.

To a normal person my father's actions would be madness but my father wasn't normal. His lack of emotion and practical thinking would allow him to tolerate the deceit as long as the end result was my safety.

"It doesn't matter, really," I said, feeling the coldness seep into me as I closed off my hurt. His eyes narrowed at my sudden change.

"It wasn't like things were serious between us," I added, belittling what we'd had. "I suppose it was fun while it lasted, but it's time to move on."

He looked at me with a guarded look.

"Move on?" he questioned. I raised an eyebrow. Did he honestly think we could have continued on after I discovered the truth?

"I don't want things to be awkward. This isn't your typical break-up, now is it?" I asked. "I could ask my father to replace you."

Then I wouldn't have to face him and be reminded of his deceit.

"I'm the best at what I do. You won't find anyone better." He crossed his arms.

"How old are you?" I asked. There was no way he was nineteen like he had told me.

"I'm twenty-three." And there it was, more betrayal.

"Was anything you told me true?" I asked, feeling raw inside.

"Yes."

I frowned, knowing my father wouldn't allow me to replace Matthew if it would mean someone else less capable. My father would not budge when it came to my safety.

"Well then we'll have to make do with the situation." I dropped my arms to my sides, pretending I was in complete control of the situation.

He gave me a contemplative look. I hadn't behaved the way he'd expected and he wasn't sure how to handle me. He was good at reading people.

"You will continue to protect me, so we need to make sure we keep things uncomplicated," I said to him in a light tone, and I got my first glimpse of a moment's hurt in his eyes before he masked it over. His eyes hardened.

I felt a rush at the fact I'd been able to inflict some pain his way—but he would need to experience a lot more before I called it even.

"I expect you to be professional," I added, and his jaw tightened.

He studied me for a moment before he gave me a brief nod.

"Your father has insisted I move into the apartment to be in a better position to keep you safe," he informed me in a businesslike voice. It was like he was talking to a stranger. His coldness had taken me by surprise. I was taken aback for a moment before I recovered.

"Whatever," I said with a shrug.

I hadn't expected to be forced into such a confined space with him, but with a bit of planning I could use it to my advantage. I was already formulating a plan.

"I'm not the only one," he revealed. *Just when I didn't think there was more*, I thought with disgust.

I frowned as my eyes shot to his. There was only one person who came to mind. "Mark?"

"Yes." It felt like another betrayal.

The idea of bodyguards wasn't appealing, but even I had to admit that if my parents had gone to these lengths to protect me, the threat had to be real.

"Fine," I agreed. It wasn't possible for him to watch me all the time.

"I will work out all the details," he assured me.

I could feel my strength start to slip and I wanted to be alone to lick my wounds. I'd never had to deal with heartbreak before, so this was all new to me.

"I'm tired," I told him. "I'm going to lie down."

"Do you need me to get you anything?" he asked, still with that tone that made me want to slap him. But how could I feel angry? He was giving me what I wanted. He was being professional so that things didn't become awkward.

"No thanks," I said as I walked into my room and closed the door behind me. I let out a sigh as I leaned against the door.

I was going to make it complicated. I was going to make sure I made his life miserable. I was going to make sure he felt the same hurt I was experiencing, and only then would I be able to move on. Letting out a deep breath did nothing to diminish the ache in my chest. I hated feeling so vulnerable—and it was all his fault.

I'd never cared for a guy the way I'd cared for Matthew, so even I knew getting over him wasn't going to be easy, but I was very determined.

Closing my eyes, I couldn't stop the memory of the first time I had met him replaying in my mind—when I had spotted him across the cafeteria. Every moment I replayed I had to relive knowing the truth. Shoving the memory away, I let out a sigh. Knowing he'd deceived me marred every memory of him. Nothing would ever be the same again and I mourned the loss of what we'd had.

I felt like a fool and it wasn't a feeling I liked at all. I closed my eyes and tried to suppress any more memories of him. It hurt too much to relive those moments knowing about his lies. If I went through my memories I would scrutinize every word and action of his to see if I should have realized the truth sooner.

That's when it dawned on me. The reason he was so secretive about his phone calls, taking them only when he was in another room so I couldn't hear what was being said. I'd been played for a fool, and that only made me angrier. It was too much to think about.

I pushed off my bedroom door. Looking around my room there were so many things that reminded me of him. The truth was I'd never felt this gut-wrenching pain before and I had no idea how to cope with it. I'd seen my friends experience heartbreak over and over again and up until this point I hadn't been able to understand it. I'd thought they were being overdramatic when they had wanted to curl up and cry. I now understood the debilitating pain.

While my friends had been falling in love and dating, I'd gone from one guy to another, seeking physical satisfaction and nothing more. I'd never formed an attachment to the guys I'd been with and I had liked it that way. It still blew my mind that when girls enjoyed sex like guys did we were given mean names, but guys weren't. I liked sex but for whatever reason any guy I'd been with hadn't stirred anything more.

I was so bad Courtney had nicknamed me "playgirl," her female version of a playboy. I would just shrug my shoulders. I lived my life the way I wanted to without any apologies to anyone. What other people thought didn't matter to me. It didn't matter that girls who were jealous of me called me a slut.

I was so mad at myself. How could I have let him in? But it wasn't like there had been a choice. Caring for someone wasn't a decision you made, it was something that just happened—and by the time I'd realized what was happening it had been too late.

I felt so strongly for him, but I refused to label the feeling. Now I had no idea how to stop the pain and carry on without him. I needed to concentrate on his betrayal every time I felt the hurt—it would be enough to stir up my anger to mask the pain.

It wasn't going to be easy to be around him, but I was convinced it would help me get over him. I was too stubborn to show he'd hurt me, so being around him would make me cover it up with my usual confidence and indifference. If I hid it enough it would eventually disappear and I'd be over him.

That was part of the plan. The other part was ensuring he felt the pain he'd inflicted on me. I wanted him to look at me with longing and remember that his betrayal had cost him *me*. He would eventually walk away. I knew it—and when he did I would make sure I was the one who was okay and he was the one suffering.

Feeling better now that I'd started to formulate my revenge, I went and had a shower. Once I got changed I was going to leave my room, but then the hurt I'd managed to suppress built up, needing release. I looked to my bed. Feeling tired, I promised myself I would give myself the rest of the day to wallow in self-pity. Tomorrow I would only concentrate on making Matthew's life miserable.

I lay down on my bed and hugged a pillow as I allowed myself to think about him and what we'd shared. It was impossible to remember without tears, and I sniffled silently, not wanting him to hear. He couldn't know I was hurting; he needed to think I was indifferent to him. It was all part of the plan and I had no intention of failing.

Later that evening he knocked on my door.

"Are you hungry?" he asked. I glared at the door as I sat up.

"No," I told him.

I couldn't even think of food while I felt like this. The part of me that didn't want him to know I was upset wanted me to pull myself together and leave my room to show him I was "fine," but I didn't care what he thought at the moment.

Tomorrow I would do it. I would get up and get dressed, looking as good and confident as I usually did. I would look at him with indifference and carry on as if anything we'd shared was forgotten, like it had meant nothing to me.

"Are you sure?" he asked and I heard the concern in his voice. It made my stomach tighten and I had to allow my anger to seep through the heartbreak that wanted to hold on to the sound of his voice like a lifeline.

"Yes, Matthew. I'm sure," I told him in a stiff businesslike tone.

Caring made a person weak—and that was how I felt. Weak.

He left me alone for the rest of the night. I assumed he was moving his stuff into the spare room, because I could hear movement around the apartment.

I knew he had two sisters from what he'd told me. But then again I had no idea if even that was true or not. He'd lied, so I had no idea how much he'd actually lied about. It only intensified the depth of his betrayal.

My phone began to ring. It was my mother. I didn't answer like I usually would have. Instead I watched as it continued to ring. I had no idea if my mother had known about Matthew, but I was too raw to deal with it at the moment.

I would deal with my parents tomorrow.

Chapter Seven

That night I didn't sleep well, but I promised myself it would be the last time I lost sleep over Matthew. The next morning, still feeling tired, I pushed myself out of my bed. Emotions were pushed away as I got ready for class. I put some makeup on to hide the noticeable indications that I hadn't slept well. I didn't want Matthew to know that I had been awake for most of the night. He had to believe I was fine, going on like he had never happened to me. I pulled my dark brown hair into a loose ponytail.

I took a deep breath as I stepped out of my room. Feeling confident, I walked into the kitchen to get a cup of coffee.

Matthew was leaning against the counter with a cup of coffee in his hand as I walked into the kitchen. The sight of him made my confidence wobble and the moment his eyes met mine I felt the pain I'd been suppressing seep back to the surface like lava burning a path through me. It was going to be so much harder than I'd thought.

"Do you want coffee?" he offered, and I nodded my head, not wanting to speak. He would hear the hesitation in my voice that would reveal how unsteady I was on the inside.

I needed to be stronger than this. I wasn't weak.

He got a cup out of the cupboard and made me coffee. He knew exactly how I took it, just like I knew how he liked his. Such small things that showed we knew each other better than the business arrangement we'd put into place going forward.

He stirred cream and sugar into my coffee and handed my cup to me. I felt a shiver at the slight touch of his fingers against mine as I took it from him. He watched me as I took a tentative sip. I was trying my best to ignore the pull of him, to remind myself why I was so angry with him. Betrayal.

At the sight of him, I remembered he'd been doing a job while we'd been together, and each time it broke my heart a little more. What made it worse was the fact I'd discovered the lie. I couldn't help thinking it would have been easier to forgive him if he'd come clean, but he hadn't. If there hadn't been a slip-up, how long would he have continued to keep the truth from me? My heart hardened at the thought I'd been played so easily.

Remembering back to the moment that had torn my world apart was hard. Seeing his name in the article, realizing who he was and why he was in my life. It had been like the stable ground beneath my feet had been broken apart with the force of an earthquake, leaving me unsteady.

His betrayal had hit me hard. His secretive phone calls. From the start he'd fooled me completely and I felt like a gullible idiot.

But now that I thought about it there were moments throughout the last month when I'd seen him pull back a few times. Had it been his guilty conscience eating away at him?

But no matter how much I wanted to have seen this coming there had been no way for me to know.

Even as my eyes ran over him now, I never would have guessed he was a bodyguard. Any of the bodyguards I'd ever met had looked like one. Normally they wore dark suits and were more heavily built than Matthew. He was always dressed so casually in jeans and a shirt—but then I supposed it was better to blend in. He was lean and he just didn't give off that type of vibe. He was easygoing and relaxed: the total opposite of the bodyguards I'd encountered before, who were always serious and on the lookout for a threat.

I never imagined when I'd told my father I didn't want protection he'd go behind my back. But he had. I was still so angry with him. He hadn't tried to call me. In his mind he had already reasoned it out. He wouldn't be feeling guilty.

"So how is this going to work?" I asked, setting my half-empty cup down on the kitchen counter as I crossed my arms.

I liked to be in control, so I wanted to know how he planned on protecting me. I didn't want any surprises. So far I'd had enough surprises from this sinfully gorgeous man standing in front of me. Despite my anger and hurt, I still felt the flutter of awareness when his eyes met mine. I hated that he still affected me, but I couldn't seem to control it. Apparently it didn't matter that he'd lied and betrayed me.

"Your father wants me to continue to attend all your classes," he informed me in a cool tone.

It was disconcerting hearing him talk to me without the warmth I was used to. I wondered it if hurt him when I treated him the same way.

"For your own security it would be best not to reveal to anyone who I really am," he added, and I arched an eyebrow at him.

"Why?" I asked, feeling my entire body tense as I waited

for his answer.

"I need to keep a low profile. If they know I'm your bodyguard it could complicate things," he revealed in a serious tone. His words brought back the reality of my situation.

"So if you're not my bodyguard, who exactly are you going to be?" I asked, even though I had a pretty good feeling of where this conversation was headed and I didn't like it one bit.

"Look, I know you're upset with me and you have every right to feel the way you do. I need you to know I didn't mean to hurt you when I didn't tell you who I really am," he began, and I put a hand up to stop him from continuing, not sure if I could stomach another word.

"No amount of apologizing or explaining is going to justify what you did," I said to him tightly as my temper began to rise. I was still too hurt to look at anything logically or even be open to any explanation he could give. "You lied to me. I thought you were someone I could care about."

I stopped when I felt the lump in my throat. There was no way I was going to cry in front of him. He held my eyes, giving nothing away. A heavy silence settled between us. There was a part of me that wanted him to justify it, but the other part of me knew there was nothing he could say that would make his actions acceptable.

"Keeping you alive is all that counts," he said fiercely, which took me by surprise. "I'll do whatever it takes."

"My father must be paying you well." It didn't make me feel any better and my confidence took another hit.

He didn't confirm my assumption. Instead he pressed his lips together tightly as if he were trying to keep control of his temper.

"Your father wants you to call him," he told me. I shook my head, not even contemplating his request.

I expected him to press the issue, but he let it go. Maybe he saw a glimpse of the stubborn glint in my eye. I was not ready to speak to either of my parents.

"This threat..." I began to say, but hesitated. "Is it bad?"

I asked the question already knowing the answer—but I needed to hear confirmation from him.

He nodded.

"My job is to protect you and I need you to keep the fact I'm your bodyguard a secret," he explained. "You can't tell anyone."

"Fine," I said in a clipped tone.

"It would be a good cover if I continue as your boyfriend," he added, and my jaw dropped open in shock.

"You've got to be joking!" I said in disbelief.

He couldn't be serious, could he? His calm expression as he waited for me to calm down told me he was very serious.

"I need to do everything I can to keep you safe," he said, "and if it requires us to pretend we're still dating, then we have no choice."

To do that I'd have to allow him to be affectionate with me, and did that include kissing? How on earth would I be able to cope with my feelings of hurt when I'd have to kiss him? It would be like reopening the wound again and again. Eventually it would be unable to heal.

"So you want us to just pretend to still be together despite all the lies, just so you can protect me?" I asked, feeling betrayed at the thought of pretending to be something I didn't want anymore.

"Yes," he answered while he watched me. He drained his coffee before he set it down on the table.

"I can't," I said, shaking my head. I couldn't be close to him and be affectionate when I felt the way I did. It hurt so much now that it would be unbearable.

I couldn't even look at him anymore so I spun around

and left the kitchen, needing space, but his footsteps behind me told me he wasn't going to give me the space I needed to wrap my mind around what he was asking. I turned to face him. Trying to hold on to what little control I still had left, I dug my nails into the palms of my hands.

"I won't," I reinforced.

"You have to," he said with a steeliness in his voice that left no room for negotiation. This side of him was so different. It was my first glimpse at the person who had the control and discipline to be a bodyguard.

I shook my head. There had to be another way. Racking through my muddled thoughts I tried to come up with a reason why it wouldn't work, but the only argument I had was that it would be difficult because of my unwanted feelings. I couldn't let him know I still cared about him.

"This threat is real. Your life is in grave danger," he said, trying to use fear against me, but I wasn't going to allow it. Six months after my father had been promoted to district attorney, he'd started receiving threats. At first it had only been toward him, but later the threats had started to include my mother and me. None of those threats had ever materialized.

I had made it clear when I had started college that I refused to have a bodyguard. The fact that my father had gone behind my back and hired Matthew to protect me told me the threat wasn't to be dismissed like they had been before. There was no use fighting my father on it—he would do as he wanted. He would hold paying for college over my head. My father was ruthless at getting what he wanted. And I would be stupid to put my life in danger if there was someone out there determined to harm me. I swallowed the fear that rose up in me.

"No," I said stubbornly, with no logic behind my words. I was making decisions purely based on the pain I was feeling.

"Unfortunately you don't have a say in it," he shot back. I glared at him, knowing he was right.

I wasn't one who allowed myself to get bullied into something, but I knew he had the backing of my father, and my father could make my life very difficult if I refused.

"No one is going to believe it," I said with new determination. I lifted my chin and glared at him defiantly.

"And why not?" he asked, looking at me with mild curiosity.

"Because there isn't any chemistry between us anymore," I informed him, feeling smug that I'd thought of this. "No one will be fooled."

He looked at me with challenging eyes.

"No chemistry?" he questioned softly as he took a step closer. I refused to back down and I nodded, determined to prove him wrong.

He reached for me and before I could react he had pressed his lips to mine. I pushed against him but as his tongue swept into my mouth I found that I was unable to stop myself from responding. My mind was screaming at me to stop and pull away, but my body refused to obey. I held on to his shirt, pulling him closer as I groaned against his lips and deepened the kiss.

Then he pulled away and looked down at me.

"No chemistry?" he questioned with a knowing smile— daring me to lie.

It had been a lie and he'd proved it. I was left breathless and even angrier with myself for my reaction to his kiss. He knew I still wanted him and no amount of words could change the truth revealed by my actions only seconds ago.

I was still fuming. I refused to look at him as he drove us to the college; instead, I kept my eyes on the scenery out of my window.

How was I going to pretend he was still my boyfriend when all I wanted was to throttle him? I pressed my lips together as I fought the urge to refuse to allow him to tell me what to do. A voice in my mind reminded me that he was just doing his job, but kissing me hadn't been necessary.

I was also mad with myself. The moment his lips had touched mine all my self-control had evaporated into thin air and I had been putty in his hands. What made me feel disgusted with myself was the fact that if he hadn't pulled away I wouldn't have stopped him from taking me. I hated myself for being weak. It didn't matter what I said—my actions spoke louder than my words.

I snuck a sideways glance at him but his concentration was on the road ahead of us. Now and then he would look in the mirror to check if we were being followed. It was something I'd never noticed before; but now that I thought about it he was always quieter when driving. It was like he'd always been so preoccupied that we didn't really talk while he drove. Was he more careful because the stalker who had been after Taylor had caused an accident to get her? I tried to remember back to what I'd read. Matthew had been injured in the accident and had been knocked unconscious. He'd been unable to stop the crazy guy from kidnapping Taylor.

For a moment my curiosity got the better of me and I turned to face him. He gave me a quick glance before concentrating back on the road.

"Is that why you're always so quiet in the car?" I asked.

"What are you talking about?" he asked, not taking his eyes off the road.

"Taylor and the accident," I answered, and I watched as his lips thinned and his hands gripped the steering wheel more tightly.

He took a while before he answered. "What do you know about it?" he asked.

"Everything I read in the article," I said. "It said something about her going missing and the only other person who was found at the scene was you, her security."

His face had no emotion as he took in the information.

"It was the first and only time I'd ever failed," he said softly, still not looking away from the road. The guilt in his voice made me want to reach out and cover his hand with mine.

For a moment I got a glimpse at the true person Matthew was rather than the lie he'd been portraying.

Chapter Eight

"I'm sure you did the best you could," I said. I couldn't imagine what it had felt like being in his position with the guilt he carried.

"It was my job to keep her safe," he said firmly. He still blamed himself despite it not being his fault.

"She's fine now," I said, still watching him.

He remained silent. He shook his head, eyes still on the road. I don't honestly know why I cared that he was allowing the guilt to eat him up.

"She doesn't blame you, I don't know why you still blame yourself," I added.

It was the truth. You just had to see the way Taylor looked at him when they were together. Anyone could see she cared deeply for him, more than someone should care about someone who had been paid to keep them safe.

The car slowed down as he did a scan of the parking lot. I'd been so absorbed in our conversation I hadn't realized we'd arrived at the college. He pulled up in the nearest parking space and turned off the car.

I'd been expecting him to ignore what I said but to my surprise he turned to face me. His expression was closed off and I had a feeling I wasn't going to like what he was going to say.

"I'm your bodyguard. You don't have to worry about my baggage. I can deal with that on my own," he said curtly and I felt my temper spark to life.

His cold tone and words cut right through me and I felt hurt. I'd been trying to help him. I could feel my temper rise and the anger I felt toward him rose too. I looked at him, refusing to pull my eyes away and show how much his words had affected me.

The pain I felt pushed me to hurt him right back. Without even thinking I opened my mouth and said, "Just make sure you don't make the same mistake with me."

As soon as the words were out of my mouth I regretted them but there was no taking them back. His jaw tensed. My comment had hurt him but somehow I didn't feel better like I'd hoped. In fact I felt a little worse.

"I get paid a lot of money to make sure I keep you safe," he said before he got out of the car, slamming the door shut.

His words hurt me because it reminded me of all the lies and betrayal. To him I was just a job he got paid to do, but to me he was so much more. More than anybody had ever meant to me. My anger and hurt trumped any sympathy I had for him. I felt the determination to make him pay dearly for hurting me as I opened the door and got out. Matthew was waiting for me beside the car but I ignored him as I slung my bag over my shoulder and walked to the entrance of the building.

I wouldn't show him any more weakness. He hadn't cared about lying to me so I shouldn't care about the guilt he carried. Like he'd said, he could deal with his own baggage. He had enough money to pay for a shrink.

When I spotted my friend Courtney, I plastered a fake smile on my lips.

"Hey," she greeted as she gave me a hug.

"Hi," I greeted back. I felt Matt's presence beside me. I wanted to ignore him but we were supposed to be playing a part.

"Hi, Matt," Courtney greeted him and he gave her a warm smile.

"Hi," he replied as he put an arm around my waist, a possessive touch I'd liked before but was now unwanted. I stiffened for a moment at the sudden touch. We needed to keep up the facade but all I wanted to do was yank myself out of his grip. It took all my self-control to lean in to him like I would have before.

"I can't believe the two of you are so loved-up after being together for a month already," she said, shaking her head.

She didn't know the truth. Matthew smiled and pulled me closer into him. I let him and he pressed a kiss to my cheek.

"Enough," Courtney said playfully. "I can't take any more."

I tensed under his grip but he didn't seem to have any problem playing the part he needed to. He smiled and hugged me closer. He was so good at it I could have believed he was still besotted with me even though I knew better.

"I still can't believe you settled down. I never thought I'd see it happen," she said.

It was true—I'd gone through guys and I'd never really dated any of them. I'd kept some for a couple of weeks but that had been the extent of it.

I looked to Matthew, who was still playing the part of the smitten boyfriend so well. He'd been different—with him

I'd wanted so much more. But where had that led me? Straight to a betrayal, and I wouldn't allow him the power to do that to me again.

Without being too obvious about it, I pulled away gently. He released but he made a point of holding my hand in his, threading his fingers through mine. It would be obvious there was something wrong if I pulled my hand out of his, so I reluctantly allowed him to maintain the hold.

"I need to get to class," I told Courtney. "I'll see you in the cafeteria for lunch."

"Sure, see you then," she replied as she gave me a quick hug.

I walked away holding the strap of my bag and Matthew still held my hand in his, refusing to let go. Just as we got out of view of my friend, I yanked my hand from his and I made a point of walking a little bit away from him, needing to put some distance between us—but he closed the distance and his hand reached for mine again.

"We need to keep up the facade for everyone, not just your friends," he whispered angrily into my ear and I shot him a quick glare. I knew he was trying to protect me, but did he really have to go this far to make sure nothing happened to me?

I was tempted to stay confined to my apartment so I wouldn't have to "pretend" to be anything. It was too much to be so close to him, too difficult to keep my feelings at bay.

In my first class I sat down in my seat and dropped my bag on the floor beside my table. Matthew slid into the seat beside me. It was suffocating having him around all the time. It was a constant reminder of what I'd lost, and the constant pull to my heart hurt. It took more effort than I could muster to keep my true feelings of heartache away from his watchful eyes.

I snuck a glance at him and watched as he scanned the

classroom. I saw a room full of rowdy college students, and I wondered what he saw. His eyes set upon a new student I'd never seen before. It was a guy with brown hair that reached his ears. Just as I let my eyes run over the guy, he turned and winked at me.

I smiled, liking that I could still get the attention of other guys. Out of the corner of my eye I saw Matthew tense and move his seat slightly closer to me. He hadn't liked it one bit. The guy who had been flirting with me gave me one last smirk as he noted Matthew's response and turned to face the front of the class.

"You're really going to cramp my style," I whispered angrily to Matthew.

"I don't care," he whispered under his breath.

I liked to do what I liked when I wanted to. I didn't like restrictions. I wasn't used to being told what I could or couldn't do. Even my parents had treated me like my own person from a young age. I thought it was one of the reasons I was more mature than most people my age.

The rest of the day flew by. I tried to keep my concentration on my classes and not on the brooding presence who had attached himself to me. He was close all the time and it was driving me nuts.

By the time I got into my apartment I was in need of some space, so without a word I went into my bedroom and slammed the door closed, letting him know I didn't want to be around him anymore. I leaned against the door and dropped my bag on the floor. Letting out a deep sigh, I let my head fall against the door as I contemplated how I was going to survive another day with him so close that I could feel my body's reactions to him. Just the smell of him was enough to get my hormones to swirl to attention.

It was getting harder to be around him—letting him hold me, touch me—without it leading to more and without wanting more. We'd never had problems with the physical side of our relationship. He knew his way around a girl's body and he knew exactly what I liked and what I didn't. For a brief moment I remembered how he knew exactly where to kiss me just below my ear to make me groan.

I pushed off the door and went to sit down on my bed. With him pretending to be my boyfriend there was no way I could meet someone else. I enjoyed the physical closeness of being with a guy. I got gratification when I wanted it and I didn't like suppressing it because there was no other way to ease it at the moment.

Then I had the most absurd thought.

It was so ridiculous I couldn't help laughing at myself for even thinking of it. But after thinking about it for a few moments, my laughter stopped and I began to truly contemplate it—as crazy as it was, it could work.

He wanted to pretend to the outside world we were still together and loved each other up to the point we couldn't keep our hands off each other. It was an arrangement. With the pretense, there was no way I could hook up with other guys or move forward with my life. And who knew how long we would have to keep it up?

I smiled as I continued to think my idea over. It could be just like an arrangement, physical benefits with nothing else. Lots of people had that arrangement, although I struggled to remember any of my friends who had done it without other complications creeping in. I had real feelings for him and there was a good chance those feelings could get caught up in this arrangement; but then on the flip side this might be exactly what I needed.

Making our relationship purely a physical one might make it easier to move on when the job was over and he moved on to his next client. It was a ludicrous idea but I loved it. But the question was, could I get Matthew to agree to it? I was pretty sure he was still physically attracted to me even though there was no way to know if his feelings toward me had been real. It wasn't like we had professed our love for each other but he'd definitely given me the impression he'd cared about me.

My phone rang. I checked it and it was my mother. I ignored it; I still wasn't ready to speak to her or my father. Once the phone stopped ringing I tried to decide which was the best way to approach the conversation with Matthew.

I wasn't sure words were going to do the trick. I had to make sure there was no room for refusal on his part. If I didn't give him a chance to say no, I could get him to do what I wanted. I smiled to myself as I began to formulate how I was going to get him to agree to what I wanted.

The sound of the TV in the living room told me exactly where he was. I wasn't one to back down from a challenge, so before I could second-guess my plan, I stepped out of my bedroom.

He was sitting on the couch and at the sound of my door opening he looked back. Our eyes met. I could feel our attraction in that one look. I could do this. As I approached him I felt a flutter of excitement at what I was about to do. He looked at me expectantly as I came to a stop in front of him.

"I need help undoing a button," I said as I turned around. I moved my hair out the way. He stood up behind me.

I felt the soft touch of his hands as he undid the button, even though he knew I could undo it on my own. Did he know I was playing a game? I turned to face him. He was watching me like a hawk and his eyes watched while I slid my tongue across my bottom lip seductively.

Reaching for the hem of my shirt I pulled it over my head and dropped it to the floor. His eyes ran over my semi-naked form. He was still in control, and I needed to break it. The only reaction was the slight darkening in his eyes.

"I need help with this button," I said as my fingers settled on the top button of my jeans.

For a moment I waited to see if he'd do what I wanted. His eyes lifted to mine and I held his gaze.

One moment became two and I held my breath, waiting in anticipation for his reaction. Then I felt his slender fingers unbutton the top button of my jeans. I smiled seductively and slid the jeans to the floor.

I was only dressed in my underwear as I stepped out of the jeans. Matthew's eyes took in my half-naked body and I knew I'd hooked him. He eyes slid over me.

"You want to kiss me?" I asked softly, letting my eyes drop to his lips. I wanted him to kiss me. I'd intended to be in complete control but the need to reach out and pull him closer made me ache with want.

He smiled, but there was no mistaking the way his eyes slid over me and then lifted to mine.

"Do you want me to kiss you?" he asked huskily. His eyes dared me to answer truthfully.

My jaw tightened. I hadn't expected him to turn the tables on me and I was taken slightly by surprise. I'd expected him to grab me and kiss me like he couldn't get enough of me. But instead of doing what I wanted him to, he was watching me with a knowing smile. The jerk. I'd gone from being the seducer to the poor victim who couldn't control her body's reaction to the thought of what he could do to me.

I studied him for a moment, keeping my turmoil hidden from him. I couldn't allow him to see he could get to me. My plan was about to fail and I needed to do something quick to keep it on track. I smiled to myself as I considered my next move. I had way too many clothes on and it was time to remedy that, so I turned around slowly.

"I need help with this," I said, looking back at him over my shoulder as I waited to see if he'd unclasp my bra. We stared at each other for a moment before his eyes went to my bra strap.

And I waited for him to make his decision.

Chapter Nine

He wanted to, but the question was: would he? For a second I thought he might turn me down. I could feel a sinking feeling in my stomach at the fear I might have lost the ability to seduce him. Did he not find me attractive anymore? Had he only been doing me to keep close enough to protect me?

The moment I felt the soft touch of his hands on the clasp of my bra, I knew I had won. I stood still, holding my breath as he undid the clasp. His fingers slid the bra straps off my shoulders and I savored the way my skin tingled with excitement under his slight touch.

He kissed my one shoulder softly as I allowed the clothing to fall to the floor. His hands rested on my arms. The feel of his mouth against my skin made me tremble. He pressed another soft kiss to my other shoulder before he turned me around. My arms were at my sides, giving him full view of my semi-nakedness. His eyes swept over me and I felt the heat of his gaze.

Gone was the man with the control and in his place was the man who wanted me and would have me. His one hand reached and cupped the nape of my neck as he pulled me gently to him. His lips covered mine and I pressed my body against his. My open hands splayed against his chest as his lips moved against mine.

It felt so good I groaned against his mouth, which allowed his tongue access to my mouth. My tongue swept against his as his arms encircled me and my arms snaked around his neck. Any logical thinking went out the window and all I could concentrate on was how I felt being thoroughly kissed by him.

The next minute his hands dropped to my bottom and lifted me off my feet. Instinctively my legs wrapped around his waist and he carried me. Our kiss deepened as our tongues caressed each other. My body shivered in anticipation of what we were about to share. I wanted him so badly.

Once we were inside his room he set me down on my feet. Our lips broke apart long enough for him to pull his shirt off and throw it down onto the floor. My hands were already undoing the buttons of his jeans when he kissed me again, cupping my cheeks so he could tilt my face upward to gain better access.

He was so good—he knew exactly what I wanted and what I needed. There were times when I needed him to take control but there were also moments I wanted him to be gentle and loving. I don't know how he knew, he just did. And right now I didn't want gentle.

He broke away and dropped his jeans to the floor. I looked down at the tent in his boxers and smiled. Emotions didn't matter. Feelings and betrayal didn't matter. I wanted him and there was no denying he wanted me.

He reached for the sides of my panties and slid them

down my legs. The slight touch of his hands trailing down my skin was so erotic. He shrugged out of his boxers. I let my eyes run the length of his naked body, taking in the contours of his six-pack. He let his hungry gaze do the same to me.

Our eyes met.

"Come here," he commanded and I hesitated for a moment, still trying to hold on to some sort of control. He reached out to me and pulled me closer. He kissed me hard, stoking the fire inside of me. My mouth opened up, inviting him. The ache between my legs was starting to intensify. I didn't know how much longer I could stand it.

"Please," I whispered against his mouth as his hands brushed down my sides and settled on my hips. Being in control didn't matter anymore. I needed him to take me and ease the ache.

I didn't have to ask again. His intent was clear as he walked me back to the bed. When I felt the sheets on the back of my legs he laid me down on the bed. I was squirming beneath his hungry gaze. He lay down on me and I opened my legs so he could lay between them.

"You feel so fucking good," he whispered as he pressed against me. His hand guided my leg around his hip. I was still on the pill so there was no need for protection. He'd been the only guy I'd ever taken without a condom.

He brushed his tongue against my bottom lip, taking me in gently between his teeth as he slid into me. My breath hitched as I felt the gentle bite as he withdrew. My hips lifted to meet his next thrust as he pulled his lips from mine.

He took my arms and guided them above my head. His hands held mine securely as our bodies began to move against each other. His fingers intertwined with mine as he began to move in and out of me. My mouth opened slightly as I wrapped my legs around his waist, holding him closer. I liked the feel of being unable to touch him as he slammed into me, each thrust harder than before.

"Oh, my God," I gasped as I felt the first tremors of my orgasm hit me. His mouth covered mine and then my orgasm hit full force. I gasped against his lips and he thrust into me, releasing my hands as he held onto my hips. He pushed harder into me like he wanted to bury every inch of himself inside of me.

He body began to tense and he came with one hard thrust back inside of me. He held me so hard I was pretty sure I would have bruises, but I didn't care.

He slumped over me and I felt the heaviness of him pin me to the bed for a few moments as he tried to catch his breath. I loved the feel of his masculine body pressing mine into the mattress. He pressed a kiss to my lips. Our bodies were slick with sweat as we lay connected for a few more minutes. I wanted it to last longer, but he eased out of me and rolled onto his back beside me.

There were no words. What did you say after sleeping with the guy who had betrayed you and turned your feelings for him to hate? I felt his eyes on me, but I refused to look at him. He reached for a blanket and covered us up. It was time to talk about what happened and what it meant to me. I didn't want him to think that one fuck erased the betrayal between us.

I turned onto my side to face him. He was watching me.

"That was great," I said with a satisfied smile.

Sex had always been earth-shattering with him. No one had ever made me feel the way he did. I always thought the sex had been better because we had an emotional connection, but I hoped it wasn't the case. I wanted to work him out of my system without emotions. I wanted to place him back into the sole category of someone I had awesome sex with.

He remained quiet. Maybe he was trying to figure out where I was going with this.

"I have needs," I began to say. "And you take care of them very nicely."

I saw a flash of anger before he masked his features.

"What game are you playing?" he asked, trying to keep his temper under control.

"We were always good together when it came the bedroom," I reminded him as I sat up, not bothering to hide my nakedness. He'd seen it all before. He knew every inch of my body and there was no reason to pretend he didn't.

"So you just want sex?" he asked, showing no emotion. It was like we were talking about the weather.

"Why not?" I asked him with a shrug. Loads of people did the friends-with-benefits thing. I thought it was a brilliant plan. He knew what I liked and what I didn't, which made him a great candidate. Besides, it wasn't going to be possible to find someone else to screw if I had to pretend he was my boyfriend.

"We can enjoy each other until this arrangement is over," I said, laying out the terms of what I wanted.

He stared at me with an unreadable expression.

"Think about it," I said as I got out of his bed. I didn't look back as I walked out of his room.

I wanted to be sure he would do as I wanted, but I had no idea if he would. I hated the uncertainty of it. That was the thing about Matthew—I never fully knew where I stood with him.

I went into the living room and picked up my discarded clothes. I thought about my panties still lying on the floor of his bedroom and smiled to myself. He could keep them. They could be a reminder of what he could have if he allowed us to enter into the arrangement where we could find physical release with each other.

Back in my room I showered and changed. It didn't surprise me that Matthew was busy in the kitchen cooking when I finally came out of my bedroom. I was happy the effects of my orgasm had made me feel happy and relaxed. Whatever he was making smelled mouth-watering and I leaned against the kitchen doorway as I watched him.

"Are you going to stand there forever or are you going to help me?" he asked, still concentrating on the task of cooking.

"Sure. What do you want me to do?" I asked. I walked into the kitchen before standing beside him. Sex between us had taken away some of the uneasiness that had been caused by my hurt and anger.

"You can make the salad," he instructed, giving me a glance. I nodded and tried to keep myself from thinking about what we'd been doing just half an hour ago.

Being so close to him made me super aware of him and I felt my body tingle where he'd touched me. It was unbelievable I could want him again so soon after we'd been together. It shouldn't have surprised me because our physical side had always been good.

The problem with us had been the truth.

Silence settled between us as we both got on with our tasks. I set the table and he brought the food over. He sat down and dished up some salad onto his plate as I watched him. The anger I'd felt before had slowly began to dissipate. It probably had something to do with being physically close to him and being unable to keep my feelings out of it.

It wasn't love. It was sex and nothing more. It made me believe this was the only way forward between the two of us.

"So did you think about it?" I asked out of the blue. I didn't have a lot of patience and I wanted to know where he stood on the subject.

He looked at me and set his knife and fork down beside his plate.

"Yes, I thought about it," he said, holding my gaze. He had that poker face on again and I didn't have a clue which way he was going to go.

I stopped what I was doing and gave him my full attention.

"No," he said, and I felt my jaw drop open from shock. I hadn't expected that. Maybe it was because I was always used to getting what I wanted and at the moment I wanted him on my terms.

"What do you mean, no?" I asked angrily when I got over the initial shock.

"You heard me," he stated calmly like he was in full control of the situation.

It wasn't something I could comprehend. We'd just had the best sex and here he was telling me he didn't want to sleep with me again? He had to be lying, because there was no way it was true.

"You don't want me?" I said out loud, trying to wrap my mind around it.

"That wasn't what I said," he said, and I looked at him, more confused than before.

"I want you," he stated. The way his gaze swept over me assured me of that. "But I don't just want one part of you."

I frowned.

"I want all of you. I want the hot sex and I want you naked beneath me," he began to explain, and I felt my stomach flutter at the thought. I could feel his hands running across my body like he'd just been doing. Beneath his imaginary touch my skin tingled. "But I also want you with all the strings attached. I don't just want the physical side—I want everything."

I looked at him like he was crazy. How could he expect me to want that with him again? I'd let him in before, and look what happened. He'd hurt me deeply.

"Even if you only hate me, I need it all," he finished.

I remembered his betrayal and how every sweet moment

we'd shared had been marred by the deceit. I pressed my lips together as I felt my anger return. How could he expect that?

He watched me carefully as I tried to figure out how to tell him it would never happen.

"You had me," I said. "And you lost me."

The finality in my voice summed us up. He'd had it all— and look what he'd done. He'd betrayed me. There was no way I could trust him enough not to hurt me again.

"I don't believe that," he said, looking at me confidently. All I felt for him at the moment was the physical need to be close to him; the emotions he was talking about were being smothered by the anger I still felt at his actions.

"It doesn't matter what you believe," I snapped back, hating the way he thought he knew me better than I knew myself.

If those were his terms, then there would be nothing between us. I wasn't going to chance getting hurt again and if he didn't want me without the strings then he couldn't have any of me. It would be hard to resist the physical attraction I felt for him, but I could do it.

But I wondered if he could. Then I smiled to myself. I could push him to see how he far he would go. In my mind there was no way he would be able to resist me if I tried to seduce him again like I just had.

"Anything I might have felt for you died the moment I found out you'd been lying to me," I reminded him.

He studied me for a moment.

"What I did was wrong, and I'm sorry," he said, sounding genuine. I hardened my heart. "But how I felt about you wasn't a lie."

His "sorry" didn't erase his actions.

"You have every right to feel angry and upset with me, but I know you will forgive me," he added.

I hated how he was so sure of the outcome, because I

couldn't see the same picture.

"What if I don't?" I asked him.

"You will."

He was so sure of himself and it annoyed me. There was no other option to him and it was why he thought it was possible to have all of me.

"Why are you being difficult about this?" I asked him. What guy turned down good sex because he didn't want it without the emotions?

"I'm offering you sex. You know how good we are together and you can have it for as long as you are my bodyguard," I reminded him, feeling exasperated he wouldn't do what I'd expected and wanted him to do.

"It's not enough."

I frowned as I felt my frustration with him rise.

"You really think it's possible to resist me?" I asked, approaching the problem from a different direction.

He nodded his head.

"If you could, you wouldn't have fucked me earlier," I said bluntly, trying to get a reaction out of him. I got nothing. He had that damn poker face on again.

"That proves nothing," he said.

I glared at him.

"The next time I take you, it will be on my terms," he promised.

I pushed my chair back as I felt my temper rise.

"It won't happen," I assured him as I put my hands on my hips. "You can say what you want, but we both know you won't be able to resist me."

He remained silent and I threw him one last glare before I left and went to my room, slamming my door as hard as I could.

I hated that he wouldn't take what I wanted to give; he wanted more. I wanted to be with him physically—I liked sex and I loved it with him—but I couldn't give him what he wanted.

Pacing up and down my room, it took me a while before my anger began to die down and I slumped down on my bed. I was stubborn and I knew he wouldn't be able to resist me. It was one thing saying the words, but it was a different thing to follow it up with action.

I would win this.

Chapter Ten

The next day when I got dressed for school I made sure I chose the best outfit to show off my figure. I was out to break Matthew so that he would agree to my proposition. I would make sure it was impossible to resist me. Smiling at my reflection in the mirror, I admired the short miniskirt that showed off my long legs. The top I wore hugged my figure and showed off my cleavage. With only a small amount of makeup, I looked good, and Matthew was going to find it hard to turn me down.

My phone rang and I looked at the identity of the caller. It was my father. I'd been ignoring him because I was still angry with him.

I pressed my lips together and let it ring a few more times before I gave in and answered it.

"Sarah," my father said. His voice was hard and unyielding.

"Father," I said, keeping my temper from flaring up as I

ground out the words.

"You finally took my call," he said, sounding annoyed.

I'd been avoiding his calls since I'd found out the truth.

"What do you want?" I asked. My voice sounded sharper than I'd meant it to.

"I know you're angry with me—"

"I don't want to hear it," I cut him off. No amount of apologizing was going to erase what had happened or the hurt it had caused me.

"I did it for your own good," he said, but I was already shaking my head. In his warped logic it made perfect sense where emotions had no place.

"You knew I didn't want a bodyguard and you agreed. You went behind my back and hired one anyway." I was breathing hard as my anger flowed to the surface. I gripped the phone against my ear, even though I knew there was no point in arguing with him.

"You made him *lie* to me," I said, feeling all the hurt I'd felt at the betrayal wash over me.

The fact that my father had made Matthew lie to me didn't let Matthew off the hook, though—he'd still had a choice and he'd made the wrong one. In my book they were both wrong and both to blame.

"What is done is done," my father said. I felt my frustration with him grow. He just couldn't understand what he'd done was wrong even if his intention had been good.

"I was concerned about your safety."

It wasn't a reason to be deceptive but I knew it wasn't something he would understand.

Letting out a frustrated sigh I sat down on my bed.

"I can't let your work dictate my every move," I told my father. "I want to lead a life of my own."

"I take your safety very seriously," he said. "With the promotion the threats I've been receiving have increased."

I bit my lip. "I know that, but if you'd needed to put a bodyguard on me to watch over me you should have said something. I might not have liked the idea but I would have understood."

He was silent because he knew I was right. I couldn't help the nagging voice in the back of my mind telling me there was more going on than he was telling me.

"You're right." That was unexpected coming from my father. "In the future I'll be more honest with you about my concerns."

It wasn't an apology but it was the most I was going to get out of him.

"Did Mom know about Matthew?" I asked.

"No."

I felt relieved that my mother hadn't known. Betrayal from her would have been harder to swallow.

I left my room, still thinking about my conversation with my father, as sounds coming from the kitchen led me there. Matthew was dressed and making coffee. I stood in the doorway watching him. It was hard to keep my hands off him after our last romp but I was determined to have him on my terms.

As if sensing me, he looked over his shoulder at me. I smiled as his eyes swept over me. There was no doubt he liked what he saw, but he pulled his eyes away from me and turned back to the task he was busy with.

"You really think that is appropriate for class?" he asked softly, and I folded my arms.

"What's wrong with it?" I asked, wanting him to tell me it made him want to tear my clothes off.

"It doesn't leave a lot to the imagination," he said as he busied himself with making coffee.

He stopped and turned to hand me a cup of coffee. I took it from him and tried to hide my smile. I could taste the victory of breaking him.

I set my coffee down on the counter as I took a step closer to him. I was the hunter and he was the prey.

"You don't need an imagination," I reminded him seductively. "You know exactly what I look like underneath this."

His features were masked. He took a sip of his coffee as his eyes fixed on me. I took another step closer and I took his coffee cup from his hands and put it down on the counter. He dropped his hands to his sides as my eyes fixed on his lips while I ran my tongue against my bottom lip.

"You know you want me," I whispered as I leaned closer, looking up at him again. "Why fight what you know you can have?"

Silence, but he kept his eyes on me.

"You want me," I reminded him. I was so close—but not enough for us to touch. "Take what you want."

He studied me for a moment, masking his emotions so well I had no idea what was going through his mind. I wanted him to reach for me and kiss me, but he stood still, not moving.

Then he leaned forward, and I smiled, knowing I'd won.

"No," he whispered softly and so close to my lips that I felt his breath.

I frowned and pulled away. I had not been expecting that.

"Why are you being so stubborn?" I asked, throwing my hands up in the air. It was so frustrating he wouldn't do what I wanted.

"I told you what I wanted," he said, and I glared at him. "My terms are non-negotiable."

His rejection hurt even though it was because he wanted more of me than I was willing to give.

"If you can't do it then I'll have to find someone who

will," I threatened him and for the first time I saw a flash of emotion cross his face.

"We agreed to keep up the pretense of dating so it would explain why I was always with you. So no one would suspect I'm your bodyguard," he reminded me, but I didn't care. The hurt from my rejection was stronger than any logical thinking.

"If you won't satisfy my needs you leave me no choice," I shot back as I took a step back.

"Don't push me," he warned softly as his hard eyes fixed on me. He was angry. I was okay with that—anything was an improvement on the indifference I'd been dealing with before.

"The choice is yours," I told him. "Either it's you or somebody else."

I gave him one last look that took in the slight twitch in his jaw before I took my coffee and left the kitchen.

I went to the living room to look out the window as I drank my coffee. He didn't follow me. My heart was hammering inside my chest and it took me a few moments to calm myself down. He made me so angry. I didn't want anyone else, but if he wouldn't break and do as I wanted, I would have to find someone else to take care of my needs.

I let out a frustrated sigh. I wouldn't allow him to get to me. We weren't anything. I just wanted great sex with him. It was nothing more than that.

In silence, Matthew drove me to campus. I ignored him. He knew what the options were and he'd made his decision, which meant I was now on the prowl for someone who would do as I wanted. We were pretending to date but it didn't matter to me. I didn't care what people would say about it.

Besides, I'd try and find someone who could be discreet about it.

Once he parked the car and turned it off, I made a move to get out, but his hand on my wrist stopped me.

"Don't do something stupid," he warned. I pulled my hand from his grip.

"I gave you a choice and you made your decision," I reminded him as I get out of the car. I didn't wait for him— instead I walked away quickly. It was childish and also pointless, because moments later he'd caught up with me anyway.

Usually we met up with Courtney before class, but today she didn't have any classes so I went straight to our first class. It was the same class we'd had the day before. Then I remembered the new guy who had winked. He would be perfect as a replacement for Matthew.

"Remember we're supposed to be pretending to date," he said. I stopped and looked at him.

"I can be discreet about it," I assured him, watching him for a reaction.

"Fine," he said, sounding indifferent. That took me by surprise. It was like the wind had been taken out of my sails.

I'd expected him to fight me harder on this. It was like he'd given in too easily. Why?

He didn't wait for me. He walked into the class and I followed behind him. I was disoriented and confused. Pushing the emotions down, I sat down beside him and shot him a sideways glance.

His eyes swept over the classroom but he ignored me completely. He was different. Gone was the guy I had come to know and in his place was a stranger I didn't recognize. Was this part of the game or was he truly ready for me to move on to someone else?

It made no sense. How did he go from wanting it all to

just letting me go? Was it a ploy or was it that easy for him to switch off his feelings for me? I felt like I'd had the wind knocked out of me as I tried to get myself together. I was stronger than this.

Sex had always been my way to keep my emotions at bay, and that was the only way I could get rid of any unwanted feelings or emotions that still tied me to Matthew. It was time to take control of my life and move on. My threat to him hadn't been empty; despite my confusion at his indifference, I was determined to carry it out. If he wasn't going to give me what I wanted, I would get it from another guy.

I pulled my gaze away from Matthew. My eyes went straight to the guy who had flirted with me the day before. My eyes met his across the room and I gave him a flirty smile. His smiled widened and I felt the appreciative sweep of his gaze.

His brown eyes were darker than his dark-brown hair. He liked what he saw. This would be a piece of cake. My confidence was restored and I began to think of ways to get what I wanted without blowing the cover Matthew needed.

I shot him a glance but his attention was on the lecturer, who had started the lesson. It was hard to believe he'd told me he wanted all of me and now he was letting me go without a fight. I shook it off. I had no idea if he was playing me or not but I was determined to move on. It was what I always did. I didn't get attached...well, until Matthew.

If he didn't want what I was prepared to give, then I would give it to someone else. My eyes drifted to the cute guy in the class, who had turned his attention back to the front of the room.

In my mind I began to try and figure out a way to contact the cute guy without making it obvious to anyone who could be watching. On more than one occasion I'd wondered if the whole bodyguard thing wasn't just an overreaction on my father's part. There had been threats but no one had harmed me. It made it difficult to believe my life was in danger.

I decided to write a note to the cute guy. I would shove it in his hand when I got a chance and the decision would be up to him.

In my note, I wrote:

If you want to meet up sometime, call me.

I wrote my number at the bottom of the paper.

Even if it did somehow get out that I'd been unfaithful to Matt, it wouldn't be a big deal. People cheated on their partners all the time and they moved past it. I was determined to go through with my threat despite everything.

It was disconcerting that Matthew never looked in my direction for the entire class. I was used to being the center of his attention and I didn't like the fact that I wasn't.

Once you move on, it won't matter anymore, I kept reminding myself over and over again.

At the end of the class I got up and made my way down to the guy I had my eye on. He turned to me when I reached him. I never said a word, but I gave him a knowing smile as I shoved my folded note in his hand before I walked away. I made my way back to the exit of the class where Matthew was waiting for me. He surprised me when he gave me a smile as we walked out of the classroom together.

I frowned. I hadn't expected him to go, like, caveman jealous—but I had expected *some* reaction to seeing me shove a note into some other guy's hand. It was puzzling and it gnawed at me for the rest of the day. Could it be he was playing me so well I had no idea what he was up to? He was usually so open about what he wanted.

For the rest of my classes I was preoccupied with my thoughts, but by the time I got back to the apartment I was frustrated with his being indifferent to me. I had no idea why it affected me so much. Was it that I wanted him to care about me? I wanted him to be jealous and I wanted him to fight for me. But he wasn't.

Feeling tired, I went straight to my room when we entered the apartment. I needed some time away from him to sort through my thoughts and feelings. He was so composed that it was frustrating to watch. I had no idea how I would feel about him giving his number to another girl. Well, that was a lie—I wouldn't like it and I knew it.

Despite everything he'd put me through I still cared about him and that wasn't going to change overnight. There was no guarantee the guy I'd given my number to was going to call, so that left me with only one option. I took a deep breath, trying to get some of my confidence back. I could do this.

Smiling to myself, I wondered if he would be able to keep the indifference going if I seduced him like I'd threatened to. Just thinking of how I'd gotten to him the day before boosted my fragile ego. I went to my wardrobe.

It was getting closer to dinnertime and I could hear him busy in the kitchen. I got into the shower intent on pulling out all the stops to make sure I was successful. There would be no failure and I was going to get what I wanted on my terms.

I decided on some sexy red silk pajamas, the color screaming out my intention to seduce him. I pulled out the shorts and top. I wasn't going to go overboard with makeup but I did put on my favorite perfume. I knew he found it to be irresistible.

By the time I had made it out of my room he was already sitting at the dinner table eating. My food was already placed in front of the chair opposite him. I wasn't interested in the food, I was interested in him.

At the sight of me he stopped eating and his eyes fixed on me. There was no doubt I'd taken him by surprise, and for a moment I saw the want in his eyes. It pushed me forward.

In front of him I stopped. He pushed out of his chair and stood up. I looked up at him as I stepped forward, not touching him.

"I want you," I said to him, watching him. His gaze swept over me and I felt the heat of it brush over my skin. "And you want me."

He remained silent and still. The sight of his hands fisted by his sides told me he was fighting it.

"Take me."

Chapter Eleven

He didn't touch me.

"I want you more than anything," he said softly as his eyes caressed my face. I felt my heart flutter at the admission. "But I will only take you if I can have all of you. Sex I can get from anyone, but I want back how you made me feel."

I felt like someone had slapped me and I took a step back. Hurt he'd turned me down, I turned and fled back to my room. Slamming the door behind me.

Tears slid down my face as I sat down on my bed and wrapped my arms around my waist, trying to cope with the pain and the bewildered feelings I was dealing with. My heart ached like it had been wounded. I'd trusted him totally and somewhere in the last few weeks he'd crept into my heart and made a place there that would always belong to him. Then when I'd found out about his deceit, that place had become a source of pain.

I didn't want to feel the hurt. I wasn't good with dealing with emotions. It was so much easier shutting it out and only concentrating on the physical side I'd shared with him. It had to be just about that because I couldn't allow him back in. I didn't trust that he wouldn't hurt me again.

People hurt the people they loved even when they didn't mean to. It was just human nature. Being stupid enough to allow someone in was my mistake and I didn't plan on repeating it.

Brushing my tears away I stood up and began to pace up and down the length of my room. As if answering my inner turmoil, my phone began to ring. I picked it up and looked at the screen. It wasn't a number I recognized, which meant it was probably the cute guy I'd given my note to. I took a deep breath to calm myself down as I put my phone to my ear and answered the call.

"Hi," I said.

"Hey, gorgeous," the guy said.

I could already feel myself talking myself into doing what I needed to do to get rid of the feelings I had for Matthew.

"What's your name?" I asked, trying to make a little conversation. It didn't matter what his name was; I wasn't interested in getting to know him. I didn't need to know his favorite color or any details like that. I liked what I saw. He was good-looking and fit. I knew it was shallow but that was enough for me.

"Zac," he answered.

"Do you want to come over?" I asked bluntly. There was no time to beat around the bush. I knew what I had to do and the sooner I got it over with the sooner I could move on.

"Message me your address and I'll be there as soon as I can," he said.

"Okay. Bring condoms," I told him and then I ended the call. I was only interested in one thing.

I quickly sent my address to Zac. Feeling like I was back in control, I wiped the remains of my tears.

There wasn't a need to seduce Zac because I was pretty sure he was a given, so I shoved my sexy silky clothes into my dresser. Just the sight of them reminded me of Matthew's rejection and it hurt. I got dressed in jeans and a tight top. I slipped on some sandals.

Matthew, I thought uncomfortably.

I'd given him an ultimatum and he'd made his choice. There was no going back now. He had to live with his decision. I had to tell him about Zac coming over. He was my bodyguard and he needed to know. But it wasn't the only reason I wanted to tell him—I wanted to see his face when I told him I was going to go through with what I'd told him. Some part of me wanted to see him hurt like I had.

He was sitting in the living room watching TV when I entered. I let my eyes take him in for a moment. Just the sight of him was enough to quicken my heartbeat.

Hearing my footsteps he turned to look at me. For a moment I wanted to give in and not care about the consequences. It would be so easy but the hard part would be allowing myself to be hurt again.

"I have someone coming over," I said, studying his features for his reaction.

"Who?" he asked, even though I could see from his expression he knew exactly what I was talking about.

"The guy from our class," I revealed, wanting to see his expression change from mildly curious to deep hurt. But I got nothing. He nodded his head and turned his attention back to the TV.

"I did a background check on him and he's harmless," he informed me.

Harmless? That was it?

I backtracked out of the living room and went into the kitchen. I poured myself some water as I tried to work through my emotions. Of all the reactions I'd expected, that hadn't been one of them. It was like he didn't care what I was going to do with some other guy. I rubbed my forehead as I tried to figure out what he was up to. Did he really feel nothing? Or was it a ploy to force me back to him?

Confused and annoyed, I took a couple gulps of water. The doorbell went and I waited for Matthew to answer it.

I don't know why but I needed to see his reaction at seeing my visitor. I stepped out of the kitchen and watched Matthew greet Zac with a nod of his head before he stepped back to let him in. He acted like nothing was wrong and it took a moment for me to pull myself together. Zac stopped in front of me and smiled as his gaze swept appreciatively over me.

"Hey," he greeted me and I smiled back at him. It was forced because I wasn't feeling happy. Things weren't going as I'd planned but there was no way I was going to back out now.

"Do you want a beer?" I asked Zac and he nodded his head.

Matthew walked past us back to the living room. There was no emotion, no jealousy and no hurt on his face. Had he not cared for me at all? The questions raced through my mind while I got Zac a beer and handed it to him. He opened it and took a sip, his eyes on me.

I took a step closer, holding his gaze. It was time to erase the deceptive bodyguard from my heart. Zac was leaning against the kitchen counter and watching me lazily. I ignored my emotions as I allowed him to pull me between his legs and kiss me. His soft lips pressed to mine but his kiss didn't sear me like Matthew's did. I pushed him from my mind as I slid my tongue into Zac's mouth and caressed his. His hands cupped my face as our kiss deepened.

I was physically attracted to Zac but he didn't turn my world around like Matthew did. Pulling away, I looked at him seductively as I pulled him by his hand to my room. There was no stopping myself from seeing Matthew sitting on the sofa facing the TV. What was I expecting? I was sure Matthew knew exactly what I was doing. There was no reason for me to expect he would try to stop me, but somehow I did.

I let Zac enter my room and then I closed the door, leaning against it as my eyes traveled over the hot guy who was going to help me over my heartache. There didn't need to be emotions—it was just going to be good, gratifying sex and nothing more. It was all I needed.

I came up to Zac, who was standing beside my bed. I reached for his shirt and pulled it up. He helped me take it off and then threw it on the floor. His mouth covered mine as his hand reached for the bottom of my shirt and lifted it. I broke the kiss long enough to remove the item of clothing. The feel of his hand cupping my breast did nothing for me. I didn't feel any excitement or anticipation.

Frustrated, I pulled away for a moment and turned my back on him. What the hell was wrong with me? I put my hand to my forehead. I had a sexy guy in my bedroom ready to tear my clothes off and do wicked things to me, but something didn't feel right and I couldn't place what it was.

"Are you okay?" Zac asked and I closed my eyes for a moment.

My determination to move past the block made me take a deep breath and release it as I turned to face the hunk who was looking at me with confusion.

"I'm fine," I assured him as I reached for his face and kissed him, trying to make myself feel something.

His arms wrapped around me and he held me while our mouths fused together. I groaned, trying to force the chemistry I so badly wanted to feel. I just had to keep going and it would work.

Slowly he trailed kisses along my throat. The longer I let

this go on, the more frustrated and angry I was becoming. Despite all my attempts to move on, it wasn't working. If Matthew did this I would be in a frenzy of need. I allowed it to continue for a little while regardless. I was down to my bra and panties. Zac was down to his boxers and we were lying on my bed, making out.

"You sure you're okay?" he asked as he pulled away from me and lay on his side. Even he could sense I wasn't fully into it.

I wanted to continue to lie to him and myself but it wouldn't hide the lack of want on my part. This was Matthew's fault.

"This isn't working," I said as I sat up. There was no more pretending.

"Is it me?" he asked, raking a hand though his hair.

I shook my head.

"There's nothing wrong with you," I assured him. I was the problem. It was hard to admit but there was no ignoring it anymore.

Zac shifted off the bed and began to get dressed. I pulled my knees up to my chest and watched, feeling vulnerable that something fundamentally had changed and I couldn't just make it go back to the way it had been before.

"Well, if you change your mind you know my number," he said just before he opened the door and left.

For a while I stared at the closed door, trying to figure out what was wrong with me. The more I thought about it the more I began to get angry and upset. I knew who'd done this to me: Matthew.

If it had been him instead of Zac, I would have responded to every touch differently. He was the one who could make me come alive and I hated that. Was it because I'd felt something for Matthew? Was it because I had connected with him on a deeper level that I couldn't physically be with another person?

Eventually a while later I got out of my bed and took a shower. For some reason I felt dirty and the need to wash Zac's touch from my skin seemed to be important.

I'd always been able to do what I wanted when I wanted and the fact a certain boy had changed me so much so quickly was scary. I got dressed into my pajamas before I left my room. I wasn't ready to face Matthew yet, but I was hungry.

The TV was going but Matthew wasn't in the living room. For a moment I hesitated, wondering where he was.

I went into the kitchen. My plate of food from earlier was untouched and sitting on the counter. I touched the plate and thought of Matthew. Letting out a sigh, I leaned against the counter and rubbed my hands over my face. Emotions tied to my actions began to build up in me. I felt guilty and lost. I'd never felt like this before and I had no idea what to do.

Before I could even think about what I was doing I went looking for Matthew. I needed to see him. Maybe it would give me the answers I needed. I stood outside his bedroom. His door was closed but I could hear movement, which meant he was still awake.

Suddenly I felt nervous so I knocked softly on his door.

The silence on the other side of the door made me hold my breath. A few moments went by and I was convinced he wasn't going to open his door. Then the door opened and I was looking into his face.

His emotions were masked but the tightening in his jaw was a dead giveaway of the anger boiling just below the surface.

"What do you want?" he asked tersely.

His tone didn't surprise me. As far as he was concerned I'd screwed someone else just a few feet away from him. I was at a loss for words as I stood silently trying to figure out what to say.

"Do you need something?" he snapped, and I took a step back.

My guilt became overwhelmed by the anger at his actions.

"Yes," I said back as my temper rose and I took a step forward.

"I don't have all night. Spit it out," he ordered, looking at me like he couldn't stand the sight of me.

That jolted something inside of me.

"I want you!" I yelled at him and he pressed his lips together.

He shook his head.

"I want you the way we were," I added quietly, feeling the pain return. My eyes scanned his features, looking for an answer of how to fix it. And knowing if he hadn't lied that we wouldn't be in the mess we were.

"You lost me the moment you fucked someone else," he told me and took a step back, slamming his bedroom door.

The stubborn part of me that didn't give up banged on his door. He opened it up and I met his glare with my own.

"Did you hear me?" he asked angrily. For the first time he looked at me with hatred and I wavered for a brief moment.

"I don't want you anymore," he said firmly, telling me exactly where we stood. He didn't know I hadn't been able to go through with it, but his words still cut right through me.

"I..." started to say but he shook his head again.

"I gave you every chance I could, but no more," he said. I could see the hurt in his eyes. "I'm done. You can move on now."

He wasn't giving me a chance to say what I had to, which was making me even angrier.

"I can't," I managed to get out.

"You moved on just fine with your fuck-buddy."

He made another move to close the door but I wasn't going to let him shut me out before I could tell him everything. I pressed both my hands to the door and pushed against it. It took him by surprise and he took a step back. He had every right to be angry with me and feel the way he did.

I had to set the record straight and tell him.

"I need you to shut up and listen to me," I told him, putting my hands on my hips.

My anger and determination began to wane as the vulnerable side of me only he saw was about to open up.

"Nothing you say will change anything," he added, shaking his head, instead of allowing me to explain.

"I didn't," I said softly, trying to build up the courage to admit I hadn't been able to move on because of how I felt about him.

He looked at me with a confused expression.

"I didn't screw Zac," I admitted quietly, feeling like I was open for him to see straight inside of me.

He studied me for a moment.

"Nothing happened?" he asked me in disbelief.

"We kissed and stuff, but..." I took a deep breath. "I couldn't go through with it."

He kept his eyes on me as I took a step closer.

"Why?" he asked. His tone was softer than it had been before.

I didn't like that my feelings for him made me so vulnerable to him, but there was no hiding how I felt about him now.

"He wasn't you," I admitted in a whisper.

I was scared of how he would react. His feelings for me might not be strong enough to look past the fact I'd tried to move on—even if I hadn't been able to fully go through with it.

Chapter Twelve

He kept silent while studying me. There—I'd done it. I'd opened up, and he was doing nothing! Anger flared up in me and my temper snapped.

"This is all your fault!" I yelled at him, putting a hand to my chest to ease the ache inside.

"What's my fault?" he asked softly, still watching me. Why wasn't he yelling back? Instead, he was calmly watching me with hooded eyes.

"Because before you...I'd never felt this way!" I screamed. I felt like I was going to explode from the emotions and pain I was suffering through.

And then he had the stupidity—or audacity—to smirk at me. I fisted my hands at my sides, not allowing myself the pleasure of wiping it off his face.

"You still care," he said. Shock hit me when I realized in the heat of the moment I'd admitted to still feeling something for him. *Damn it!*

"What does it matter?" I asked hoarsely, suddenly feeling tired from the emotional rollercoaster I was riding.

"It matters."

He moved closer and I looked up at him nervously. Before, it had been easier to care for him, but it was different now. I'd trusted him and he'd hurt me.

"So what do you want?" he asked. His eyes pierced me right down to my soul. I could lie but he would see through it. I didn't want to say the words out loud. I pressed my lips together, not wanting to admit it.

After a minute's silence I still refused to answer.

"If you can't tell me what you want I can't give it to you," he stated firmly and crossed his arms. He was being an asshole and I wanted to storm out of his room, but I couldn't ignore my feelings anymore.

Why did he want me to admit it out loud again? I already had.

"You know what I want," I said. I crossed my arms as I glared at him.

"I need to hear you say it," he said.

Annoyance and determination mixed together in my mind. I squared my shoulders and lifted my chin slightly. I wasn't one to back down and I wasn't going to start now.

"I want you," I ground out. There—I'd said it. He smiled and took a step closer to me.

"Just physically?" he asked. I felt my stubborn streak kick in, refusing to let me answer him.

"You want what we had before," he reminded me.

He was right. As much as I didn't want to admit it I did want what we'd shared.

"I want you," he admitted. I could see the emotion in his eyes. He closed the distance between us.

I looked up at him as his eyes searched mine. He hadn't touched me yet but I felt the chemistry between us make my heart quicken. He reached out and took my hand in his. His touch made my skin tingle and my stomach flutter.

"We have to build something new and the only way we can do that is if you can forgive me," he explained. I bit my lower lip as I contemplated what he said. There was still too much anger for me to simply say "You're forgiven" and mean it. It would take time to be able to truly move through it.

"Can you forgive me, Sarah?" he asked me softly. His eyes searched mine.

"I want to but I don't know if I can," I answered, trying to be as honest as possible.

"I'm sorry I hurt you," he said, pulling me closer so he could wrap his arms around me to hug me. I breathed him in as he hugged me tight. For a moment I allowed my walls to come down and to enjoy the reassurance his closeness gave me.

"I will never lie to you again," he assured me, pulling away slightly. I could see he meant what he said but the problem was that he'd hurt me already.

"It will take time," I said. I didn't want to spoil the moment we were having but I couldn't just lie and say everything would be okay; there was a chance that despite all our attempts we wouldn't be able to put ourselves back together.

"I can live with that," he said with a broadening smile. He hadn't looked this happy in a while, and it was strange that it made me happy.

He leaned closer and kissed me gently. I reached for the sides of his face, holding myself close so that I could control the kiss. Slowly he pulled away and leaned his forehead against mine.

"You put me through hell," he whispered. I got a glimpse of the havoc I'd caused in him over the last couple of days and I felt a bit guilty I'd caused his sadness. But then I remembered how he'd deceived me and it was difficult to stop myself from allowing the hurt to pull me away from him again.

"But we're still not square," I said, and he gave me a questioning look.

"What you did was horrible and you hurt me," I added softly.

"I never meant to deceive you the way I did. Circumstances made it inevitable. I'll make it up to you," he assured me.

"You'd better," I said, trying to lighten the heavy atmosphere. "You can start now."

He gave me a knowing smile. I felt the impact of it on me as I tingled under his gaze.

"And what exactly do you want me to do now?" he asked coyly.

"There are a lot of things I want you to do to me," I said, confident in what I wanted and needed. "But you can start off with kissing me."

He didn't need to be told twice. He pulled me closer and his mouth covered mine. I groaned as his lips moved against mine. I reached up on my tiptoes to put my hands around his neck as his tongue slid into my mouth. Pulling him closer, he deepened the kiss and I was left breathless when he broke it.

"I've missed you," he whispered against my lips.

His eyes caressed me as his fingers touched my cheek. He couldn't have missed me physically too much, because we'd been together not so long ago. But emotionally I'd frozen him out since I'd discovered his secret—was that what he meant?

"Don't fuck it up, Mr. Weiss," I said to him in a slightly teasing tone that didn't mask the seriousness of what I was saying. "No more lying."

"No more secrets," he assured me.

Even though it couldn't be completely wiped clean I did

feel some of the burden I'd been carrying lift off my shoulders. For the first time since our relationship had unraveled, I felt hope that we would make it back to where I'd been at my happiest.

I reached out and touched his cheek. I didn't do affection often—but in that moment, standing in front of him with our gazes locked together, I needed him to know I cared. At times, more than I wanted to.

"No more secrets," I echoed.

He cupped the nape of my neck as he brought his lips against mine. I sighed, loving how he made me come alive beneath his touch.

"I want you," I rasped when his lips broke from mine. My heart was hammering in my chest and my body vibrated with a need for him.

"You have me," he whispered before he lifted me off my feet and carried me to his bed.

This time wasn't the same as the last time we'd been together. The previous time I'd concentrated on more of the physical side of things and my raging hormones. This time it wasn't like that. His actions were soft and gentle—like he didn't want to break me—and I savored every moment of it.

After, when we lay breathing hard next to each other, I couldn't stop the pull at my heartstrings when I looked at him.

I wanted this to work so badly but the fear he would hurt me again kept me from allowing that feeling to grow.

Time. I needed time.

The next couple of days passed. The sex was awesome but being able to try and work through our issues made me more relaxed than I'd been since our breakup. We didn't need to just pretend to be together anymore. We were still far from being completely past the betrayal, but I was willing to give him a chance to show me I could trust him again.

Zac gave me a couple of interested looks and he flashed me a seductive smile that did nothing for me. He couldn't compare to how Matthew made me feel. I ignored him until he eventually lost interest. He hadn't been my best decision and I wouldn't be knocking on that door again.

Matthew watched Zac like a hawk initially—and a couple of times he openly glared at him—but when he realized I was only interested in him and no one else, he began to relax. We were making our way back to how we used to be, except this time we were sharing the same apartment. We'd gone back to sleeping in my bed. I hadn't realized how much I'd missed it until I woke up snug in his arms.

That morning I didn't want to get up and go to school. I was in bed with Matthew, my head resting on his chest with his one arm around me.

"Can't we just stay here?" I asked, not wanting to get out of bed. It didn't help that it was slightly overcast.

He pressed a kiss to my forehead.

"You have class today," he reminded me. *As if I could forget*, I thought. I peered up at him and rested my chin on my hands.

"I know. But I'd rather stay here with you," I explained to him, giving him a seductive smile to ensure he knew we would be doing many more activities if we stayed.

A laugh rumbled through his chest and he kissed me.

"Come on," he said, shifting out of bed. The loss of warmth made me glare playfully at him.

"I could make it worth your while," I tried—one last attempt to persuade him to stay. He shook his head, flashing me a smile as he pulled up his jeans and fastened them.

"You're no fun," I told him as I sat up. He walked over to the bed and for a moment I thought he might change his mind, but he leaned down to kiss my cheek.

"You have thirty minutes to get dressed," he instructed me before he left my bedroom.

Realizing I wasn't going to be able to change his mind, I got out of bed. I got some clothes out of my wardrobe and had a shower before I got dressed. I was busy putting on a little makeup when I felt eyes on me. My eyes connected with Matthew's in the mirror.

"You know you're beautiful without all of that stuff," he said. I smiled at him.

My heart warmed at his words. It was ridiculous how a comment like that could make me feel so much for him. My feelings for him seemed to grow every moment I spent with him.

"Thanks," I said. I didn't use a lot; I put on some lipstick and mascara. Once I was finished I surveyed myself in the mirror.

"Beautiful," he whispered from behind me. I turned to face him.

"You're not too bad yourself," I said with a teasing smile.

"Say what you want. I know I rock your world," he said confidently. I bit back a laugh.

He was right. But not only did he make my world tilt when he kissed me, he also made my heart swell with emotion. There were still moments when I thought about his betrayal and it was difficult to completely forget about it. It was going to take time. It was strange—I trusted him with my life and yet I couldn't trust him with my heart. Some wounds couldn't be fixed with bandages and medicine.

On our way to college I felt his hand cover mine. I smiled at him. As hesitant as I was to give him a second chance I was glad I had. But there was still a part of me that held on to doubt.

Matthew was his usual reserved and occupied self, paying attention to every detail. When we got to the campus we got out of the car and walked to the spot we normally met up with Courtney. I glanced down at my watch to check the time. Courtney wasn't in the usual spot waiting for us. That was unlike her; I figured maybe she overslept or was running late.

Matthew glanced down at his watch before his eyes scanned the sea of students moving around us. He looked agitated and preoccupied, but I didn't ask questions.

Once we were seated in our first class of the day, he grabbed his phone and typed a message. I frowned. There was definitely something up.

"What's wrong?" I asked in a hushed whisper, watching him anxiously. Did it have to do with Courtney being a no-show? I couldn't stop the anxiety from building up in me.

He looked at me, masking any emotions he may have been feeling. He didn't have to answer my question. His eyes said everything. There was something wrong.

"Courtney?" I questioned, trying not to let my thoughts go wild before I knew there was something to worry about.

"I'm not sure," he whispered.

I swallowed as the lecturer started the class. Any questions I had would have to sit until the class was finished.

I tried to concentrate on what the lecturer was saying— but it was impossible. My thoughts were already starting to run wild with possibilities. I threw a couple of glances at Matt, hoping to be able to read his expression, but I couldn't. I was annoyed and agitated by the time the class had finished.

Just outside the classroom I pulled him to one side.

"Tell me," I demanded. His eyes held mine reluctantly. He didn't want to tell me, but I wasn't going to let this slide.

"I don't know anything yet," he revealed, and I felt

myself tense up.

"You're worried about Courtney," I said, and he nodded.

"I've sent Mark by to check on her at her apartment," he told me.

"How do you know where she lives?" I asked. He'd never been to her place.

"It's my job to know."

"She could just be running late—or...maybe she overslept," I rationalized. I didn't want to think that something worse than that could have happened to her.

His phone started to ring and he got it out and answered it.

"Okay. Stay there," he ordered.

I felt my stomach fill with dread. He wasn't revealing any emotions but it didn't take a rocket scientist to figure out something wasn't right.

He paused. "She isn't there," he said slowly.

"But that doesn't mean something happened to her—" I started.

"We need to go back to the apartment," he said, cutting me off. He took me by the hand and led me toward the exit, ignoring the looks from the other students. Still feeling a little stunned, I allowed him to tug me by the hand to the car before I yanked my hand out of his grip.

"Stop it," I said, refusing to move another step.

He sighed out loud and then ran a hand through his hair.

"It might have something do with you or it might not. We can't take any chances," he explained.

I didn't have a good feeling about this, so I allowed him to secure me in the passenger seat before closing the door and going around the car to get into the driver's side.

A heavy silence settled between us on the way back to the apartment. Did Matthew really believe this had something to do with me? Was that why he was so quick to get me back to the apartment safely? Had something really bad happened to Courtney? Did this have something to do with the people Matthew was protecting me from?

I bit down on my nail as I gazed out of the window, trying to keep control over my overwhelming thoughts. I had to think positive and I had to believe this was a coincidence.

Thinking it could have something to do with me made me feel guilty. For the first time I was glad to have the protection of a bodyguard.

I glanced at him for a moment. A bodyguard I couldn't let anything happen to.

Chapter Thirteen

Time seemed to slow down as we anxiously waited for any news about Courtney. Ten minutes felt like an hour and I kept glancing at my watch, but it wouldn't speed up the wait. Matthew prowled around the apartment like a caged lion and I sat on the sofa biting my nails. He held his phone in his hand, waiting for news.

"Do you think the people who are after me might have taken her?" I asked quietly, trying to wrap my mind around what was happening.

He stopped pacing and turned to face me. He knelt in front of me and took my hands in his.

"They might have," he answered.

"But...I don't understand," I mumbled, feeling the guilt that something might have happened to her because she was my friend. It was hard to comprehend.

He reached up and caressed my cheek with his hand.

"We don't know anything at the moment. Let's wait

until we find her before we start speculating," he suggested, but I could see he didn't believe for one moment her disappearance didn't have something to do with me.

He gave me an encouraging smile. I tried to return the smile but I could barely force the tips of my lips upward. It was hard to pretend on the outside what I didn't feel inside.

"She might have gone out and met someone and stayed over at their place," he said dubiously. That didn't sound like Courtney at all.

Instead of arguing with him, I nodded my head. Courtney wasn't one to go out during the week. I'd known her since high school and this was completely out of character for her.

In our tight-knit group from high school we were the only ones who had attended the same college. Although we still kept in touch with our other friends, Courtney and I had always been closer to each other than we had been to the rest of our group.

Matthew stood up and began to pace again. Unable to watch him walk up and down the length of the room one more time, I got up.

"Are you okay?" he asked.

I nodded tiredly. "I just need to lay down a little," I said. The truth was I needed space—and watching him worry wasn't helping me.

Inside the quiet of my room, I slumped down on my bed. I tried to think back to the last time I'd seen her and I tried to remember if she'd said anything about going away. But I couldn't remember anything. The last time I'd seen her I'd been too consumed with my own situation with Matt. Feeling bad I'd been so wrapped up in my own life when my friend may have been in danger, I lay down on the bed and covered my eyes with my arm.

I had to believe she would be okay when we found her,

because I couldn't think of a different scenario. It was too hard to.

My phone rang, and I sat up quickly. It was my father.

"Hi," I answered softly.

"Sarah," he said in his usual deep tone. Did he know about Courtney? "Matthew called."

I kept silent, not trusting myself to keep it together.

"I'm sure Courtney will be fine," he assured me when I kept quiet.

"I hope so." I said the words not believing them at all, but the other options were too terrible to contemplate.

"Your mom wants to talk to you," he said. I heard some background noise as he handed the phone to her.

"Sarah." Her voice brought my emotions back up to the top and I took a deep breath. "She'll be fine."

I couldn't answer her. I pressed the phone tighter to my ear, refusing to allow myself to cry.

"Mom..." I was struggling to keep myself calm.

"I know."

Our call ended soon after that. I was too upset to try and continue the conversation. For a while I lay on my bed, staring at the ceiling, hoping we were all overreacting and that Courtney would show up finding it hard to believe we'd all worried so much.

The sound of Matthew's phone ringing made me hold my breath as I strained to hear what he was saying. I couldn't make anything out so I shifted off the bed and walked into the living room.

His expression said it all. I felt like someone had ripped the carpet from beneath my feet. I couldn't breathe as I waited for him to say something. His phone was still pressed to his ear.

"I'll see you there," he said, and I began to feel a little dizzy because I couldn't exhale.

He disconnected the call and walked to me.

"You found her," I croaked out.

He nodded.

"Is she alive?" It was the most important question. Was my friend alive? It felt like I had a vise gripping my heart and squeezing it tight.

"Yes," he said and I felt my knees weaken. He wrapped an arm around my waist and pulled me close as I fisted his shirt in my hands, holding on to him desperately.

"Sit down," he instructed, and I felt him sit me down on the sofa. I felt dazed and shocked.

He bent down in front of me.

"I'm going to get you something to drink," he said. His voice sounded like it was coming from far away, as if he were in a tunnel. I nodded my head. I didn't really take what he'd said in. Moments later he shoved a glass into my hands. "Drink."

It tasted like water with some sugar. It didn't taste very nice but I forced myself to gulp a couple of sips down.

"It'll help with the shock," he soothed as he sat beside me. I took a couple more sips before I handed it back to him.

I had to pull myself together. Questions were racing through my mind but the most important thing was if I could see her.

"I need to see her," I said, standing up. My need to make sure Courtney was okay made me pull myself together and discard the shock and confusion.

"Sure," Matthew said, leading the way to the front door. He led me to the car. He helped me in and fastened my seatbelt before he got into the driver's side.

I could have asked Matthew more questions about how Courtney had been found but honestly I didn't think I could handle the answers. There wasn't time to break down and get emotional. My friend needed me, and I had to hold myself together for her. I would be able to deal with the answers and my feelings later.

Every few minutes Matthew would look at me, but I refused to acknowledge him. When he pulled up in front of the hospital I began to shake. It was all so real and I wasn't sure I had the strength to do what I needed to.

"I'm here." Soft words and an arm around my waist gave me the strength to put one foot in front of the other and walk into the hospital.

Matthew knew exactly where to go.

The sterile smell of the building hit me as the elevator's doors opened. I was numb. It was a reminder people died all the time, and it wasn't something I wanted to be reminded of at the moment.

Mark was there, standing in a small waiting area. His worried look did nothing to ease the fear building up inside me.

"Where is she?" Matthew asked him.

"The doctor is examining her."

My focus was on the red stains on his shirt.

"Is that...?"

I reached out and nearly touched the red mark on his shirt. I couldn't finish the sentence. *Oh. My. God.*

It was blood. It was Courtney's blood.

The realization hit me in the chest and I stopped breathing. My heard started to spin and it felt like I was hearing voices echoing from down a tunnel. That was the moment I felt everything start to spin out of control, and the panicked voices in the background disappeared as I fainted.

When I started to come around, I felt disoriented. I groaned as my hand touched my head.

"It's okay," someone said soothingly. It was Matthew, his voice strong and comforting.

I opened my eyes to see his concerned expression.

"You're awake," he said softly and he gave me a smile, showing his dimples as he looked down at me. *I love those dimples*, I thought absently.

I tried to remember what had happened. When I remembered that Courtney had been missing and the blood on Mark's shirt, I suddenly tried to move.

"Take it easy," Matthew instructed as he shifted me off his lap and slowly helped me upright. He stayed beside me as I tried to get my bearings.

A quick look around the room revealed that we were still in the waiting room. Mark had gone.

"Where's Mark?" I asked, feeling panicked.

"He went to find out if there is any news on Courtney," he explained, watching me carefully.

Courtney. The blood.

I felt a feeling of dread spread through my stomach. I put my face into my hands, unable to deal with the guilt that something had happened to her because of me. What if she didn't make it? I shook the thought from my mind. There would be no way for me to deal with that. Matthew's hand rested gently on my back. I looked at him.

"I can't..." I began to say, and then I felt the sting of tears and I was unable to complete the sentence. He put his arm around my shoulders and pulled me close. I rested my head against his strong chest, allowing myself to feel all the emotions that were swirling up inside of me.

"She'll be okay," he said, consoling me even though we hadn't heard from the doctors yet.

I took comfort in his words even though there was no possible way he could know that. It was easier to fixate on the positive possibility that she would be okay rather than try and process the fact she might not. I wasn't a coward by nature but this time I was taking the easier route.

Mark appeared in the waiting room and I pulled away. My eyes fixed on him, making sure not to focus on the bloodstains on his shirt. I was too scared to ask, so I waited for him to say something.

He looked serious as he came to stop in front of us.

"How is she?" Matt asked with his arm still around me.

"She has been beaten up pretty good, but the doctor reckons there aren't any serious injuries, only superficial wounds," he explained. I felt better immediately—never in my life had I felt so relieved.

"She'll have to spend a few days in the hospital just for observation," he added.

"Can I see her?" I asked, standing up. I needed to see her injuries with my own eyes.

"The nurses are just cleaning her up so you will have to wait to see her," he said.

I nodded. "Thank you," I said.

"You're welcome."

"What happened?" I asked, needing more details although I was scared to know the full story.

Mark looked to Matthew and Matthew gave him a slight nod as he stood up beside me, as if to give him permission to tell me the details. Maybe he was concerned with how I was going to handle it because so far I hadn't handled things well at all.

Fainting had made me seem so weak.

"I can take it," I added, straightening my shoulders, preparing for the added weight of the guilt.

"When I didn't find her at her apartment, I started to call the nearby hospitals to find out if anyone with her description had been admitted. When they told me a girl with that description had been brought here I came straight through."

Oh, my God! Where had they taken her from? More importantly, what had they done to her? I wanted to be brave enough to ask, but I wasn't. Maybe it was a good thing I couldn't see her yet. It gave me time to pull myself together.

"Did anyone see who brought her in?" Matthew asked. Mark shook his head.

"I've spoken to hospital security and I'm trying to get access to their video surveillance."

In most cases any normal person would have been too freaked out to be able to take note of the type of stuff that they would. I sat down, finding it difficult to process what he'd just told us. Why on earth would they take her only to hurt her and then leave her at the hospital? It didn't seem to add up.

Matthew and Mark began to talk softly between themselves and I was still trying to wrestle with my feelings of guilt when the nurse walked into the waiting room.

"You can see her now," she said to Mark.

"Thanks," Mark said.

I took Matthew's hand and held on tightly as we walked to her room. When we got there, I released Matthew's hand and I hesitated in the doorway. I wasn't sure how bad her injuries were going to be and I was trying to mentally prepare myself so that I didn't get hysterical or too upset. *Be strong for Courtney*, I thought as I took the first step into her room.

The sight of her hit me like a brick wall and I tried my best to keep my emotions hidden from my face. She looked so fragile in bed. Her eyes were closed. It was hard to look at every bruise that marred her skin. Instead of fear, I felt anger at the actions of the people who had done this to her.

Mark stood on the other side of her bed with his attention fixed on Courtney. I reached for her hand gently and held it, trying to swallow down my shock at the sight of her. I felt Matthew standing behind me and I was relieved he was there. Even though I'd been independent for most of my life, I liked having someone to lean on.

My eyes went to her face and her eyes fluttered open.

"Hi," I said softly, my eyes stinging.

Her eyes began to water, too, and I leaned close, trying to hug her without hurting her more. She sobbed and I held her, feeling her pain vibrate though me. Every tear tore through me reinforcing the weight of my guilt on my shoulders.

Finally her tears eased and I let her go.

"You're safe now," I said softly.

"I don't know why they did this to me," she said in a hoarse whisper, and I looked over my shoulder at Matthew. He had an unreadable expression.

I had no idea why the same guys who were threatening me had gone after my friend. Was it their way of getting to me? Was there something else behind this? Not wanting to draw this out in the open in front of Courtney, I turned back to brush the remains of her tears away from her face.

"You'll be okay," I said, trying not to think of the faceless people who could have done this to an innocent girl. The only reason they could have gone after her was because of me.

Courtney was so shaken up by the events that the nurses decided to sedate her. I didn't want to leave her but Matthew steered me out of her room. Mark followed behind us.

"Her family has been informed and they are on their way. Mark will stay here with her," Matthew told me when I tried to pull free from him.

I looked at Mark.

"You promise you won't let anything happen to her?" I asked, needing him to say the words out loud to me.

"Yes," he answered, holding my gaze without wavering for a moment. "I won't let anything happen to her."

"Okay," I said, suddenly feeling tired. The stress of the whole situation had caught up with me.

"I'll check in with you later," Matthew said to Mark.

Mark nodded and then went back into the room with Courtney. I felt dead on my feet, and when I got into the car, I yawned.

"I'll have you home soon," Matthew assured me as he started up the engine.

Chapter Fourteen

By the time I entered the apartment behind Matthew, I was exhausted. Without a word I walked into the room, kicked off my shoes and climbed onto my bed. I studied the ceiling, hoping it would help calm the fear and chaos inside. I wasn't one to be scared easily—but what had happened to Courtney had created a deep-seated fear I was struggling to cope with. It felt like my world was spinning out of control and I couldn't do anything to stop it.

The sound of footsteps outside my room made me look to see Matthew leaning in the doorway. He looked at me with concern. It wasn't something I was used to and I didn't like that I felt so weak and vulnerable.

"I need to make some phone calls," he said softly. I nodded.

He seemed to realize I needed space because he left me alone in my room. In the background I could hear the steadiness of his voice as he talked to someone. I couldn't make out the words and I wasn't sure I wanted to.

I closed my eyes and all I could see was Courtney's badly beaten face and the fear in her eyes. Suddenly it felt like I couldn't breathe, so I sat up. Feeling panicked, I breathed in deeply and my lungs opened up. I'd always been in control and to feel so scared went against who I was. I stood up and began to pace the room, needing to figure a way to get myself together. I didn't understand why the bad people who were after me had hurt my friend—why would they do that?

No matter how much I racked my brain I couldn't answer the question.

I decided taking a shower would maybe help keep my mind from concentrating on Courtney's attack. Maybe keeping my mind busy with simple tasks would push the unwanted thoughts from my mind.

Stripping off my clothes in the bathroom, I tried not to think, but it was nearly impossible. Even inside my shower with the warm water running down my body I couldn't stop the images of Courtney from flashing through my mind. I leaned my head against the cool tiles of the shower trying to get a handle on myself, but no matter how hard I tried I couldn't stop the fear from overwhelming me.

By the time I made it out of the shower, I was a mess. I wrapped a towel around my body. Being alone wasn't working so I went looking for Matthew. Still with only the towel wrapped around my damp body, I found him staring out the window of the apartment. At the sound of my soft footsteps against the wooden floor he turned to look at me.

For a moment he studied me when I stopped a few feet away from him. His hands were in his pockets as his eyes swept over my face. Water dripped onto the floor but I didn't care.

I couldn't put my feelings into words to explain to him what was going on inside of me. His eyes held mine as he watched me quietly. Maybe he was trying to figure out why I was standing in front of him wearing only a towel. This wasn't about seduction, this was about needing some sort of comfort.

He took his hands out of his pockets and he stepped forward. One step and then another brought him closer, closing the distance between us until finally he stopped in front of me and cupped my face. His eyes held mine.

"It's okay," he said gently, as if sensing my vulnerable state.

I closed my eyes for a moment, savoring the feel of his soft touch to my skin. Being so close to him had eased the destructive emotions taking control of me and it had given me a moment of peace. His thumb gently brushed my cheek and I opened my eyes. All thoughts I'd struggled to push from my mind faded into the background and all I could concentrate on was the man in front of me, and how he made me feel, emotionally and physically.

"Tell me what you need," he murmured.

In that instant I knew exactly what I needed. My hands released the towel and I stood in front of him naked. I didn't need to explain what I wanted from him in words. He released me gently, his eyes taking in the action and he stilled.

"I need you," I said. There was no mistaking what I was talking about. There was a vulnerable quality to my voice, and he looked like he was struggling with what to do.

"Is this what you want?" he asked gently.

It wasn't about sex—it was being close to someone in the most intense way. Being with him made me think of nothing else but him. He also had a calming effect on me that helped soothe the emotions I was struggling with.

"Yes," I said breathlessly.

He stepped forward and touched my arms. I tilted my face up to his as he leaned closer and kissed me.

My hands slid around his neck as his lips moved against mine. His hands moved to my waist and he pulled me closer. Gasping at the intensity of the kiss, I opened my mouth slightly and he took full advantage, sliding his tongue into my mouth. He gently swirled it against mine and I felt myself tremble.

I was still holding on to him tightly when he pulled back slightly, breaking the heated kiss. His eyes were dark as his eyes found mine.

"Are you sure?" he asked. My answer was to lift myself onto my tiptoes and press my lips to his. I needed him like I needed air; without him I could shrivel up and die at any moment.

He lifted me up bridal-style and carried me to his room. I held on to him like a lifeline that I would die without. He put me on his bed and stepped back for a moment. His eyes feasted over my naked form, taking in each soft curve.

"You're beautiful," he whispered in awe.

He stripped his clothes away and I felt my breath hitch when I looked at his naked form. He was beautiful from the hard curves of his stomach to the lean muscles in his arms. My eyes ravished him. He knelt onto the bed and I lifted myself up to meet his lips with mine. His hand cupped the nape of my neck as our mouths moved together, caressing and nipping.

My heart was thumping rapidly in my chest as his body moved over mine. His hard muscles moved against my soft curves. His mouth slid against my neck and he gently nipped below my ear. I felt the fire inside of me burn out of control, and all I could do was hold on to the hope he would end it soon. I had to have him.

His soft touches and the gentle movement of his wet tongue against my skin made me quiver with want.

"I need you now," I whispered. He stopped and lifted his

head. Our eyes met and I felt our attraction pull us closer together.

The warmth of his body covered me. His body fit perfectly against mine.

He studied me with an intense look that made me want to pull him closer to kiss him. His hardness nudged at me and I groaned as he slid into me in one hard thrust. My lips parted for a moment, feeling the fullness of his body's connection with mine. There were no thoughts, no fear. The only thing that mattered was the intense physical feeling of being thoroughly loved by him.

I savored every moment, every touch. Sweat covered our bodies as we moved together with one goal in mind: reaching the point we both craved. I gasped as I felt a wave of pleasure crash over me, making my whole body tense slightly and then tremble. Closing my eyes for a moment, I enjoyed the feel of my release.

Matthew held my hips in place with his hands and he pushed into me one last time. I groaned at the sensitive action. I felt him stiffen for a moment—and then he kissed me as he came.

Breathing hard, we stayed that way, his body pressed into mine as I wrapped my arms around him. Loving the feel of him covering me like a protective shield, I closed my eyes and let myself feel the intensity of my emotions.

It pushed the darkness inside of me away and I felt a peacefulness settle over me.

Then it struck me. I loved him. I wrapped my arms around him and held him for a moment at the realization of how much he meant to me.

He rolled off me and onto his back. His arms pulled me closer and I lay in them, enjoying the moment we'd just shared.

It wouldn't last forever, but I would enjoy it for as long

as I could. I couldn't run from my fear and I would have to face it at some point. I looked at Matt and he pressed a kiss to my lips.

But I didn't have to face it alone. He was there to protect me as my bodyguard. His job was to make sure I was safe. His feelings me for me protected me emotionally, too. The fear didn't seem too bad when he was there to carry it with me.

For most of the night I couldn't sleep. Even in the safety of Matthew's arms and with his soothing deep breathing I couldn't seem to relax enough to nod off. I stared at the ceiling in the darkness, trying to calm my thoughts down. I needed to put my mind at ease long enough to get some much-needed sleep.

Finally, in the early morning, I fell into a troubled sleep.

I was standing outside one of my classes waiting for Matthew. It was strange because he was usually in every one of my classes. I looked up and saw him walking toward me.

He smiled as he walked, slowly coming closer to me. My heart filled with my love for him; I felt it lift me a little higher and make me happy. He was so hot and he was all mine. A smile that reflected my inner feelings spread across my face as I held my books to my chest.

Then suddenly the atmosphere changed, and the light started to darken. Matthew, just a few steps in front of me, stopped. Something nagged at the back of my mind, telling me something wasn't right.

Fear gripped me when I looked at him. In that same moment I heard a loud bang. Unsure of what the noise was, I looked around, not seeing anyone else but the two of us. My eyes shot back to Matthew.

Horror filled me at the sight of a dark crimson stain that marked his shirt. It continued to grow as he dropped to his knees. I ran to him. Dropping to my knees beside him, I laid him on the cold floor, not understanding what was happening.

"Please! Please!" I begged over and over again. My hand went to his wound to stop the bleeding but no matter what I did the blood flowed freely from his body into a pool of blood around us. I had to try and stop the bleeding—if I didn't he would bleed to death.

"Stay with me," I told him while I put both of my hands to his wound in the middle of his chest.

I looked up to see a tall, dark figure, who was faceless, holding a gun.

"That bullet was meant for you," the stranger said to me before he faded away into the darkness.

Scared and shocked, I held on to Matthew, begging him not to leave me. He took one shuddering breath—and then there was nothing. His eyes stared at me, unseeing.

"NO!" I screamed, not being able to cope with what I was seeing. I couldn't comprehend it. I threw myself across him and held him desperately as I screamed till my throat hurt. The tears began to slide down my face as I held him, not wanting to ever let go.

It couldn't be true. He couldn't be dead.

I shot up in the bed, breathing hard. It was dark and I looked around frantically, trying to get my bearings.

"It's okay, it was just a dream," a familiar voice said. Strong arms pulled me to a hard chest while my body trembled from the remnants of the nightmare I was still trying to process.

"Matthew."

When I remembered what happened in the dream, I threw my arms around him, pulling him so close, needing to assure myself he was okay—letting reality sink into my mind, which was still reeling from the horrid nightmare.

"You...w-were..." I couldn't finish the sentence. If I spoke it out loud it would make it more real.

"I'm okay," he assured me, hugging tightly.

I pulled away and in the darkness I moved my hands over his chest to make sure there was no injury. There was no wound bleeding his life source from his body. The dream had felt so real that I could still feel the blood covering my hands. I felt relief flood through me, leaving me breathless. It had felt so real.

"It was just a nightmare," he told me softly. I nodded shakily. In my dream he'd died, and that wasn't something I could shake off easily.

Afterward, Matthew held me, but I couldn't stop the image of his dead eyes staring up at me. Fear shivered through me.

It had been a dream—but he was my bodyguard and there were bad people after me. His job was to protect me with his life. Had my subconscious brought my deep-seated fears into my dreams? Matthew lay behind me with his arm around my waist, holding me close. My hand rested on his arm, I found that the small action reassured me he was still alive and beside me.

The attack on Courtney had made me fear what could happen to Matthew. The people who were after me were real and they wouldn't mess around. Just remembering how badly Courtney had been beaten left me with no doubt they would kill to get to me.

It had all become so real.

I wanted to ignore the thought, but I couldn't. If they came after me and Matthew got in their way, there was no doubt in my mind now that they would kill him. Just the thought of it made me remember the heart-wrenching pain that had felt like it was tearing me in half. That pain wasn't something I could deal with.

Matthew went back to sleep. His deep, regular breathing was comforting. Remembering the last breath he'd taken in my nightmare had been the worst sound ever.

I remained wide awake. Later I crept from the room as quietly as I could so I didn't wake him. I made myself a cup of coffee and I sat down in the kitchen, trying to figure out how I could stop my dream from becoming a reality.

It wasn't long before I heard footsteps enter the kitchen. I looked up to see Matthew standing in the doorway. He looked so effortlessly gorgeous with his messy bed-hair and his sweats hanging low on his hips. My eyes swept over him and I felt the pull he held over me. The physical attraction I felt mingled with my love for him.

"Did you get any more sleep?" he asked, walking to me. I shook my head, still holding my mug with both hands.

He pressed a kiss to my cheek and I felt a flutter of my attraction to him. Even with my heavy thoughts it was hard not to respond to the way he made me feel with one intense look.

"What did you dream about?" he asked with a slight look of concern on his face as he scanned my features.

I didn't want to be reminded about my nightmare. Even hours later it was still hard to think about. When I didn't answer, he lifted my eyes to his with his finger to my chin. I put my mug down.

"It really freaked you out," he said, a crease forming in his forehead.

I pulled away from him, needing to distance myself from him. I turned my back to him while I gripped the kitchen counter.

"Don't shut me out," he said, standing behind me. He was so close I could feel his presence. "Talk to me."

He reached for me and turned me to face him.

"Tell me," he said firmly. His eyes held mine.

"You died," I whispered, feeling the emotions I'd felt when the moment had played out in my nightmare.

Understanding spread through his features.

"It was just a nightmare," he reminded me. He wrapped his arms around me, and I held on to him. I wanted him to be able to wipe the horrors from my memory, but he couldn't. The dream had tapped into my subconscious thoughts that had been planted by the attack on Courtney.

Just thinking of her made the guilt fill me. It was my fault she'd been attacked and I was struggling with that. No one I cared about was safe, especially not the bodyguard I'd fallen for. What had happened to Courtney was only the beginning.

I leaned my head against his chest while he rubbed my back gently. In my mind I was already making the decision to keep him from getting hurt. I would never be able to live with myself if something happened to him while he was trying to protect me.

Chapter Fifteen

I pushed my decision to the back of my mind. My fear made me want to get as far away as possible from Matthew but my heart wouldn't let me let him go. I'd struggled with what to do, going around in circles, unable to make a choice.

The selfish part of me wanted me to hold on to him with both hands and never let him go, but the part of me that loved him and wanted to keep him safe made me want to push him away, so he wouldn't get hurt.

The choice was hard.

The guilt of Courtney's attack stayed with me as we went to the hospital the next day. I had to mentally prepare myself before I could face her again. To see her bruised face and know I was the reason why she looked how she did was a lot to contend with.

"You okay?" Matthew asked me when I hesitated for a moment before we entered the hospital.

I nodded my head, trying to keep the guilt from

overwhelming me. The slight pressure of his hand on the small of my back gave me the courage to walk into the hospital.

Mark was in the waiting room when we arrived.

"How's she doing?" Matthew asked him.

He shook his head, and I felt my blood run cold. Why was he shaking his head?

"She doesn't remember anything about the attack," he clarified when he saw my horrified expression. What did he mean she didn't remember anything? Just the day before they had given her a sedative to knock her out because she'd been so hysterical.

Matthew frowned.

"How's that possible?" I asked, not believing that the attack could have been forgotten overnight. Had she bumped her head?

"Sometimes when someone is experiencing a traumatic event that they can't handle," Matthew began to explain, "it's easier for the mind to block it out than to try and deal with it."

I needed to sit down. Matthew steered me to a seat and I sank down in it. I rubbed my temple, trying to pull myself together.

Matthew and Mark talked beside me while I took in the news. Then a thought popped in my mind.

"If she can't remember the attack, how do we know who did it?" I asked, feeling helpless.

"I got the hospital surveillance tapes, but I can't get a clear shot of the guy's face," Mark told me. That was no help at all.

"Do you actually know who is after me?" I asked, needing to give a face to the person who wanted me dead. This time my eyes were on Matthew. They shared a look before Matthew turned to face me. His expression wasn't a good sign.

"Yes," he answered, and I waited for him to elaborate. "We can talk about it once we've been to see Courtney."

The only reason I agreed to delay the talk was that I didn't want to get all worked up about it just before seeing my friend.

"Okay," I agreed.

"Her family is with her at the moment," Mark added, looking down the passage to where her room was located.

"Get someone to cover for you," Matthew instructed Mark. From what I'd gathered they ran their own security company with a handful of other bodyguards. They were probably going to get one of them to watch over Courtney so Mark could have a shower and get some sleep.

"I'll call you later," he said before he gave me a brief nod. He left and I turned my attention to Matthew.

"This is so messed up," was all I could say. My friend had been attacked because of me and it had been so bad she'd blocked out the memories. I couldn't imagine going through something like that, and it made it even more difficult to build myself up to face her.

We waited another five minutes in the waiting room to get a chance to see her—and then her parents walked into the waiting room.

"Mrs. Young," I said as I stood up to embrace her mom. Her mom hugged me. Her father gave Matt a brief nod before he gave me a hug of his own.

"She doesn't remember what happened," Mrs. Young told me.

"It might be for the best," I said, trying to look at the good side of forgetting her ordeal. Seeing her hysterical had been difficult. If forgetting the memory made it easier for her to handle it then I was all for it; although I was pretty sure she couldn't suppress it indefinitely. There would be a time it would come to the surface and I worried she wouldn't be able to cope with it then either.

"We don't have any idea what happened or why?" Mr. Young asked. The stress had made him look well beyond his age.

I looked to Matthew, unsure of what her parents had been told. I didn't want to say anything in case I revealed something I shouldn't. Matthew shook his head. I wanted to be honest with them and take responsibility for what had happened to their daughter—my friend—but I bit my lip and followed Matthew's lead.

"I'm so sorry," I said.

Her mother looked at me with a kind expression. "It wasn't your fault," she assured me, and I felt worse. She was wrong.

We left Courtney's parents when we went to the room to see her. I took a deep breath and released it just before I entered her hospital room. It was a total turnaround from the last time I'd seen her. Instead of being scared and shaking, she was sitting up and smiling as we entered.

"Sarah," she said and she beamed. I rushed over to her and hugged her gently enough to avoid aggravating her injuries.

"Courtney," I whispered as I held her for a few moments, making sure not to hug her too tight.

"I'm okay," she assured me, pulling away. "I'm a little bruised but other than that I'm fine."

It wasn't okay. She shouldn't have been attacked and landed in the hospital. I wasn't even sure if she'd been told any of the details about the attack before she'd pushed the memories from her mind. There was no point in discussing something she didn't remember—or, more importantly— didn't want to remember.

"Hey," she greeted Matthew, who was standing at the

foot of the hospital bed. He smiled at her.

"I'm glad you're okay," he said and walked to stand on the other side of the bed.

If I hadn't known he was a bodyguard, there was no way I would have suspected he was anything other than what he appeared to be. I couldn't stop the pang of betrayal at the fact he'd been good enough to fool me for a month. I tried to forget about it. We were starting off fresh and I had to learn to let go of it if we were ever going to make it.

"The doctor said I'll be out in a few days," she informed me. "This place is so boring."

I didn't want her to get out. I don't know why, but I felt she was safer inside the hospital than walking around where she could be taken again. My alarmed eyes found Matthew's. He shook his head slightly.

It was another thing we had to talk about when we were done at the hospital. My list of questions had formulated in my mind and Matthew had some answering to do. We spent another half an hour before the nurses informed us visiting hours were finished.

"I'll be back tomorrow," I assured her.

"Bring me some chocolates and something to read," she asked, and I smiled.

"I will."

One last hug and I walked out of the room feeling a little better. Maybe the fact she hadn't been so upset had eased my guilt a little.

"You handled that well," Matthew said, taking my hand into his as we walked to the elevators.

I shrugged. I wasn't so sure I had.

"We're going back to the apartment and you're going to answer some questions," I told him with a determined look. He nodded his head, accepting it was time for him to tell me everything he knew. There was no more avoiding it. I wanted to know who was after me and why they'd attacked Courtney.

I also needed to make sure Matthew was going to keep Mark watching over her. I wouldn't be able to live with myself if something else happened to her. The fear started to seep into me, and I tried to ignore it. It was one thing having a threat that never materialized, but after seeing what had been done to Courtney there was no way I could ignore it anymore.

I felt anxious and nervous when we got back to the apartment. The drive back had been quiet as we'd both been preoccupied with our own thoughts. It was time for all of my questions to be answered. No more ignoring the fact someone was after me and determined to get to me in any way they could. On the outside I was calm, but on the inside I was a mess.

Seeing my friend in the hospital, her face battered and bruised, had been enough to bring reality home.... I shuddered.

Matthew was quiet as I sat down on the sofa. He remained standing, watching me carefully. I could already see his mind ticking over what to tell me and how to tell me so I wouldn't freak out.

"It's time to tell me everything," I said, trying to keep myself calm. If I showed how truly scared I was, Matthew might not give me the entire truth—and that wasn't an option.

"Your parents didn't want you to know all the details," he began, and I listened intently, trying to calm my inner fear. There had to be a good reason my father had kept it from me and that scared me even more. He wanted to protect me like any father would want to protect his daughter.

"A new level of threats arose when your father took his new position."

I understood that. It was something my father had spoken to me about before he'd taken the promotion.

"You're not telling me anything I didn't know before," I said, wanting to hurry him up. He just needed to stop beating around the bush and tell me who was after me. I had to put a face to the person who'd taken my friend and beaten her up. I still didn't know the reason behind the attack, either.

"Your father put away a big-time criminal who had his hands in everything from illegal prostitution to selling narcotics," he said. "Marcus Cole was convicted and sentenced to a lifetime in prison."

I raised my eyebrows.

Seeing my questioning gaze, Matthew said, "He was also convicted on a murder charge."

It was like my life was playing out in some sort of crime movie about mob bosses and stuff. Murder—taking someone's life!

"Is he the one who is after me?" I asked, needing to know that information already.

He shook his head.

"There were so many threats before and obviously they'd increased with your father's profile. At first we weren't sure who was after you but we believe we have narrowed it to the most likely person."

"So who is it, then?" I asked, holding his gaze. I wouldn't show how scared I was on the inside.

"His son," he answered. "Nicolas Cole. We think it's about revenge."

And I was the object of his revenge. He was after me to get back at my father. It wasn't a surprise, but it still shook me to my core.

"So now that we know it was him, what do we do about it?" I asked. Surely there was a way to protect me and the people close to me, including Matthew.

"It's complicated and it'll take time," he answered.

I looked at him incredulously.

"How complicated can it be?"

I could feel my temper rising at the unfairness of the situation. People were responsible for their actions. They shouldn't be allowed to get away with what they'd done to Courtney—it had been so bad she'd blocked it out.

"We have no concrete evidence that links him to the attack. We can't identify the person who took Courtney to the hospital. There was no surveillance of her kidnapping, and without her memory we have nothing," he answered.

This couldn't be happening. I threw my hands up in the air in frustration. Standing up, I began to pace.

"Do we have to wait for him to be holding a gun to someone's head before we can convict him of anything?" I asked, feeling like I was drowning in the hopelessness of the situation.

"Something like that," he said. He didn't look happy about it either.

"And what happens if by some miracle that does happen? How do I know someone won't decide to take revenge for putting him behind bars?" I asked, my anger evident in the tone of my voice. It could be an endless circle with no end in sight, which meant I may never be safe.

"If Nick gets convicted then you'll be safe," he assured me. "Family is the only link in this revenge and if Nick is taken out of the picture, the next guy to take his place won't care about revenge. They'll be happy to take over his position. It's all about money and power."

I rubbed my head, trying to wrap my mind around what he'd just revealed to me.

"So you're saying as long as this Nick guy is walking the streets, my life and the lives of the people close to me are in danger?"

He nodded.

I let out a deep breath as I walked over to the window that overlooked the street in front of the apartment block. It was a lot to take in.

"But can't they still get their revenge from prison?" I asked, turning to face Matthew.

"Not likely if they don't have the people on the outside to carry it out."

"But this could go on for ages if my father can't get a conviction on him." I felt the hopelessness again at the idea that I could be a target for a long time. I would become a prisoner, not wanting to live my life for fear of him getting to me. And for fear of the people I loved being attacked.

"Why do you think they hurt Courtney?" I asked. I had a good idea of why but I needed him to confirm it.

"To scare you."

They had succeeded. I was petrified. I rubbed my hands over my face. It was so much to take in.

"I won't let anything happen to you," Matthew said, his voice moving closer to me. I lifted my eyes to see him standing in front of me, his expression concerned.

And that scared me as well. He could get caught up in this. I couldn't imagine how I would feel if anything happened to him while trying to protect me. It couldn't happen—somehow I had to make sure of that.

I let him take me into his arms and hold me close. He comforted me as my mind began to figure out how to keep him out of the mess I was in. I wouldn't be able to do that for my family—they were in as much danger as I was—but I had the ability to keep the guy I loved from getting caught up in it.

He pulled back slightly and lifted my chin. My eyes met his.

"I promise I won't let him get you," he assured me softly

with a confidence that told me he would put himself in harm's way to keep me alive. But I couldn't live with that. If something happened to him and I was responsible for it, I would never recover from it.

He pressed his lips to mine gently and I closed my eyes, savoring the feel of his lips against mine. I loved him. But did I love him enough to do whatever it took to keep him from getting hurt? Already my mind was trying to figure out how to take him out of my life.

He looked at me with the same love I felt for him. There was no way he would just walk away because I asked him to. Either I had to drive him away or make it impossible for him to stay. I could sleep with someone else and tell him he didn't mean anything to me anymore, but after everything we'd been through I knew I couldn't do that to him. I wanted to save him—not crush his heart. There had to be another way to do it.

"Do you trust me to keep you safe?" he asked, scanning my features.

I trusted him with my life.

"Yes," I answered.

That wasn't the problem. The problem was keeping *him* safe.

Chapter Sixteen

"I want to see a picture of him," I told Matthew. He seemed to contemplate my request for a few moments before he stood up.

I couldn't explain why I had the need to see the guy who was after me. Maybe it was because he might not seem as scary as the unidentified monster I had in my mind. I hoped it would make him less scary.

Matthew went into his room and he came out with a folder.

"Are you sure?" he asked me, and I frowned.

"Yes, I want to see him."

He reluctantly opened the folder and handed me a picture.

Any hope of it easing my fears vanished. Initially he hadn't been what I'd been expecting, but the closer I looked the more I realized it was worse than I could have imagined. Nick looked just a few years older than me, but the hardness in his features made him look much older. He was tall with dark black hair that reached just below his ears. Dressed in a suit, the photograph had been taken just as he was about to get into a limo. Even just looking at a picture of him made a shiver run through me. His eyes were his worst feature. The dark brown depths were empty.

It was like looking into the soul of someone who would do the worst things you could think of and not feel an ounce of guilt. There was no sign of humanity in him and that scared me the most. What was a human without a conscience?

I held the photo for a few more minutes before I gave it back to Matthew. When he went back into his room to put the folder away, I began to pace the room. I was agitated. I wished I hadn't seen a picture of him now.

"You'd better call your mother," Matthew said when he came back out of his room. "She's worried about you."

I turned to look out the window for a moment, taking a deep breath to push the fear from my body when I exhaled. A few more deep breaths eased the negative emotions and I turned to face Matthew, who was still standing behind me.

"I'll call her," I said before I walked past him to get my phone.

I went into my room and sat down on my bed as I searched for my mom's number in my phone and hit dial. It rang a few times before she answered.

"Hi, baby," she said. I could hear the relief in her voice.

"Why didn't you tell me?" I asked my mother as I held the phone against my ear. I wasn't sure if I'd known all the details before if it would have helped me keep my friend safe —and I was still angry my parents had lied and kept all of this from me.

I heard her sigh.

"We didn't want to scare you," she answered, sounding

tired.

"I know you think by keeping me in the dark you were protecting me, but you have to be honest with me," I told her angrily. "You can't keep stuff like this from me."

"I know. We love you and we just want you to be happy and safe," she said. *I'm an adult*, I thought with irritation. They had to understand that they couldn't shield me from all the bad things in the world.

I let out a deep breath as I rose up. Since the attack on Courtney, I'd been nervous and scared. I wasn't used to feeling this way, and it was tiring. But I was determined not to let the fear make me give up my life and go into hiding.

I looked up to see Matthew watching me from the doorway of my room. The fear I had for my own life was nothing compared to the fear of something happening to Matthew.

"You haven't been keeping anything else from me?" I asked, needing to know everything.

"No, that's everything."

I rubbed my forehead to try and ease the jumbled thoughts in my mind.

"You have someone watching you and Dad?" I asked.

"Yes," she answered, and I felt relieved.

There was no way to give protection to every close friend but I couldn't shake the fear of something happening to my parents. Or to Matthew, who was still watching me.

"Maybe it's best for you to come home. At least until this blows over?" she asked.

That would be the easier option but I felt like a coward. Besides I had no idea how long it would take before Nick made a mistake and my father could build a case against him. It could take months. I wouldn't allow the thought that it could take years to stay in my mind.

I didn't want to think that this could take over my life

but there was little else I could think about at the moment. I doubted it would get easier to handle it.

"No," I answered.

Matthew crossed his arms as he watched me.

I wanted to keep him safe. Keeping him close wouldn't keep him out of harm's way but I wasn't sure I was strong enough to push him away. The way he made me feel was unlike anything I'd ever experienced and I couldn't imagine giving it up.

I was so undecided on what to do. My mind told me to let him go, but my heart refused.

"I have to go, Mom," I said.

"Okay, baby."

"I love you," I told her softly.

"I love you too," she said and I ended the call. I let out a sigh.

"Everything okay?" Matthew asked as he pushed off the doorframe.

I nodded. I hated for people to see me when I was vulnerable, but there was no way I could hide the way I was feeling. Everything wasn't okay, and until Nick was behind bars nothing would be. I put my phone down beside my bed. Matthew stood beside me. I lifted my eyes to his and he put his hands on either side of my face as he scanned my features slowly.

"How are you doing?" he asked softly. He was one of the few people who could see through the facade I was trying to portray. When he looked into my eyes he saw right down to the truth I couldn't hide from him. I was scared and confused.

"I won't let anything happen to you," he promised me.

I knew he meant every word, and it scared me. There would be no limit to what he would sacrifice to keep me safe, even giving his own life to save mine. I closed my eyes for a moment when a wave of grief washed over me. I swallowed hard, trying to get a handle on the feeling of despair at the thought of something happening to him.

"Talk to me," he said, and I opened my eyes. Staring into the depths of his, I wanted to hold on to him so badly and never let go.

"It's nothing." I brushed off his concern, not wanting to give voice to my fear.

His thumb brushed over my lip.

"If you talk about it, you'll feel better," he said.

I shook my head. Talking about it would only make me face the reality that I had to let him go and it wasn't something I was prepared to do just yet.

My hands covered his, still cradling my face.

"What can I do to make you feel better?" he asked softly. His eyes searched mine for the answer.

I dropped my hands to my sides and reached up on my tiptoes, pressing my lips to his. I needed to be close to him, as close as two people could physically be. My hands reached up and slid around his neck, pulling him closer as my tongue swept into his mouth, deepening the kiss. At that moment nothing else mattered but what we were doing. I wasn't thinking about Courtney, Nick or the fact my life was in danger. Only Matthew mattered.

He broke the kiss before he looked down at me with darkened eyes that told me he wanted me as much as I wanted him. He was breathing hard while he stared at me. My chest rose and fell with my deep breaths.

I swallowed and nodded my head at his unspoken question. I needed him.

He didn't hesitate. He took my hand in his and led me to his room. Inside his room he turned to face me, pulling me closer to kiss me so hard it made my toes curl. Tongues and caresses stirred me up. I broke away, my chest rising and falling with my deep breaths. A fire of desire shone from his eyes as they swept over me, and I shivered with anticipation.

I'd always used sex to deal with difficult stuff but this was different. With Matthew it wasn't just about a physical act that connected us, it went way beyond that. It was love. My feelings were open to see as my gaze swept over his face.

His hands reached for the bottom of my shirt, and he pulled it over my head and discarded it on the floor. The feel of his gentle touch swept down the sides of my body until his hands rested on my hips. I felt like I'd been lit on fire.

I reached for the edge of his shirt and helped him remove it. It landed on top of mine. Our mouths met again in a frenzied kiss that swept me through me. My hands reached the back of his neck and pulled him closer, needing more. His kisses were hot and deep.

There was no better feeling than being kissed by him. It made me feel like the most important person in his world. I loved that. His hands drifted up my back to unclasp my bra. He continued to kiss me while his hand pushed the straps of my bra off my shoulders. The bra hit the floor and then he pulled me close. His hard chest pressing against the softness of my breasts was such a turn-on. Skin to skin.

My hands moved to his chest. The feel of his hard, defined muscles sent a thrill through me. He had a perfect body that was lean and well defined.

He stared down at me with want, and then he moved to unbutton my jeans. I wiggled out of them. His hands trailed gently down my legs. My skin tingled beneath his touch. Once the jeans were gone, I was standing there in my panties. I stepped forward and unbuttoned his jeans. They dropped to the floor and he kicked them off.

The touch of his hands on my lower back pulled me up against him. He kissed me again before his mouth slid against my skin down my throat. I groaned at the sensitive touch.

The back of my mind nagged at me. If I were stronger I would do the right thing, but I wasn't. I couldn't push him away to keep him safe. I wasn't strong enough to do that.

He gave me exactly what I wanted, up against the wall. Our bodies connected and together we reached our peaks. Sweaty and out of breath, I kissed his forehead.

He opened his eyes and looked at me adoringly. I loved him. The words were on the tip of my tongue but I bit my lip to stop myself. I wasn't ready to tell him that yet. He released me and my legs felt weak as he set me down on my feet. He picked me up and put me into his bed before climbing into it himself. I closed my eyes for a moment as he hugged me from behind.

The sex had been awesome, and for a few brief moments I'd forgotten about all the difficult things in my life that had been constantly on my mind. His arms tightened around me and I felt the guilt tear through me. I closed my eyes for a moment. I couldn't think about losing him.

Then the memories from my nightmare resurfaced and I remembered the horrible terror that I'd felt when he'd taken his last breath.

The next day, Matthew accompanied me to visit Courtney. He waited outside with Mark, giving me a chance to visit with my friend alone.

She smiled when I entered with a pile of magazines and her favorite chocolates.

"Now I remember why you're my best friend," she teased when she got her hands on the large box of candy.

Guilt tinged the affectionate smile I gave my friend. The quickest way to her heart was chocolates.

There was a part of me that wanted to come clean for

being the reason why she'd been taken, but she didn't remember anything. Telling her wouldn't absolve me of my guilt, and it would cause her more pain. Not remembering was better, I knew that. I would keep it from her and wrestle with my guilt on my own.

"How are you feeling?" I asked, sitting beside her in a spare chair pulled up next to her bed.

She lifted her shoulders and let them drop. Her usual happy demeanor dropped for a moment. "I don't remember any of it."

I kept silent as I reached out and covered her hand with mine, giving it a slight squeeze.

"They say blocking out a traumatic event is my mind's way of helping me cope." She frowned. "But it still scares me that I can't remember a thing."

Feeling emotion clog my throat, I just nodded as I listened.

"A policeman dropped by to get a statement from me but I couldn't remember anything. All I can remember was leaving campus after classes on Thursday afternoon. Everything after that is a blank. All they told me was I went missing for a while and someone left me at the hospital." She shook her head slightly. Her eyes went wide and I saw them water a little. "What if they come back for me?"

I gripped her hand tighter. "They won't."

Mark had been assigned to watch over her but now I didn't think it was the best idea. She knew Mark and if she found out who he really was it would raise questions I didn't want to answer. What if it triggered her memories before she was ready to deal with them? I would ask Matthew to assign someone she didn't know so their secret wouldn't be revealed.

"My father has assigned a bodyguard to watch over you."

She shivered slightly.

"It's just a precaution while the police investigate it."

"I don't know how they'll be able to solve it if I can't remember anything."

"I'm sure they have their ways." That seemed to reassure her enough and she smiled as she looked down at the box of chocolates on her lap.

"You really know how to make me feel better." She began to open the box.

"Best friends know this stuff."

We'd been close friends since high school. I still remembered the moment she'd taken the seat beside me in the cafeteria on our first day of school and we'd been inseparable ever since.

She was on her third chocolate when the doctor came in to check on her. He was an older man with gray hair. She offered him a chocolate but he shook his head.

"I see you're feeling better," he said while he checked her chart.

She nodded and ate another candy. "Chocolate heals everything."

The doctor smiled and shook his head slightly. "I think it has more to do with the sugar and endorphins." He looked at the chart. "You should be able to leave tomorrow."

I had some questions about her condition but I couldn't ask them in front of Courtney, so I excused myself for a moment after the doctor put her chart back and left. I told her I was going to get some coffee. I caught the doctor just outside her room.

"Sorry, Doctor, but I wanted to ask you some questions." Matthew watched from a few feet away as I spoke.

"Sure."

"Will she remember the memories she's blocked out?" I asked.

"Every person and every situation is different but the likelihood is that she will. It could take months, or years," he said. "It could be triggered by a smell or sound. I think she will remember when she's ready."

There was no surety in his voice, and I didn't like that.

"Thanks," I mumbled.

"You're welcome." The doctor left to continue his rounds.

Chapter Seventeen

I gnawed my lip as I thought over his answer. It was then that it struck me. If Courtney remembered what happened to her, she might be able to tell us who did it and there was the slimmest chance she could link it to Nick. But I refused to even entertain the thought of trying to get my friend to remember something that would have a huge impact on her just to be able to save myself. No—I couldn't do it. And there was no guarantee that telling her what had happened would actually make her remember anything anyway. It could all be for nothing.

"What are you thinking?" Matthew asked, studying me. His hand touched my arm.

I shook my head, trying to clear my current thoughts. They were a waste of time. "It doesn't matter."

"Tell me," he insisted, cocking his head to the side with a slight frown as he studied my features. He had a way of making me open up.

"It just occurred to me that if Courtney remembers her attack, she might be able to tell us who was involved and it could be the information we need to link Nick to her abduction."

Matthew inclined his head. "Yes." He'd already thought about it.

"But I can't do that to her." I looked at him, feeling bad I had even considered it for the briefest moment.

"I know." He reached out and caressed my face. "Like the doctor said, she'll probably remember on her own when she's able to handle it better."

I nodded in agreement. "Besides, there's no guarantee that even if we reveal the details that she will remember."

If I were in her shoes I wouldn't want to remember. Other than the physical wounds there was nothing else that hinted at her ordeal. I pushed the thoughts away, not having the energy to deal with them. There was no way to ease the guilt I felt at being responsible for what had happened to her.

"Where's Mark?" I asked, remembering what I had thought about replacing him so it wouldn't lead to questions I didn't want to answer, in fear of what they would cause.

"He went to get something to eat."

"We need to get someone else to protect her." I rubbed my forehead slightly.

"Why?" he asked, frowning.

"As far as Courtney knows you are my boyfriend, and Mark is your friend. If she discovers Mark is a bodyguard, she'll be suspicious. It could lead to a whole bunch of questions I would rather not have to answer at the moment."

He nodded. A serious expression was on his face. He got his phone out and made a call to assign a replacement for Mark. While he spoke, I waited, wanting to make sure everything would be organized. I didn't want to leave anything to chance. It was the least I could do to make things up to her.

I hated keeping secrets, but this time it was necessary. Being truthful was easy—lying required a lot of hard work. Remembering the lie, and who you told and who you didn't, wasn't easy. It was just easier to be honest but this time it wasn't an option. I would have to lie to my friend.

"It's done," Matthew assured me once he had hung up. "You okay?"

I rubbed the back of my neck slightly and nodded. "I'm fine."

I couldn't complain. I wasn't the one lying in a hospital bed. I composed myself, taking a deep breath before releasing it and going back into her room. By the time I hugged my friend goodbye and exited her room I was tired and emotionally drained.

Mark and Matthew were talking when I left her hospital room, both looking serious like they were discussing something important.

"The replacement for Mark will be here soon," Matthew said.

I nodded at the information. "We need to keep to the same script as before. You're my boyfriend and Mark is your friend." It was important to keep up the facade for her wellbeing. After everything that had happened, I owed her at least that.

"I've already cleared it with your father," Matthew assured me, putting an arm around me. I leaned against him, feeling exhausted.

"So we carry on like before," Mark reaffirmed. "I'll be assigned to you as Matthew's backup."

I was agitated and nervous. I was pacing the length of the living room while Matthew watched from a seat on the sofa. He stood up and walked over to me.

"You're wearing a path into the carpet," he said in a teasing tone. But I was too wound up to smile.

I shrugged. "I don't know how to deal with all of this."

It wasn't like I had ever been in this type of situation before, and I simply didn't know how to work through the array of feelings I was experiencing.

"What do you do?" I asked, tucking my hair behind my ear.

Unlike me, Matthew had had experience in stressful life-and-death situations. While my world felt like it was spinning out of control, he was calm. I wanted to feel calm, but other than taking some drug prescribed by a doctor...

"I go to the shooting range when I need to blow off steam," he admitted.

Shooting a gun. My father had tried to get me to learn how to use a gun, but after the first couple of initial lessons, my mother had put her foot down. She hated guns and the thought of me handling one was too much for her to deal with. And truthfully I hadn't minded—I was never completely comfortable holding a gun either.

"Do you think it might help me?" I asked. I needed to find a way to release the building pressure, and if I needed to shoot a gun to do so I would.

"You want to go to the shooting range?" he asked, looking a little taken aback.

"If I don't find a way of dealing with this the only option will be a prescription."

He studied me for several seconds before he took my hand into his. "Let's go."

I let him take control and before I knew it I was safely buckled into the car and we were on our way.

"There's a small shooting range nearby," he told me.

I nodded, feeling apprehensive and hopeful. I reminded myself that it wasn't like I had never handled a gun before. I just needed a little bit of a refresher and then I would be good to go.

I glanced at Matthew. His full focus was on the road as usual. Every now and then he would do a sweep of his gaze, taking in the surrounding cars. Was that his training as a bodyguard that had kicked in? Was he looking out for any potential dangers? His eyes lifted to the rearview mirror before he concentrated back on the road in front of him.

It took a twenty-minute car ride before he pulled up in front of a small shooting range. The one my father had dragged me to had been much larger. I felt a bit nervous as I closed the car door.

"You still want to do this?" Matthew asked, taking in my visible apprehension and giving me an out.

I wiped the sweat from my palms on my jeans. "Yes."

Matthew took my hand in his and led me to the entrance. The sound of guns being fired increased my nervousness. It wasn't long before Matthew and I were looking at a bull's eye target, ready to start.

"You ready to do this?" he asked from beside me.

I didn't want to reveal my inner anxiety so I nodded my head instead of answering.

"We just need to go over the basics."

I listened and nodded as he ran through everything. He showed me the best way to hold the weapon. It wasn't like I wanted to own one of my own. This was just an exercise to help see if it could help expel the negative emotions that had been plaguing me since we had discovered Courtney at the hospital.

Matthew was a handsome man already, but there was something about seeing him in bodyguard-mode with the gun in his hand that made me swoon despite the turmoil inside. He'd never looked sexier.

"You ready?" he asked.

"Yes," I lied. I wasn't sure that I wouldn't end up shooting something I wasn't supposed to.

He handed me the gun and I tested the weight as I pointed it down at the floor. It was heavier than I had expected. My father had taught me never to point it at something you didn't intend to shoot.

"Remember. Only point it at the target." Matthew sounded so much like my father.

"Mr. Weiss," I said in a teasing voice, "you worried I'm going to shoot you?"

"A little." He positioned me so I was facing the target.

I lifted the gun with two hands. He moved my left hand to support the gun.

"Anytime you're ready." He put the protective ear muffs on me to protect my ears.

I inhaled and exhaled slowly as I lined up the target. I could hear the slight echo of my heartbeat in my ears.

The first pull of the trigger was sudden—I completely missed the target. I held the gun and tried to aim it closer to the target. My second shot, I hit the bottom right of it but I was getting the hang of it. Movies made it look so easy but hitting the mark in real life was so much more difficult.

I tried to calm the chaos inside me by thinking of nothing but the target in front of me. I lined up the next shot and slowly squeezed the trigger. By the end of the round I was feeling less emotional and even a little proud. I was no sharp-shooter, but I managed to hit the paper three times.

I couldn't quite put my finger on what had helped. Had it been the control I felt holding the gun? Or the smell of the gunshot? Or maybe using all my concentration on aiming had left little room for any other thought, for guilt or feelings of fear.

I pointed the gun the floor as I passed it to Matthew. I was smiling as he put the safety on while I removed the protective ear muffs.

"That was awesome," I said. It had worked. My earlier nervousness and agitation were gone.

"You're pretty good for someone who hasn't had a lot of practice."

"Thanks," I said, loving the fact I was feeling lighter. "I feel better." I couldn't explain how shooting off a couple of rounds at a stationary target had helped release the negative emotions that had been building up earlier.

The image that stayed with me was one of Matthew holding a gun. When we finally arrived back at the apartment, I only allowed him enough time to put his weapon away before I walked to him and pulled him into a kiss.

I wanted him right here, right now.

Despite me taking him by surprise, he kissed me back hard, pulling me closer as his arms wrapped around me, keeping me up against his body.

He pushed me up against the wall and I leaned my head back as his lips trailed against my jaw.

"Now," I whispered hoarsely. My hands fumbled against the top button of his jeans. There was no time to go to the bedroom or foreplay.

He pulled away only long enough to help me discard my jeans before he ripped my panties down. I kicked them away. His fingers brushed against me as I opened my legs and I groaned with need.

He lifted me up against the wall. My legs wrapped around him, securing him as I felt him against me. With one powerful thrust he filled me and I hung on to him. I panted as he did me, hard, up against the wall.

It was raw and sexual. And so hot.

He kissed me as I began to feel the familiar nearing of my orgasm—the tightening of my body as he rocked against me. I groaned as I came. Still riding my high, and my body still sensitive, he thrust into me before his body trembled and his head fell against my shoulder. His breathing was as uneven as mine.

It had been intense. And the best sex we'd ever had.

Going back to school after the attack on Courtney wasn't easy. I'd never feared much before but I couldn't help fearing the people who wanted to hurt me. I constantly watched everyone around me, wondering if they could be working for Nick.

Just remembering his face in the picture would send a shiver of fear through me.

"You okay?" Matthew asked with concern. We'd just gotten into our first class of the day and I'd been preoccupied with my thoughts.

I nodded. But he knew me well enough to know I was lying.

Even paying attention to the professor was almost impossible. Had I returned to college too soon? Would another couple of days make me less fearful? The answer was no. No amount of time was going to make this easier to deal with.

The only way to make me feel safe again would be putting Nick behind bars so he wouldn't be able to carry out his revenge, but realistically I knew that even with evidence it would take time.

I felt the heat of Matthew's gaze on me. He knew what was getting to me and he was trying his hardest to assure me he would protect me. The problem was I knew he would do anything to keep me safe, which included putting his life on the line for mine. I didn't want that. My life wasn't more important than his.

The class ended and I packed my notes away in my bag and slung it over my shoulder. Matthew followed close behind me out of the class. Just outside of the room, he pulled me to one side.

"Maybe you're not ready to be back yet," he said, his eyes scanning my face for confirmation.

I shrugged. I didn't want to hide away like a coward but I wasn't brave enough to be out in the open with the fear I felt.

"Do you want to go home?" he asked softly.

I swallowed as I contemplated his question. A part of me that I wasn't used to wanted me to say yes and give in to the fear. But the part of me that was strong and refused to back down wouldn't allow me to take the cowardly way out of this situation.

I took a deep breath and released it. And with a look of determination, I shook my head. I could do this and I would.

For the next couple of hours I persevered through my fear, refusing to let anyone intimidate me. By the time we were headed to our last class of the day I was feeling tired and I couldn't wait to get home.

Matthew stood beside me with a hand on my lower back. When he saw me hesitate for a moment he would touch me to remind me he was with me. The smallest of touches from him could give me the strength to go on when all I wanted to do was give up.

We had to walk across campus to get to our class. A few groups of students loitered around us as we made our way to the car.

Beside me, Matthew stiffened slightly. I looked at him

but his eyes were looking toward the road in front of the building. The fear I felt had only been there for a split second before I heard a loud bang. As if in slow motion, Matthew shoved me down, and there were a few more bangs. My ears rang as I landed on the ground, feeling the pain jolt through me at the hard landing on my side. The force of Matthew's body covering mine pushed the air from my lungs.

It took seconds to try and figure out what was happening. Then there was silence and Matthew groaned. I looked into his eyes. He had a pained expression. There was the sound of an engine revving and tires screeching. He turned to look toward the street closest to us.

What had happened?

Matthew hissed as he lifted his body to take the weight off me and rolled onto his back. I didn't understand until I saw the deep red stain on his shirt by his side.

Oh. My. God.

I began to panic. It felt like I was living my nightmare. Matthew had been shot.

Chapter Eighteen

The panic overwhelmed me as tears blurred my vision. Matthew groaned and clutched his hand over the wound. I wanted to close my eyes and push the horror scene away. I wanted it to be a nightmare I would wake up from. But I wasn't dreaming.

A crowd gathered around us. One guy had a phone out and he was calling an ambulance.

"You can't die on me," I whispered to him as he closed his eyes. His breathing was labored. A pool of blood had started to form around him. There was so much blood.

"Please," I whispered.

He opened his eyes.

"Call Mark," he said, his eyes pleading with mine.

Call Mark. The instruction echoed in my mind. Then I remembered he'd programmed Mark's number into my phone in case I needed it. Somehow I got my phone out and searched for Mark's number. My hands were shaking so bad it took me a few tries before I found it and I hit the call button. Blood stained the screen.

"What's wrong?" he asked.

"It's... It's Matthew," I tried to explain as I gripped the phone.

"Where are you?" he asked, the light tone gone after he heard the panic in my voice.

"Front," I answered. My thoughts were so jumbled it was easier to stick to one-word answers.

"I'll be there in three minutes," he said and the call disconnected.

"He's on his way," I whispered to Matthew.

His face was etched in pain and I wanted to be able to take it away. I would suffer it for him.

"I need you to keep pressure on the wound," he whispered to me, still with his eyes closed.

There was no arguing. I gritted my teeth and as he removed his hand on the bullet wound, I pressed my hand down on it. The warmth of his blood wet my hand.

"It'll be okay," I said to him. "It'll be okay." If I said it enough times out loud, it would make it a reality. I tried to swallow the emotion clogged in my throat as I fixed my eyes on his pale face.

I couldn't lose him.

If I'd been strong enough to let him go, this wouldn't have happened. Guilt overwhelmed me as tears slid down my face. I had been too weak to do what had been best for him. He was in pain because of my inability to put him before myself.

In that moment, I hated myself. I hated that I'd been so selfish. There was a chance he could die and that I would lose him forever.

Please let him live, I thought over and over again. If he lived I promised I would let him go. Even if it killed me, I would put his life above mine and I would walk away.

Matthew's eyes fluttered closed and I squeezed my eyes shut to stop the hysteria from rising. When Mark arrived, I felt a little relief.

"How bad is it?" he asked as he rushed through the crowd and bent down to examine his wounded friend.

"I don't know," I answered honestly. I had never seen anyone get shot before.

"Hang in there," he said to Matthew, but he didn't respond.

He lifted my hands for a moment and examined the wound before applying pressure to it. I wiped the blood on my hands on my clothes, but nothing would wipe the guilt away.

There was a rush of activity when the paramedics arrived. They began to work on him and I stepped back to let them do their job.

"He'll be okay," Mark assured me as he put an arm around me to keep me steady. I didn't know whether he was telling the truth or just saying it to make me feel better. I leaned against him and closed my eyes for a moment.

"We'll follow them," he said as the paramedics put Matthew in the ambulance.

I shook my head. There was no way I was leaving him alone.

"No, I'm going with them," I said and walked away from him and to the ambulance.

He grabbed my wrist. "I can't protect you in the ambulance," he tried to reason with me.

Wild horses couldn't have kept me from getting into the ambulance to be with Matthew. There was no way Mark was going to stop me. I turned to look at him.

"I'm going into the ambulance with him," I told him in a firm tone that told him it wasn't up for discussion. "You can follow behind."

Maybe there was something in my eyes that told him I wasn't going to back down, because he shrugged and nodded his head. I held Matthew's hand all the way to the hospital. He was unconscious. The paramedics told me that he'd lost a lot of blood and would need surgery. Staring down at his peaceful face, I prayed he would make it through. I promised I would do the right thing if he survived.

Once we got to the hospital Mark was by my side. I watched with fear and anxiety as they wheeled Matthew away for surgery and I stood outside the door. I felt so hopeless. There was nothing I could do. His life was in the hands of the medical staff. I paced up and down.

Each time someone came through the doors my heart would stop and I would hold my breath, hoping they had news on Matthew. Mark made a call as we waited in the waiting room. He'd called my father to tell him what had happened.

"How are you?" my father asked, sounding concerned when Mark handed me the phone.

"I'm fine," I assured him. Matthew was the one in surgery. He'd put his life on the line to save mine. If he hadn't put his body in the way of the bullet, it would have hit me. He'd saved my life.

"How is Matthew?" my dad asked. I took a deep breath and released it.

"I don't know."

I handed the phone back to Mark unable to concentrate on the phone call as I turned my attention back to watching the doors. Each minute that passed with no news made me worry more. Mark continued to talk to my father for a few minutes more. From the bits and pieces I heard, Mark was going to organize more bodyguards to watch over me.

Once he was off the phone he came to stand beside me as

I watched the doors with my arms crossed. He seemed to sense I didn't want to talk because he kept silent. He leaned against the wall, watching me pace up and down the hallway. He didn't have to say it—I could see he was worried about Matthew as well. He just seemed to be dealing with it better than I was.

"This wasn't your fault," he said unexpectedly. I stopped to look at him. How had he managed to read what was going on in my mind?

I shrugged. It was. I should have stayed at home today instead of going to class. But my stubbornness and inability to back down had led to this.

"It's his job to keep you alive," he reminded me.

I didn't say anything, I just kept staring at him. Matthew had been employed to keep me safe but our relationship went beyond that. I loved him and I was pretty sure he cared for me. I'd messed up so bad up to this point that I swore I would do whatever I had to do to keep him safe. He would make it through this and then I would let him go. It would hurt, but I would do it, because it was the right thing for him. I would never be able to live with myself if he died to save me.

But first he had to make it through the surgery.

I turned away from Mark. My eyes fixed on the doors when they swung open. The surgeon, still dressed in scrubs, walked to me and I felt my world stop as I tried to read the outcome of the surgery from the look on his face.

The time it took for the surgeon to walk up to me felt like forever. My eyes scrutinized his features for any indication on the result of the surgery, but I couldn't decipher anything. I clasped my hands together and tried to keep myself from going into a full-blown panic.

"He's stable."

I felt relief flood through me. Mark relaxed beside me.

Mark asked the surgeon some questions, but for me all that mattered was that he was alive and stable. Nothing else mattered.

After the surgeon left, Mark pulled out his phone and made some calls. From what I could hear they were to Matthew's family, telling them what had happened. When he finished the call he shoved the phone back into his jeans.

"Why didn't you call them before the surgery?" I asked.

"He wouldn't have wanted them to worry," he explained.

I'd worried enough for everyone. The adrenaline that had been carrying me began to wane, and I felt tired. I looked down to my hands. I'd managed to wash the blood from my skin but the memories of what had happened would stay far longer.

"This is all part of the job," Mark began to explain to me. I looked at him.

"It was my fault," I said quickly. "I didn't want to let fear make me too scared to live my life. I should have stayed at home and none of this would have happened." The burden of responsibility weighed heavily on me and no amount of words was going to change what had happened. I was the reason Matt had been fighting for his life. Just the thought of what had nearly happened took the breath from my lungs.

"The thing is, if it hadn't been today, it could have been tomorrow," he said softly, watching me. I swallowed hard. "And you never know. On a different day, things might have worked out differently."

That scared me even more. Matthew had survived this attempt, but what if he didn't survive the next one? And there was no doubt in my mind there would be a next one.

"He did his job today. If he hadn't, you would be the one in surgery or worse. Don't beat yourself up about it," he said. I knew he was trying to get me to realize it wasn't my fault and that it was part of the job Matthew was employed to do. But Matthew wasn't just a bodyguard employed to keep me safe; he was the guy I'd fallen head-over-heels for. I rubbed my forehead, trying to ease the barrage of thoughts that were hitting me.

"You'll feel better once you've seen him," Mark added. I didn't respond. I didn't think anything would ease the burden of Matthew being hurt because of me, even if it had been his job.

We waited another half an hour before we were allowed to see him.

"I'll wait outside for you," Mark said. He was giving me an opportunity to visit Matthew on my own. Feeling the way I was, it was probably best I did this alone.

Outside the door, I stopped for a moment. I took a deep breath and released it before I opened the door and stepped inside. The room was quiet except for the sound of a heart monitor.

Nothing could have prepared me for what I saw next. My heart stilled at the sight of Matthew lying asleep in the bed. I took another step into the room and closed the door behind me.

He looked so peaceful and fragile. It was so different from the way I always saw him. He was always strong and in control. I took another step toward him.

My eyes washed over him and I felt a lump in my throat as the first sting of tears hit me. The first tear slid down my face when I came to stand beside him. My eyes fixed on his handsome face. I lifted my hand and brushed my fingertips across his cheek. Another tear slid down my face as I leaned down and gently pressed a kiss to his cheek. I brushed the tears away before I took his hand into mine.

Memories of his face etched in pain as he held the wound, the blood pooling where he lay, filled my mind. My stomach clenched.

"I'm so sorry," I whispered to him, needing him to know I held myself responsible for what happened to him. I squeezed my eyes closed as the overwhelming feeling of guilt swept through me, shaking me down to my core. I held his limp hand in mine.

"I love you," I said to him softly, pressing a kiss to his hand. "I don't want to let you go, but I have to..."

Another bout of tears hit me.

"You are everything I want. I can't let anything happen to you."

I swallowed hard as my emotions bubbled to the surface. I breathed in deep and released the heavy breath.

"You're going to be angry..." I continued. "And you're going to be hurt."

I looked down at him for a few seconds.

"But I'm doing this because I can't lose you," I admitted softly.

I wanted to hold on to him and never let him go. I wanted so many more days with him. All the times I had woken up in the morning beside him and saw him smile had become the most precious memories I had. But there would be no more.

Our time had come to an end. My heart cried out for me to wait to walk away until he woke up, but I was scared that if I had to look into his beautiful green eyes I wouldn't be able to. To keep him safe, I couldn't allow him in my life in any capacity. He couldn't be the guy I loved and I couldn't allow him to be the bodyguard paid to protect me.

If I gave myself more time to contemplate my decision I would find some reasoning to back out of it. This was the best thing I could do for him. I loved him and had to let him go.

I kissed him one last time, this time on his mouth. I made myself take a step backward as I released his hand from mine.

It was one of the hardest things I'd ever had to do. By the time I made it out of the room, a few tears had escaped down my face. Mark pushed off the wall across from me and walked toward me. I tried to push my emotions down so I could deal with them later in private, without prying eyes.

"He's going to be okay," Mark assured me when he took in my red puffy eyes. There was no mistaking how upset I was.

"I need to make a phone call," I said to him hoarsely. I took my phone out and walked a few feet away from him. He gave me space but watched me pace up and down the hallway as I dialed the number.

It rang once before my dad answered.

"Sarah," my dad said. I could hear the worry in his voice.

"I don't want Matthew as a bodyguard anymore," I instructed him with a calmness I didn't feel.

"He's injured but he should make a full recovery," my father began to explain. "I've already spoken to his doctors."

"I want you to replace him with someone else," I said with determination. I didn't want to have to explain to him why I was making the decision to cut Matthew from my life. No one needed to know why I was making the decision I was.

There were a few seconds of silence before my father replied, "Okay."

"And I want a bodyguard posted outside his hospital room until he leaves the hospital," I added.

There was no way I was going to leave Matthew unprotected while he was recovering. I had no idea if they would come after him to finish him off.

"Fine," he agreed. "I will have to call Mark and make the necessary arrangements."

"Here, you can speak to him now," I said, walking to Mark and handing him my phone.

I crossed my arms and watched Mark's face as he took

instructions from my father. His eyes held mine as he nodded, saying, "Yes, I will arrange that."

A few minutes later, the call ended and Mark handed me back my phone.

"I understand why you did this," he said softly. "But I'm not sure he will."

I looked down at the floor as I contemplated what he said. It would hurt him—but at least I was keeping him alive.

Chapter Nineteen

I didn't want to leave the hospital until Matthew's family arrived. It was like I didn't want to leave him without leaving someone to watch over him. It was hard enough, I couldn't leave him alone. Leaning against the wall I looked up to the ceiling. I wanted to go back inside his room and watch him while he slept peacefully, but I was scared it would make it impossible to leave him. A nurse walked out of his room and gave me a friendly smile, which I tried to mirror but failed.

"They'll be here soon," Mark said from beside me.

I nodded. There was so much going on in my mind. My heart was screaming for me to put myself first, but my mind and the guilt made me stay exactly where I was.

A nervous knot developed in my stomach at the thought of briefly meeting Matthew's family for the first time. Had he ever told them about me?

I pushed the thought out of my mind. It didn't matter. Whatever we had I was walking away from to protect him, and thinking about things that weren't relevant anymore was a waste of time. Every sound at the entrance of the floor made me look up but each time I saw people arrive, they would walk in another direction.

But the moment his family arrived, the resemblance left me with no doubt of who they were. An older couple alongside two young women who looked younger than me stepped out of the elevator. Their worried looks pulled at my guilt.

Matthew looked just like his father. They had the same features and they were similarly built. My eyes moved to the lady walking beside him. Matthew had the same color eyes as who I assumed was his mom.

Mark walked to meet them and I stayed where I was. I felt like this was my fault and I wasn't sure how they would react to my presence. Would they blame me, even if it had been his job to protect me?

"Where is he?" his mom asked Mark with a worried expression.

"He's recovering from surgery in his room," he informed them.

One of his sisters looked at me with a questioning glance. Mark turned to me.

"This is Sarah," he introduced me to them. "He was protecting her."

I gave them a nervous smile, unsure of how to respond to them.

Matthew's mom walked to me and took my hands in hers.

"I'm so glad you're okay," she said. Her reaction took me by surprise and all I could do was nod.

Only two people could visit at a time, so Matthew's parents went into the room and his sisters remained outside with Mark and me. I don't know why I was still waiting around. I'd told myself that once his family arrived I would leave, but actually walking away from him was harder than I'd expected.

Mark introduced me to Matthew's sisters.

"Sophie," he said, giving a nod to the youngest-looking one who had a similar coloring to Matthew. She stepped forward to hug me. I returned her hug.

"It's nice to finally meet you," she said with a genuine smile that reached her eyes. I gave her a questioning glance.

"He told us all about you."

"Really?" I said, feeling a little taken aback. She nodded.

I wasn't sure why that surprised me. Maybe it was because he'd lied to me about who he really was?

"And this is Tracy," Mark said, introducing me to the other sister. She was fairer than Sophie, with long wavy dark blonde hair and the blue eyes.

She didn't hug me like Sophie had, and her smile never reached her eyes. The dislike was evident in her expression.

"Hi," I said, but it didn't seem to ease her tight features.

She wasn't as forgiving as the rest of her family. She was pretending to be fine with my presence, but I could tell she wasn't. I couldn't blame her. She was reacting exactly the way I'd expected.

Mark seemed to notice because he pulled her to one side by her elbow. Tracy gave him a glare and pulled her arm free from his grip. They spoke in hushed tones, so I struggled to hear exactly what was being said, but I could tell it was getting a bit heated.

"Don't worry about her," Sophie piped up beside me. I glanced at her. "Tracy doesn't approve of the whole bodyguard-thing."

It was something I could understand. If I had someone I cared about take on a job that risked their life every day I would probably feel the same way. Our situation was different

—it hadn't just been about the money.

"I get it," I said with a shrug.

My eyes went back to Mark and Tracy, who were still having the same heated discussion. Mark, who was usually calm and reserved, was clearly angry. Tracy glared at him as she crossed her arms.

I couldn't help feeling there was more to their discussion than Matthew and the fact he was in hospital. I watched them with interest. Mark shook his head at something she said, looking like he was struggling to contain his anger.

"I swear they should just screw and get over it," Sophie said out of the blue. My jaw dropped. I gave her a look of alarm and she giggled.

"There's been something going on between those two," she explained with a shrug. "I don't know why they don't just get together."

I smiled at her honesty.

"Really?" I questioned as my eyes went back to them.

"Yeah, it's been going on for a while."

With this new information I studied them, looking for any sign of an attraction I might have missed before. Mark said something to Tracy and she pressed her lips together. She looked so angry. Mark gave her one more silent hard look before he walked away from her. Her eyes followed him. Then I saw something deep in her eyes when she didn't think anyone was watching. I saw a glimpse of something there. A slight vulnerability.

Sophie was right. There was something definitely going on between the two of them. When Tracy noticed my eyes on her she pinned me with a glare and any softness that had been there a moment ago vanished.

Mark walked to where Sophie and I were standing.

"Let me know when you're ready to leave," Mark said, and Sophie gave me a curious look.

The time had come to follow through on my decision. No more thinking or wrestling with it. Nothing good would come from me remaining at the hospital. The longer I stayed the more difficult it would be to leave him.

I looked to the door of the hospital room Matthew was in. What I wanted more than anything in this world was in that room, but I had to do the right thing. Remembering the pain and the blood when he'd been shot was enough to give me the strength to turn to Sophie.

"It was nice to meet you," I said, and I gave her brief hug.

"You're not staying?" she asked, looking a little confused by my actions.

It was hard for me to understand why I was doing what I was, so it would be almost impossible to explain my actions to an outsider. So, instead of answering her question, I shook my head.

Tracy, who was standing alone a couple of feet away from us, gave me an indifferent look.

"I'm ready," I said, pulling my attention back to Mark.

I walked down the hallway to the elevator and Mark followed beside me. It felt like a part of me inside was dying. Walking away from him went against every fiber of my being...but I had to. No matter how much it hurt, I had to keep reminding myself that I was doing this for him. I had to keep him safe, and the only way I could do that was to keep him out of my life.

He wouldn't understand. My decision would hurt him, but at least it would keep him alive and that was all that mattered. How much it crushed me to put one foot in front of the other and leave him didn't matter.

"You still think this is for the best?" Mark asked from beside me when we got into the elevator.

My gaze fixed on Matthew's two sisters, who were

watching from outside his hospital room. The doors to the elevator closed and I nodded, even though I could feel the sting of tears. This was going to hurt Matt, and that worried me more.

I knew it was going to be hard to turn my back on him and walk away, but it was so much worse than I'd ever imagined. Time seemed to slow down and every second felt like a minute.

Being back at the apartment was worse. Every room I stood in had memories of happier times when we'd been loved-up and happy. Earlier we had both been okay, and now we weren't. Now, without him, every happy memory was tainted with the blood he'd shed trying to save my life. I closed my eyes for a moment and tried to erase the memories pulling at my heartstrings.

I had to find a way to make it through this without him. I loved him enough to let him go and now I had to pick up the pieces to my life and try to carry on as normal, even though there was a threat of death that was even more prominent than it had been before. It would be so easy to hide away and let him scare me but I wasn't built like that. Backing down wasn't part of who I was. Even with the reality of my situation, I wasn't going to hide. I was going to carry on as normal.

I sat down in the living room and slumped backward on the sofa, looking at the ceiling and trying to organize my thoughts. The slight rustle of movement could be heard from Matthew's room. Mark had gone in there when we'd arrived. He was packing up Matthew's stuff.

Unable to keep my mind from moving back to thoughts of Matthew, I put the TV on. I had hoped it would distract me, but it didn't work. Nothing worked. No matter how much I didn't want to think about him, he was seared into my thoughts. There was no ignoring or forgetting.

Frustrated, I switched off the TV and stood up just as Mark exited Matthew's room with his bags packed.

"His sister insisted on coming to pick up his stuff," he informed me.

I was about to ask which one, but before I could, he answered.

"Tracy."

Great, I thought bitterly. It had to be the one with the death glare who would rather have seen me in the hospital bed rather than her brother.

I rubbed my forehead.

"Don't worry about her," he said quietly. "She's more bark than bite."

I didn't believe him. I was pretty sure she hated me and I couldn't really blame her. It was my fault her brother was in the hospital.

"I'm going to take a shower," I said.

He nodded as he set the bag next to the sofa. I went into my room and closed the door. For once, since the start of this whole ordeal, I was alone. One deep breath in and out, and then I walked into the shower and stripped my clothes from my body. I shoved them in the trash. There was no way I would ever be able to wear those clothes without being reminded of Matthew's blood pumping from the bullet wound that had been meant for me.

I got in the shower and opened the taps. The icy-cold water streamed over my body. I gasped as the water chilled me. It was like it was numbing me. It helped me to concentrate on the moment rather than the crazy thoughts in my mind.

Eventually the water warmed slightly, and I picked up some soap. I washed my whole body, and when I looked down I saw there was a slight pink tinge to the water as it ran from me. Blood. Matthew's blood.

I scrubbed my body harder, trying to remove the memories that came with the physical evidence, but no matter how hard I washed, it couldn't wash away what had happened. My skin was raw as I got out the shower and dried off. I got dressed quickly.

There was something else nagging at me and I wanted to ask Mark about it. I found him by the window looking out to the street below.

"Is there someone watching Matthew?" I asked.

Mark stood still, but his head turned slightly and his eyes met mine.

"Yes. I have one of my best guys posted outside his room."

That made me feel better.

"Thanks."

I don't know why I felt the need to thank him but it made me feel better he had one of his best bodyguards watching over Matt until he recovered.

"I'm not doing it just for you," he explained. "He's my friend and I don't want anything to happen to him either."

I nodded my head. I understood.

"I've organized a couple more bodyguards to watch you from a distance so that they won't be detected," he informed me.

I wasn't sure if having more people watching over me made me feel any safer. All it took was one lucky shot getting past their defenses and I was as good as dead. "I'll be moving my stuff into Matthew's room."

It wasn't a surprise but I couldn't help the way my stomach squeezed at the thought of him taking over Matthew's room. It was stupid—a totally emotional way of thinking. It was just a room, and he needed to stay with me in the apartment to keep me safe. It was a logical move.

I gave him a brief nod before I turned to go back to my

room. I needed some time out away from prying eyes.

Lying on my bed, I stared at my phone. I wanted to call the hospital to find out how Matt was doing. Was he awake yet? Did he know I'd left and cut him out from my life? The urge was too much to overcome. I dialed the number. It led to a brief conversation—they couldn't tell me anything more than the fact that he was awake and his vitals were good.

"Thank you," I said before I disconnected the call.

He was awake. I wanted to be with him, holding his hand and taking in the fact that, despite taking a bullet, he was safe and alive. I had to fight the urge to throw caution to the wind and go to the hospital to be with him. I kept reminding myself I was doing the right thing, even if it sucked. Loving someone sometimes made you have to make the difficult decision to put their own wellbeing above your own.

There was a brief knock at the front door and I got up to see who it was. Mark was already opening the door as I stepped outside my room. Tracy's glare hit me full force as her eyes met mine.

"Come in," Mark told her, and she stepped past him. He closed the door while I stood and watched her approach me.

"How's he doing?" I asked, trying to break the ice.

"How do you think?" she said angrily. She put her hands on her hips and turned to face me. "He took a bullet to save your life and when he woke up, you were gone."

"That's enough, Tracy," Mark told her, a crease on his forehead. She gave me one last glare before she turned it to Mark, who was standing beside her.

"It's the truth," she said, but he shook his head.

"You don't know everything," he said with a hard look in her eyes.

It was better for her to hate me, because revealing the true reason I'd shut her brother out of my life would give him hope, and he would fight to become a part of my life again. I couldn't let that happen. All that mattered was keeping him alive; my heartbreak was a small price to pay for that.

"Then tell me everything," she challenged. Mark gave me a look, but I shook my head.

Let her believe I was the horrible person who had abandoned her brother when he was most vulnerable. It didn't matter. Tracy saw the look that passed between us, but she didn't say anything.

"I packed Matt's stuff," he said, and then he walked away from the two of us and into the living room. Tracy followed him and I stayed where I was.

He handed her the bag and she took it from him.

"Thanks," she said. Their eyes met for a moment before she pulled her gaze away from him.

She made her way to the front door. Just as she passed me, she stopped for a moment.

"Stay away from my brother," she warned. "He deserves better than you."

Her words cut right though me, and I wanted to explain my actions—but I didn't. I kept my composure as I watched her leave the apartment. Mark closed the door behind her and then turned face me.

"She doesn't understand why, but I do," he said, his eyes sympathetic.

His words should have made me feel better, but they didn't. I felt like the worst kind of person even though my intentions had been for the best.

Chapter Twenty

A week later I was sitting on the sofa, flipping through the channels but unable to find anything to keep my attention longer than a few seconds.

"You're giving me headache," Mark said from the chair beside me. "Pick something."

I shot him a glare. I was feeling moody from cabin fever. Being holed up for a week in my apartment was driving me nuts and I could feel myself becoming bitchier than usual.

"If you think this is a picnic for me, think again," he quipped in response to my death glare.

I pressed my lips together to keep from saying something that would just make things more difficult. I had to remind myself Mark was doing a job and it wasn't his fault I was in this situation.

We had already established that going back to college was too risky. Mark had upped my security. My father had organized that I could continue some of my classes from home. It was only a temporary solution for a couple of weeks. I could only hope it would be enough time, even though realistically I had a feeling it would take longer.

Mark's phone rang and he answered it. He frowned as he listened. "What does he look like?"

He nodded and then ended the call.

"Are you expecting someone?" he asked, standing up and returning his phone to his pocket.

"No, why?" I answered, confused as to why he was asking me that. I shifted to the edge of the seat, putting the TV remote down.

The doorbell rang. The sound shot through me and my eyes shot to Mark.

"How did you know?"

"Cameras."

He walked to the front door and I followed behind, feeling anxious. An uninvited guest.

"It's Ryan," he stated after looking through the peephole.

I frowned and looked through the peephole, confirming it was him.

"Ryan," I answered cautiously as I opened the door, not feeling very friendly that he was showing up uninvited. Mark stood behind me.

"Sarah," he said with a nod. I crossed my arms and refused to allow him inside.

I had already learned not to give an inch with this guy—otherwise he would take it and make it into something it wasn't.

"What are you doing here?" There was no reason for him to be here. The last I had seen he had been dating someone else, finally leaving me alone.

"I heard about what happened," he said, his eyes going over my shoulder to Mark, who was still watching from behind me, before he looked back at me. "I wanted to see how you were doing."

I arched my eyebrow at him, convinced there was an ulterior motive.

"Things didn't work out with Summer." And with that, he had confirmed my initial suspicion.

I had an uncomfortable feeling about where he was headed with this. Matthew's presence had kept him at bay, and now that he wasn't here, Ryan was trying his luck again.

"I'm sorry to hear that," I said stiffly.

His eyes shifted past my shoulder again.

"Where is your boyfriend?"

I wasn't sure what to say. I looked back at Mark, hoping he would help.

"He is recuperating," Mark answered. "He should be back in a week."

"Yeah, I heard he got shot. It's crazy."

I nodded. I don't know if it was the idea that Matthew was still a fixture in my life that made him back off. But it would only be a temporary reprieve, because I knew Matthew wouldn't be returning. It was another thing I had to worry about on top of everything else.

"Thanks for stopping by," I said coolly. I was intent on this encounter coming to an end.

"Take care," he said, still lingering.

I closed the door and leaned against it.

"He is a persistent idiot, isn't he?"

I nodded. "It's just going to get worse when Matthew doesn't show up in week."

"Don't worry about it. We'll figure it out."

The easy solution would be to pretend Mark was my new boyfriend, but I wasn't sure I could pull that off. With Matthew it had been easy, because we'd had chemistry. Besides, even though we weren't really together, it felt wrong to pretend with someone else.

I closed my eyes briefly, feeling a little overwhelmed. I hated the feeling of not being in control and being at the mercy of the actions of others.

Later that day, my father called.

"You should come home," my father instructed. "We can protect you better here."

I wasn't ready to give up on the independence I'd gained by living in the apartment away from my parents.

"Let's see what happens," I deflected without refusing outright. "I need to continue with my classes and get notes." Even though it could all be done electronically, I preferred to stay. There was also the possibility of a stalker when Matthew didn't return but I refused to allow Ryan's ill-thought-out action to push me into making a choice I didn't want.

I heard someone else talking in the background. The voice was familiar. It was Matthew. The sound vibrated through me, leaving me shaken and unsteady. I sat down on my bed.

"Is that Matthew?" I asked my father, not quite believing it. As far as I had been aware he was still recuperating from his wound.

"Yes."

"What is he doing there? I told you I didn't want him protecting me anymore!" I said, raising my voice. My anger was rising—my father had gone against what I had requested.

"He isn't a part of your security detail, but he runs the company that is providing the bodyguards. He is still supervising your protection."

It made sense, but the news winded me slightly. I rubbed my forehead. It was unexpected and I felt a mixture of feelings at the idea that he was still a part of my life even though my intention had been to cut him out for his own safety. I was momentarily stunned.

"Shouldn't he be at home resting?" It had only been a week.

"He believes his guys will protect you better if you were at home," my father said, sidestepping my previous comment.

Was he putting extra pressure on my parents to get me to move back home?

"Your mom is worried about you." I knew that already. She'd spent every morning for at least thirty minutes on our regular phone calls for the last week trying to guilt me into coming home, but I'd stood my ground.

"I'll think about it."

If Matthew was having meetings with my father, would I see him around? There was a flutter of excitement in my stomach at the thought of seeing him again.

I had tried to keep him out of my life to keep him safe but clearly it wasn't within my control.

There were bad people in the world, people who killed with no care or conscience, but it was one thing reading or watching about it and being faced with it in real life. I had tried not to think about the man who was responsible for this and I had spent a lot of time at night remembering the picture Matthew had shown me.

After everything that had happened I wasn't sure I would ever be able to go back to the carefree person I had been before, but at least if Nick were behind bars and his organization could go on with their bad dealings with someone else in charge, I could return to some kind of normal.

My father finally gave up trying to persuade me and ended the call. I put my phone down beside my bed.

"What are we up to today?" Mark asked from the doorway of my bedroom.

I pinned him with a look that told him I wasn't in the mood for jokes. He knew very well I wasn't going to step a foot outside the front door. I wasn't stupid.

"Nowhere," I said. I hadn't been able to set foot outside the safe haven of the apartment.

A couple of policemen had come by to take a statement from me about the shooting. *Did you see the shooter? Did you see where the shot came from? Did you see anything suspicious?* I had felt useless—I hadn't been able to give them any valuable information. It had all happened so fast and my only concern had been Matthew bleeding out in front of me.

Mark remained silent, watching me.

"What?" I asked, hating the attention while I was feeling weak.

"Don't push yourself too hard," he said. "You've been through a traumatic event and you need time to deal with it."

Traumatic. Someone had tried to kill me and they had shot Matthew. It had been a life-changing event.

"How is Matthew?" I felt the need to ask. He was constantly on my mind, but hearing his voice had made it even harder to keep out of his life.

He pressed his lips together, like he didn't want to tell me. "He's angry like you knew he would be."

That piece of information did nothing to make me feel better. But had I expected anything else? No. He had every right to feel that way. If our roles were reversed I would have felt the same.

"He was having a meeting with my father."

I watched him closely but he gave nothing away.

"It's his responsibility to ensure we all do our jobs to keep you safe."

So that's what I was. It felt like I'd been slapped. A responsibility. I nodded as my throat tightened. "He should be recuperating."

Mark shrugged. "He knows his limits."

I put my hand to my forehead. Would it ever get any easier? I was struggling to move on from the shooting, and the guilt I felt at abandoning Matthew in the hospital only made me feel worse. It didn't matter that my reasons for doing so were to protect him.

"Has he asked about me?" I asked, even though I wasn't ready for the answer.

I had tried to keep him out of my life, and after the decision I had made I had no right to ask about him, but I couldn't help myself.

Mark shook his head.

I briefly closed my eyes as I felt a sharp pain in my chest. It was a familiar pain, one that reminded me how much I still loved and cared about him. Would the pain ever ease?

Was he so angry that he had cut me from his life without any problems, while I was suffering constantly? There had been a few times I had wavered in my decision and it had taken a glimpse at the memory of Matthew lying on the ground with a bullet wound to give me the strength to keep my distance.

"Courtney called again," Mark told me, changing the subject.

I didn't respond to that information. I had refused to take any of her calls.

"Shutting everyone out is not the solution."

I stood up.

"At the moment I'm a target and the people around me are in danger," I argued, feeling my rising anger at the situation I had been forced into by the actions of another. "Courtney was attacked!"

I paused when I felt my rising emotion. "And Matthew took a bullet meant for me."

He leaned against the doorway with his arms crossed,

listening to me with a contemplative look.

"Don't tell me it isn't safer for them to be out of my life."

He pressed his lips together before pushing away from the doorway. "And what about you?" he asked.

"I'll manage." There was no other way. Putting the ones I loved in danger wasn't something I could live with.

What if Courtney had died instead of just being badly beaten? What if Matthew hadn't survived the shooting? So far I had been lucky that the ones I cared about had walked away with only injuries, and I knew I might not be lucky enough for that to happen again.

"You can't keep going the way you have," he said. "You're shutting everyone out."

I started to bite my nails. It was something I hadn't done in years, but the stress and emotions from the last few days were too much to handle.

"I'm scared," I finally admitted out loud. "There have been threats before, plenty. But this was the first time someone has actually tried to hurt me."

Understanding dawned in his features. "It's understandable."

Mark walked over to me and placed his hands on my arms, leveling our gazes.

"Try not to fixate on it." I nodded, feeling like a five-year-old who was being soothed by an adult. "Your parents think it would be better for you to move back home."

My parents' house was big, and the security was top notch.

"It would be easier to keep you safe there. A secure property with limited access is much simpler to secure than an apartment in a building with no way of restricting access."

I had been too stubborn to think about it logically, but I knew it made sense.

"Fine," I grumbled. "I'll do it."

Even I knew it hadn't just been what he'd said that had changed my mind. The possibility of seeing Matthew again was too tempting to resist. It wasn't like we could go back to having what we'd had before, but I wanted to see him even if he looked at me with nothing more than anger and hatred.

"Do you think we'll find something to tie Nick to the shooting?" I asked Mark. I didn't know if he could answer the question, but he had more experience with this type of thing than I did.

I just needed to know this would not go on forever. I had to believe there would be an end to it—an end which didn't include my death.

"I want to tell you it will be over soon, but I can't," he said optimistically despite the lack of information. "We've got some of the surveillance footage for the shooting. It isn't great but we have some guys working on it to see if we can get a better picture."

"But that will be useless unless there's a way to link him to the hit."

He nodded and released his hold on me.

"What if we can't?" I asked, feeling despondent.

If we couldn't link him with the information they had been able to obtain from Courtney's kidnapping and the attempt on my life, I really felt like it was impossible to stop him—until he made another attempt. I shuddered.

"Keep positive," Mark said. "We've got guys working on this."

I wanted to believe him so badly so I nodded my head and pushed out the negative thoughts that had been cycling through my mind.

"I'm going to call your father and make the necessary arrangements to move you to the house," he said before he turned to leave. Then he stopped and looked at me over his shoulder.

"Courtney is worried about you. Call her."

I nodded tiredly. I was nervous as I picked up my phone and contemplated what I was going to say to her. She still hadn't remembered anything about her attack, and she didn't know that being my friend was what had put her in danger.

It rang three times before she answered.

"Why haven't you called me back?" she asked, sounding annoyed.

I let out a heavy sigh, still struggling with what to tell her and what not to.

"I've been worried out of my mind," she said. "I heard Matthew got shot—and no one knows why?"

I swallowed hard. My emotions were still raw from the incident. I had hoped that she wouldn't have found out yet, but it had been a feeble hope.

"What happened?"

I let out another heavy sigh. "Someone's been making threats to my father. Some of the threats have been aimed at me."

"Oh, my God," she gasped.

"I was the target at the shooting, but Matthew pushed me out of the way," I said, leaving out the fact he was a bodyguard who had put his body in the way of the bullet as part of his job. It still hurt to talk about it. I could still feel the fear from when I had first noticed he had been shot and had seen the blood staining his shirt. I squeezed my eyes closed tightly for a moment as I rode the emotion.

"How is he?" she asked, her voice a little hoarse.

They had gotten close in the short time I had been with him.

"He's fine. He's recovering."

"Which hospital is he in?" she asked.

I hesitated. If she spoke to him directly, it might get out

that he was my bodyguard.

"I think he is out of the hospital."

There was a pause.

"What's going on with you two, Sarah?" she asked. I shook my head. My friend was a lot more perceptive than I had given her credit for.

Chapter Twenty-One

I was caught between a rock and a hard place. I wanted to tell her the truth but I wanted to protect her as well, and neither option allowed me to do both. There was a choice to make.

"Sarah?" she prompted.

It was time. The nervous knot in my stomach tightened. For a moment I wondered if I was doing the right thing.

"Matthew is...was...my bodyguard," I revealed with a heavy voice, hoping I wasn't making a big mistake by revealing the truth to her.

I wanted to protect her, but I didn't want to lie to her either, and I had a feeling it would just cause more problems if she discovered the truth from someone else.

"What? I don't understand."

"I was getting threats, so my father employed Matthew to protect me," I let out with a sigh.

"Wow," was all I heard her mumble as she took in what I

said. "Did you know?" she asked.

"Not at first."

"He dated you without telling you he was employed to watch you?" she asked, sounding angry.

I didn't like how that made Matthew sound.

"My parents should have told me what was going on but they didn't want to worry me. Initially he was only supposed to watch me from a distance, but then Ryan became a nuisance."

"I get it. Ryan was definitely on the verge of stalking you but I don't know how I feel about him getting involved with you without telling you truth."

I bit my nail. "I was angry when I first found out, but we worked things out."

"So you guys are a real couple?"

We had been.

"Not anymore." Somewhere there was a dull ache in my chest reminding me of the pain of what I'd lost.

"I don't understand." There was a moment of silence.

"I broke it off with him to keep him safe." I ran a hand through my hair.

"Aww, Sarah. I'm sorry," she said, sounding concerned.

"It is what it is." There was no use feeling sorry for myself. It didn't change anything.

"Is Mark a bodyguard as well?" I sighed again. There was no point in being half honest.

"Yes. They were both employed to keep me safe."

"Oh, my gosh! This sounds like something right out of a movie."

I nodded. "Yeah, something like that." Real life was much worse.

"Did they find out who was responsible?"

"Not yet," I admitted in a heavy voice.

"What are you going to do?"

I shrugged as I paced. "I'm moving back home until the threat is gone."

"It's probably for the best. Your parents have the best security money can buy," she told me. "I'm going to miss you, but you'll be safer there."

I hesitated for a moment, trying to decide if I should tell her she'd been attacked because of me. But I decided against it. If she had forgotten about it, was there any point in bringing it up? What if it just made things worse for her?

A few minutes later I finished talking to her and placed my phone down on the table.

I heard Mark on the phone in the other room. It sounded like he was talking to my father. Maybe being home would make me feel safer. If it made it easier for Mark to keep me safe, then it was the best choice. Besides, I didn't have the energy to deal with Ryan's renewed interest.

You can't hide forever. True, but I couldn't go back to my day-to-day life and hope I survived the next time they tried to take me out. Besides, putting myself in danger put Mark's life at risk as well as Courtney's, so the best thing was to retreat back to my parents and hope everything would be solved soon.

I had to hope that Mark and whoever he had working on it would be able to find a way to prove that Nick Cole was the person responsible for the attempts on my life.

"Yeah," Mark said, and his eyes met mine. I stood in the doorway of my bedroom watching him talk on the phone.

"Tomorrow... Yes, sir." Then he ended the call.

"So tomorrow I go home?" I asked, and he nodded.

"I just need to plan the route and organize another couple of guys to follow us."

I felt alarmed. "Is that really necessary?" I asked quickly, but I already knew the answer.

"I'd rather take too many precautions than not enough."

His voice sounded calm and calculated, but his words made me feel even more nervous than before.

I nodded slowly, realizing this was real. My life was in danger. There was no more ignoring it or wishing it away.

"It'll be fine," he assured me as he gave me a sideways glance. "It's just a precaution."

"I know," I managed to mumble.

I felt the fear that had started with the attack on Courtney and had grown with Matthew getting shot take hold of me like a vise inside my chest, making it harder to breathe.

Mark walked over to me and put a hand on my arm.

"Breathe," he instructed. I followed his command and inhaled sharply, feeling my panic rise.

"I didn't mean to scare you," he assured me. "I'm planning on creating a diversion just to make sure no one follows us."

Diversion? It all felt so unreal. Like Courtney had said, something right out of a movie. Except in real life people died. I got ahold of myself and shut down the panic that had been threatening to overwhelm me.

"I'm sorry," I said, putting a hand to my temple.

"Most people in the same situation would be freaking out or on the verge of a nervous breakdown," he assured me, holding my gaze.

That made me feel a little better. "Thanks." I gave him a weak smile.

"You need to go and pack," he instructed, dropping his hand from my arm. "Just the essentials. We can get everything else sent over later."

Inside my room I surveyed my closet for a few moments before I pulled a duffel bag out and put it down on my bed. I tried to keep my mind focused on what to take with me and what could be sent later on.

I reached for my red blouse. Staring at it as my fingers rubbed the satin fabric, I remembered wearing it on a date with Matthew. We'd had so much fun, and that night had ended with amazing sex. I could still smell him and I remembered how he tasted. I shook my head, trying to rid myself of the memories that would only bring me more sadness.

I had to look on the bright side: at least he was okay. And I would be going back to my parents where I wouldn't put another person at risk again.

Somehow I managed to suppress other memories of Matthew while I put my clothes in the duffel bag. I put some toiletries into a small bag and dumped that in, too.

Resigned, I sat down on the bed. I didn't want to think of Matthew but every moment I wasn't busy with something I couldn't help but think about him. I wondered how he was doing. And there was a part of me that wondered if he would ever forgive me for leaving him when he was in the hospital.

Would he understand why I had done it? I reminded myself it didn't matter. I was making the sacrifice to save his life and it wasn't going to be easy. I had to remain strong.

My eyes went to my phone. I resisted the urge to pick it up and dial his number. It wasn't like I was going to talk to him, but I wanted to hear his voice loud and clear rather than as background noise over a phone call with my father.

But he would be angry.

The next morning I couldn't ignore the flutter of nerves as I made my first attempt to leave the apartment since Matthew had been shot.

I hadn't managed to sleep much. From three that morning I had been awake, staring at the ceiling and unable to find further solace in sleep. Instead, the threat of nightmares had kept me too afraid to fall back asleep. Even after being awake for hours, it was still hard to shake the dreams that had woken me up, shivering in fear and relieved that that's all they had been.

Mark had organized a diversion. Another guy was going to drive my car out first, hopefully catching the attention of anyone stationed outside who was possibly watching me. Another car with two other bodyguards were to follow us to give me extra protection in case the diversion failed.

Thinking of someone watching me like that did nothing to ease my growing nervousness. I clasped my hands as I waited patiently for the plan to be set in motion.

Mark gave the bodyguard who was to carry through with the diversion further instructions via the phone. When he ended the call he walked up to me where I sat on the sofa with my packed duffel bag with all my essential stuff by my feet.

The sight of him putting on a bulletproof vest brought the reality of the situation I was in home. Once he'd fitted the black vest over his shirt, he turned to me with another one. In that moment he looked every inch the trained bodyguard who was being paid to protect me. And unlike before, he was a little intimidating now.

"I need you to put this on," he said, holding the vest in one hand.

I frowned when I took the object he was holding out to me. I took it from him, trying not to shake and give away the fact that I was a frightened mess.

"Is this really necessary?"

"Again, it's just a precaution." He helped me to my feet and into the vest. He strapped it to my body. It wasn't very comfortable—but then dying wouldn't be nice either. He then helped me into my jacket.

"You ready?" he asked with a raised eyebrow as he shrugged on his leather jacket.

I wasn't, but I was out of time. I nodded. He reached for my bag. I followed him to the front entrance and hesitated momentarily before I forced myself through my fear to take my first step past the doorway and out of the apartment.

He was on guard. His eyes were looking for anything out of the ordinary. It wasn't like he was obvious about it, and to anyone looking it wouldn't be anything unusual. I noticed because I had spent so much time watching Matthew in action.

The thought of him immediately increased the aching pain in the middle of my chest. Forcing myself from my thoughts to the present situation, I followed Mark into the elevator.

Everyone else was waiting downstairs in the private parking lot located in the basement of the building. Just as the doors were about to close, a hand stopped them.

"Sorry," a guy apologized as he stepped inside. He was over six feet tall and built like a tank.

Feeling alarmed, I shifted closer to Mark, giving him a wide-eyed look. He shook his head briefly, as if reassuring me the guy wasn't a threat. But to me, every stranger had the potential to be an enemy.

Finally, when the doors opened, the stranger left before Mark walked out. My legs still felt a little shaky as I stumbled slightly. Mark put an arm around me as he hurried me to the nearby car. He opened the passenger door and I got in quickly. He closed the door and walked around the front of the car.

Once inside, he slammed the door shut and got his phone out. Fear pumped through my veins as we got closer to leaving. Mark was calm and in control. There was no outward sign he was affected at all. Maybe that was a requirement to be a good bodyguard, to be able to be cool under the most pressurized situation.

"Seatbelt," he reminded me.

My hands shook so badly I couldn't get it fastened. Mark took over and clipped it in for me.

I watched my car pull out of its parking space.

It was happening. The nervousness I had felt earlier had worsened and I felt nauseous. I breathed in and held the breath for a moment, trying to calm myself. He put his phone back into the inside pocket of his jacket while his eyes followed my car out of the exit.

"How long do we wait?" I whispered.

"A few minutes."

He gave me a sideways glance as I clasped my hands in my lap, trying to fight the urge to freak out. He put his sunglasses on.

"Trust me. I'll get you home safe." His voice pulled my attention back to him. "The windows are bulletproof."

I nodded, not wanting him to hear how nervous I was feeling. Inside it felt like there was a hurricane messing with my emotions, leaving nothing remaining where there had once been stability. I was feeling frazzled and unhooked. Even the added information that the windows were bulletproof did nothing to calm my emotions. It felt like every second we waited was dragging on, and minutes felt like hours.

Finally, Mark started up the car and backed out of the parking spot. My hands gripped my seatbelt like an anchor as we slowly made our way to the exit.

The sun blinded me for a moment, so I put my hand up to shield my eyes. I slid my sunglasses down from my forehead and over my eyes to block the bright light.

Mark did a scan of the surrounding vicinity before he turned left into the street. I fisted my hands, feeling my nails dig into my skin as I tried to remain calm. Allowing myself to freak out would only make things worse. Later, when I was safe back home, I could fall apart and allow myself to deal with the negative feelings that were spinning me out of control.

I looked back momentarily to see a car pull out from the parking lot in my building to follow behind us. They were driving the same kind of black SUV with darkened windows. I couldn't see their faces.

"Are those your guys?" I asked Mark before swallowing to ease the dryness in my throat.

"Yes."

I looked back to the front and tried to manage my breathing.

Everything will be fine, I told myself. I hated feeling weak and emotional. It was all I had seemed to feel since my life had changed when Courtney had been taken. I bit my nail.

"That's a bad habit," Mark murmured beside me. He hadn't even looked in my direction.

"I can't help it." Admitting I wasn't in complete control was difficult. "I do it when I'm stressed."

When I'd been younger my mother had tried everything to stop the habit—even making me wear nail polish that tasted terrible—but none of it had worked. I had eventually grown out of it when I had made a point of looking after my nails. But every now and then I would fall back into it. It gave me a comfort I couldn't explain.

He remained quiet as he continued to drive. It wasn't a long drive to my parents' house, but because I was on edge, it felt like it took forever.

I checked my watch. We'd been on the road for fifteen minutes.

Each time we stopped at a traffic light I could see Mark watching the surrounding cars, trying to determine if they were a threat or not.

Despite all the precautions he'd taken—the diversion, the car with the bulletproof glass and the additional bodyguards following us—I didn't feel any safer. And no matter how much he assured me that nothing would harm me, I couldn't shake the foreboding feeling that something bad was going to happen. My instinct told me it had been a mistake to leave the safety of the apartment. I gripped the seats and could only hope I was wrong.

Chapter Twenty-Two

The urge to hyperventilate was difficult to fight but somehow I continued to breathe without going into a full-blown panic.

Every now and then I would look at Mark. He was calm and drove with precision. I tried to reassure myself that if there were a problem he wouldn't look as in control as he did. I was trying every excuse I could find to talk myself out of my growing fear.

I held on to my seatbelt as I turned back to see if there was anything that looked out of place. It wasn't like I would even notice if we were being followed by someone we shouldn't, but it was a way of keeping myself busy and it felt like I was helping.

As we left the busy city road, Mark picked up the speed but remained just below the speed limit. It was only when I saw him look at the rearview mirror twice in the span of a few seconds that I felt a feeling of foreboding return.

Something was wrong.

"We're being followed," Mark said, answering my unasked question.

Oh, my God!

Horror and fear gripped me like a vise. Unable to breathe, I held on to my seatbelt for dear life. Even though Mark had put security measures in place to use a diversion, it hadn't worked. Had there been more than one person watching me just in case? Was Nick so determined to get his revenge that he would do anything he could to ensure I couldn't escape him?

I checked the speedometer, but Mark wasn't going any faster. Why wasn't he putting his foot down and getting me out of here as fast as possible? If I had been in the driver's seat I would have sped up and tried to lose them. I wanted to shout at him to go faster, but I bit my lip. Yelling at him wasn't going to help. He had to keep calm and allow his training to guide him on the best way out of the situation we were in.

Unable to stop myself, I looked back. The black SUV behind us was fighting to stay on the road as another SUV tried to push it off. My mouth dropped open at such a brazen action in the middle of the day.

I closed my eyes as I faced the front again. Seeing that only made me feel more frightened. They were going to do anything they could to take me out. If they ran us off the road and caused an accident, bulletproof windows weren't going to help. And my bulletproof vest would also be useless.

Breathe in, I commanded myself. *Breathe out.* Allowing myself to spiral into a sobbing mess wasn't going to help anything. *Keep your control. You can do this.*

"Hold on," Mark instructed.

With one hand I gripped the seat and the other I held my seatbelt. Fear sped up my heart and I could feel it thump in my chest with every beat.

There was a sound of metal scraping against metal behind us. It had to be the other SUV. Had they run them off the road? I was too scared to look back again. Like if I didn't see what was happening, I could lie to myself and tell myself I would be okay.

A loud bang made my heart slam into my chest—they were shooting at us.

"Get down!" Mark commanded with one hand pushing my head down and my sunglasses dropped to the ground.

The sound of wheels squealing and then a louder sound of metal crunching made me close my eyes and start to pray.

Please, let us be okay. Please let me get home safe, I thought desperately, one prayer after the other, hoping someone would answer them.

Mark had taken a back route to my parents' house, which added an extra ten minutes onto our journey. The road was a single lane through the residential area. Now I wished he'd taken the shorter route.

I felt the car jerk slightly and realized it was caused by a car pushing us from behind. The only sound was the deafening squeal of the tires as Mark tried to shake them. Metal and against metal, the car tried again and again.

Another shot rang out, hitting the car. *Thump, thump.* I put my hands over my head.

We were going to die. They would push us off the road like they had done to the other SUV. And even if by some miracle we survived the impact they would be there to finish off the job.

I could swear I saw my life flash before my eyes. And the depressing thing was that it hadn't taken that long. I was so young—I hadn't even had a proper chance to live. All those meaningless hookups that were supposed to make me feel independent and in control had only made me feel empty inside.

How many people would care if I died? My parents would. An image of Courtney appeared in my mind. She would be devastated. And Matthew? He would mourn the loss of his friend and partner, Mark—but would he mourn for me? He was probably still upset I had turned my back on him when he'd been in the hospital recovering from the injury that had saved my life. Or had he realized my motives behind the action?

The car jolted forward and brought me back to the present situation with a thud. I held on desperately, trying to hold on as the car swerved and Mark tried to keep them from pulling up beside us.

"Call Matthew," Mark said, with the first signs of strain evident in his voice. He had both hands on the steering wheel, keeping a close eye on the car still trying to run us off the road.

With shaking hands I got my phone out of my bag, still hunched over, and tried to call Matthew. It took me a few tries before I put my phone against my ear and heard it ringing.

"Matthew," he answered after a couple of rings. His voice was distant but I felt it wash over me like a protective blanket.

"Matthew," I breathed, struggling to keep the hysteria at bay.

"What's wrong?" he asked, immediately picking up on the stress in my voice.

"Tell him Charles and Ben were pushed off the road," Mark said, pulling sharply to the left to cut off the car. Another shot rang out.

My mind was muddled trying to answer Matthew while taking instructions from Mark.

"Sarah, what's going on?" Matthew commanded.

"Matthew...we're in trouble," I managed to get out.

Another sharp swerve made me drop the phone. I had to regain my balance before I leaned over and picked it up off the floor in front of me.

"Sarah!" Matthew yelled so loud I could hear him before I put the phone back against my ear, still keeping my head down.

"I'm here! They pushed the other car off the road," I began to babble, trying to get him all the information I could. "They're trying to run us off the road too."

"Where are you?" Matthew asked. It didn't make me feel any better when I heard the worry in his voice.

I knew the area, but the adrenaline I felt made it hard to concentrate on the road names and for the life of me I couldn't remember them offhand.

"I don't know," I said, on the verge of tears. "I can't remember."

"It's okay," Matthew said, calmly now, completely different from how he'd sounded at first.

Mark rattled off the name of the road we were on and the upcoming intersection. I repeated it to Matthew.

I nodded and pressed the phone closer to my ear. I whimpered when we suddenly jolted to the side and I put my hand out to steady myself, but the force was so strong I felt a sharp pain in my wrist.

"What happened?" Matthew asked.

"I'm okay," I assured him, keeping my injured arm close to my chest.

"Stay on the line with me." He didn't have to tell me that—I didn't have the courage to end the call. It was a lifeline.

The constant swerving was making me ill and I didn't know how much more I could take.

I heard Matthew talking in the background. Mark swore

beside me and it was the first time I had ever seen him visibly alarmed.

"I've got people on the way. There's an ambulance for Charles and Ben," Matthew said when he came back on the line. "Tell Mark they'll be there soon."

"He has help on the way," I said to Mark, who clenched his teeth as he held the steering wheel like a vise grip in his hands. His arm muscles strained as he continued to fight for our survival.

"He is sending an ambulance for Charles and Ben," I relayed the information in a shaky voice.

He never answered as I held the phone against my ear, listening to Matthew on the other side. "Stay with me, Sarah. They should be there soon."

I closed my eyes tightly, trying to block out everything but his voice. He kept talking to me, like he knew how much I needed him to stay on the phone with me.

"Everything will be okay." I didn't believe a word he said. I was in the middle of a situation spiraling out of control with every minute that passed. But the sound of his voice held me together like glue.

Mark swore beside me and I knew we were in bigger trouble than before.

I opened my eyes to see a car pull up alongside us. I gasped when the driver smashed into the side of our SUV.

I screamed as the action jolted us.

"Sarah?" Matthew prompted, but fear had locked my throat closed and I was unable to say anything. All I could do was watch in slow motion as the car swerved at us again. The sound of the car scraping against ours made me gasp. The driver pulled out a gun and aimed it at me. The shot hit the bulletproof glass. My mind reeled from the action.

In the distance outside my bubble of fear I heard the faint sound of a police siren.

"Sarah!" Matthew yelled through the phone, and I pressed the phone against my ear.

"They're shooting at us," I breathed, closing my eyes tightly and trying to stop the hysteria from taking over. If I couldn't see it, I would be okay.

"Mark will get you out of it," he assured me, his voice only wavering for a split second. It was enough for me to know he was worried, really worried.

His words made my tummy feel warm. It was difficult to keep my feelings for him suppressed.

"Help is on the way. They should be there soon," he continued.

The sounds of sirens got closer and closer.

"The cops," I murmured.

The car beside me slowed before making a U-turn. The action of withdrawal was so sudden it took a few moments for it to sink in.

"Sarah?" Matthew said with concern.

I held the phone tighter against my ear as the sight of the police car came into sight in front of us.

"They're here." I swallowed the emotion that bubbled to the surface.

"They're here," I repeated, nodding to confirm I wasn't seeing things. We passed the cop car and it turned to follow us.

"Hold on a sec." I heard him talking in the background. I couldn't stop the call even if I wanted to. I don't know if it was the adrenaline or the shock that had set in but I remained fixated on the distance in front of me, still unable to process what had just happened.

Voices echoed around me. Mark touched my arm and I looked at him, still holding the phone in my hand but not against my ear. His mouth was moving but I couldn't hear anything he was saying. He frowned and took the phone from me.

He pressed the phone against his ear while he continued to drive. He wasn't stopping.

What if they come back? I shook my head, unable to contemplate that.

Dazed, I looked to the front, my eyes unseeing. My wrist throbbed.

I'd hurt myself trying to keep myself from flying around the car, I remembered vaguely. I wasn't sure how long I sat there staring at my wrist before I looked up to see the familiar gates of my parents' home swing open.

One breath in. I exhaled. I was home. I was safe.

Fear and pain throbbed through me. I began to shake, feeling my entire body tremble. The hysteria I had managed to suppress welled up in me.

I looked at Mark as the car stopped. Slowly I began to hear the sounds of doors opening.

One breath in. I tried to remember to breathe to keep myself from giving in to the emotions that needed to be released.

"Sarah," a voice breathed—it was so close.

I turned my head. Matthew pulled me gently out of the car. Emotions that had been frozen with fear began to warm and seep through me.

He winced slightly when I touched his side. Then I remembered that's where he had been shot. He was still injured.

For the last week he had been on my mind and the fact that he was really here in front of me, looking at me with fear in his eyes... I could have died today.

"Say something, Sarah," he said gently. His hand touched my face. I swallowed.

Then I realized he was scanning me for injuries. His arm wrapped around me and he led me inside. I stumbled slightly, unable to put one foot in front of the other. My feet felt like lead.

I caught sight of Mark talking to a couple of police officers as I walked beside Matthew and into the house.

"Sarah," my mother gasped. She rushed toward me.

She hugged me but I didn't have the strength to return the gesture. My arms stayed limp by my sides.

"What's wrong?" Her eyes searched mine.

It was like my mind was still trying to catch up with my body. I felt dazed and unable to process what was going on.

"She's in shock," Matthew answered and steered me into the nearby kitchen. "I need some sugar water."

While my mother hurried to get what he asked for, he sat me down.

"Are you in pain?" He spoke to me like he was talking to a child.

My wrist was throbbing. I lifted my arm and his fingers touched the darkening bruise. I winced when his fingers applied a little more pressure.

"It doesn't look like anything is broken." I nodded absently, trusting him. It hurt but once the adrenaline wore off it would be much worse.

"We might need a doctor to check her over," Matthew said to my mother as he began to check for other injuries.

I didn't want to be checked by anyone else. I was tired and sore.

One breath in. My breathing halted when a tidal wave of emotion suddenly got caught in my throat. My eyes held Matthew's as they began to water and a sob tore from me. I was coming apart at the seams and there was no way to stop it.

He put his arms around me and hugged me as I began to sob, unable to stop the tears.

"Here," my mother said as she handed Matthew a glass

filled with liquid.

Matthew held me for a few more minutes before my sobbing eased. "Drink," he instructed when he pulled away. I took a gulp and spluttered.

"Easy there," he soothed as he gently patted my back.

I wiped my mouth with my uninjured arm.

"Sarah," my mother said.

"Mom." I swallowed, trying to keep myself from crying again.

"You're okay," she soothed, gently tucking my hair behind my ear.

I winced when I raised my hand to smooth my messy hair. I didn't feel okay. Closing my eyes, I was forced to relive in flashes of memories another attempt on my life.

"How long before the doctor gets here?" Matthew asked my mother.

"He should be here any minute."

I wasn't okay. Not by a long shot. My body began to tremble so badly I messed some of the sugar water as I gulped some more down.

"Slowly," Matthew instructed.

More images flashed through my mind. I closed my eyes tightly, trying to suppress them, not ready to experience it all again. Someone had tried to kill me. The sound of metal against metal and the glass shattering reminded me they had nearly succeeded. The memory of the driver taking a shot at me echoed in my ears.

I stood up and pushed Matthew's hand away.

"No," I mumbled, backing up against the wall.

Matthew stood up and walked to me while my mom watched with concern from behind him.

"You're safe," he said in a calm voice.

I closed my eyes and concentrated on the sound of his voice, needing it to soothe me like nothing else could.

His hand touched my arm.

I kept my eyes closed. "I'm not...safe."

"You are."

His hand found mine. I hadn't realized how much I had missed his touch until his fingers threaded through mine.

"Sarah."

I opened my eyes to look up at him.

"I will keep you safe." They weren't just words. It was written in his eyes. He meant every word.

Chapter Twenty-Three

I lay on my side in my bed with the covers up to my chin. The room was dark but I wasn't alone.

He hadn't left me, not once. When he'd tried to leave the room when the doctor had checked me over, I'd become hysterical. Even my parents couldn't make me feel the safety he did.

He sat watching me in the nearby chair.

"Sleep, Sarah," he said as he shifted slightly in his seat. He looked uncomfortable but I was too selfish to tell him I would be okay on my own.

I closed my eyes and tried to keep them shut but the memory of the driver aiming the gun at me made me open my eyes. There was no way I would be able to drop off to sleep on my own so when the doctor had offered me sleeping tablets I had taken them.

The sound of a gunshot echoed through the mist. It was dark and I struggled to see anything in front of me. The mist was damp and cold.

Tires squealed and I stood, still trying to get my bearings. My heart began to speed up as I looked around but I was unable to see anything. Fear took over in an instant. Something bad was going to happen.

You'll be okay, *I kept repeating to myself.* Don't be afraid.

The mist in front of me began to clear. A man without any features wearing sunglasses held a gun loosely at his side.

"Please, don't." There was no doubt what his intention was. "Please."

In a flash he lifted the gun and shot me without any hesitation. Pain exploded in my stomach and I faltered. My hand went to my stomach and I touched the blood seeping into my shirt.

That moment I woke up with a start, frantic. My hand went to my stomach and there was no bullet wound or blood.

"It's just a dream," a familiar voice soothed. Hands touched mine in the darkness and I made a move to pull away before I realized it was Matthew.

Feeling rattled by the remnants of the dream, I gripped his shirt in my hands.

"It felt so real," I whispered, still trying to calm myself down. My one hand released his shirt to soothe over my stomach to reassure myself I hadn't been shot.

Feeling vulnerable I began to cry, unable to separate the emotions from my nightmare. It had felt so real.

"Shhh," he soothed as the bed dipped beside me. His strong arms enveloped me, making me feel safe and protected.

I let out a trembling breath, trying to release the fear from my nightmare. I leaned closer, closing my eyes as a few more tears escaped, dampening his shirt. The familiar smell of him reassured my senses. He released a heavy breath before he got into the bed beside me. I lay carefully beside him, making sure not to touch his healing gunshot wound.

"Does it still hurt?" It was a stupid question—of course it still hurt. It had only been just over a week.

"It's fine," he said stiffly. I closed my eyes when I felt the wave of guilt. There was no taking it back. I had made the decision with his wellbeing in the foremost of my mind and if I were faced with the same situation I would do it again.

I lay as close as I could to him without intertwining our bodies. This was about feeling protected and he was the only person who made me feel that way. And after my horrific day, I allowed myself to cling to him.

I promised myself it would just be for the night. When the sun rose the next morning I would have the strength to keep my distance from him like I had intended.

I breathed Matthew in, taking comfort in the familiar smell of him. He didn't hold me close like he would have before. Despite the near-death experience, we weren't back to where we had been before. Despite our physical closeness the emotional valley between us was a reminder of the betrayals that had pulled us apart.

Listening to the sound of his heart beneath my ear, I closed my eyes and concentrated on the fact that despite the shooting and the car chase, we were both alive and, for this moment, together. Tomorrow it would be different.

Even now as we lay together things were not the same.

I don't know if it was the tablets or just being with Matthew but I drifted to sleep. Sometime later I woke up with a start, sitting up in the bed.

The space where Matthew had been was empty and I looked around the room. He was sleeping in the chair with his long legs straightened in front of him, crossed at the ankles.

The memories of the nightmare still held me firmly in its grasp and it took me a few minutes to assure myself it had only been a dream and that I was safe in my bedroom.

I shoved my hair out of my face as I tried to even my breathing, clutching the sheet close to my chest while I tried to sort through my thoughts. The slight throb in my wrist reminded me how close I had come to death the day before. It was wrapped up tight. The doctor had assured me it had just been badly bruised.

There was the unmistakable feeling of loss and disappointment that sometime in the night he had left me alone in the bed. It was a reminder I had hurt him and I had to accept the consequences.

While he slept peacefully, I took the time to watch him. I had missed him so much and being able to give myself a few stolen minutes I could take him in with him unaware was something I treasured. He shifted slightly in the chair. He looked uncomfortable and I felt bad. He would rather try and sleep uncomfortably than lie beside me in a comfortable bed.

Feeling a renewed sense of hurt, I dragged myself out of my bed as quietly as I could to my bathroom. I closed the door and leaned against it for a few moments, trying to find the strength to push myself through the fear of what happened yesterday. There was nothing I could do about it. It was over, and somehow I needed to find a way to deal with it without leaning on Matthew.

My attempt to keep him out of my life had failed. All it had done was hurt him. It was complicated. Feeling frustrated with myself, I stripped and got into the shower. I washed myself as well as I could with my injured wrist. I tightened the towel around me before I entered my bedroom.

Matthew was sitting on the chair rubbing his neck.

I stopped and watched. It was only a few moments before his eyes lifted to mine. I swallowed. The soft look of affection I was used to seeing in his eyes when he looked at me was gone. It confirmed we were still back to where we were before yesterday's attempt on my life. It was something I already knew, but being confronted with it directly was different.

"Thanks for staying with me," I said quietly.

He stood up and shrugged his shoulders. "It's my job." His cold eyes held mine.

His words hurt but I tried to hide how much. "I told my father I didn't want you involved in my security anymore."

My feelings for him made me want to push him further away but that wasn't within my control anymore. I took solace in the fact that my decision to keep him safe had at least taken him out of direct line as my bodyguard.

He put his hands on his hips as he cocked his head to the side. "I run the company, so I make the decisions when it comes to your safety." His eyes were cold. "I told your father if you don't want me involved then he could hire another company."

The fact that he had been prepared to walk away made it harder to breathe but I remained calm on the outside even if it had been what I wanted. The wrestle between my mind and heart was confusing.

"But your father knows we are the best and he isn't willing to take any chances with your life."

It irked me that I had put myself through hell to do the right thing and it had all been for nothing.

"Fine," I said stiffly. "I don't want what happened between us to make things uncomfortable."

"The only way things would be uncomfortable is if I still cared," he said, his voice calm and in control. His eyes darkened. "And trust me: I don't."

There was no softness in his features, which only added to his words. He was over me. I'd succeeded. My throat tightened but I pushed through the pain.

"Good." It took all of my control to walk past him like I hadn't just had my heart wrenched from my chest as I went to open the closet. I looked back at him over my shoulder. "Get out. I need to get dressed."

He didn't linger. The door closed behind me and I felt the sting of tears. The fact that he had not slammed the door showed his calm control. If he had still cared he would have been angry and would have slammed it. I felt the loss. It was like a piece of me was missing.

Still holding on to the door of the closet, I struggled to rein in my tears. I gritted my teeth and tilted my head upward for a few moments. My heart hurt.

I had just gotten some clothes on when there was a knock at my door.

"Come in."

My father stepped into the room. "Sarah."

"Hi."

He walked to me and engulfed me in a hug. "You're okay." He breathed into my hair, taking me by surprise.

My mother had been the affectionate parent, constantly wrapping me up in hugs and dropping kisses on my cheeks. My father on the other hand had been the complete opposite. I can't remember the last time he'd told me he loved me before all this had started, whereas my mom had told me every day.

I nodded. "I'm fine."

"Someone will be over later to take a statement," he informed me.

At this rate I would be on a first-name basis with all the cops in the area. I frowned when I remembered I had seen the face of the driver clearly before he had tried to shoot me.

"I saw one of the guys," I murmured to my father, still taking in the details from my memory, his deep-set eyes and his shaved head.

"Would you be able to identify him?"

It was a moment in time engraved in my memory

because of the fear I had felt at that exact second.

"Yes."

I had the hope that somehow being able to identify the guy would lead to a link to Nick, and it would be enough to put him away.

Later that day after giving the cops a statement and going through some photos, we had been unable to link the guy I had seen to Nick. I looked out the window and across the lush gardens of my parents' estate.

The only feeling I could describe was sadness. It felt like no matter how hard I tried I would never be able to escape the situation I was in. Was it only of a matter of time before they got it right and took my life?

I started biting my nails.

"You need to stop that or you won't have any nails left," a voice said behind me. I turned to look at Mark over my shoulder.

"Biting nails doesn't seem so bad compared to a psychiatric ward." I shrugged.

He came to stand beside me.

"I feel like I'm stuck in limbo, in constant fear of what's going to happen," I murmured. I felt his eyes on me. I don't know what was making me reveal my innermost thoughts to him. "I just want it to be over with."

"I get it," he said from beside me, looking back out the window. "I wish I could tell you it will end soon, but I would be lying."

I nodded, and we stood there, silently looking out the window. A minute later, I heard a sound by the door.

"Am I interrupting something?" Matthew asked. His voice was laced with anger.

"No." I turned to face him. Mark looked between the two of us and made an excuse before leaving the room. I crossed my arms as I faced Matthew. He closed the door behind him and leaned against it as our eyes met.

"Keep away from Mark," he warned, pushing off the door.

I frowned. "That's a bit difficult when he's my bodyguard."

His eyes glittered with anger and I had the urge to make him lose control and lash out at me in some way.

"You know what I mean," he told me curtly as he stopped in front of me.

I looked up at him. "You don't get to tell me what I can or can't do."

The pull of the attraction was hard to fight even though I didn't want to feel it. And he had made it clear he had washed his hands of me.

"Don't play games with me," he said tightly.

He was dressed in a suit. It was strange and sexy to see him dressed more formally. I had the urge to slide my hands up his chest and grip his collar while I kissed him. Mentally I shook the thought away.

"I don't have time for jealousy," I said sharply, without thinking. Once the words were out of my mouth I realized I'd said it to get a rise out of him.

My mind told me to stay away from him but my heart needed to know he still cared.

He gave me a hollow laugh. "Is that what you think this is?" he asked.

I kept quiet.

"I'm not jealous." His words felt like a blow to my chest and it burned. "I know you."

His eyes held mine, like he was seeing right through me down to my inner self. "You're looking for another distraction, someone to toy with to pass the time."

I swallowed, trying to keep him from seeing how much his words affected me. The person he was describing wasn't me anymore. I'd changed.

"You'll use him and when you're bored you will move on to the next one."

The only thing was that with him it had been different. There had been more. He'd been the only one to touch me in a way that had opened me up, and before I had realized it, it had been too late. I loved him.

"So why not let me play?" I said seductively, needing to inflict the pain I was experiencing back on him. "I need something to keep me busy."

He walked closer, backing me up to the wall behind me.

His eyes darkened as he pressed his lips together. His hand wrapped around my uninjured wrist.

"I'm warning you," he threatened. He leaned closer.

I swept my tongue across my bottom lip, knowing exactly what the little gesture would do to him. He might not care about me anymore but he was a red-blooded guy and I knew exactly how to get what I wanted.

His eyes dropped to my lips and his hold on my wrist tightened, proving he wasn't unaffected.

"What are you going to do if I don't listen?" I whispered, feeling my blood heat in my veins. I remembered what it felt like to have his lips against mine, his hard body pressed against mine. I felt a shiver of anticipation.

His mouth covered mine, taking me by surprise. There was no resistance as his mouth savaged mine. It was unlike any kiss we had ever shared before. This was hot and hard.

His lips bruised mine with their pressure but I gripped his shirt, not wanting him to stop. He pushed me against the wall. His hands moved to my hips and pulled me close. There were so many reasons to stop what was happening between us, but I had no willpower.

I was addicted to him and, like a drug addict, I was powerless to resist. There was only a need to get as close to him as possible. My senses were surrounded by his smell and touch and were going wild. My breath was ragged when his hands dug into my hips. I was sure there would be bruises later but I didn't care.

He abruptly pulled away, leaving me struggling to keep myself upright. His breathing was ragged like mine; there was no mistaking the effect I had on him. He wiped his mouth with the back of his hand as he stepped back. That stung. The disgust was evident in his eyes as they held mine. He wasn't even trying to protect my feelings. This was so unlike the Matthew I had known before.

He turned and without another word left the study.

The sound of the door slamming lifted my heart. I had gotten to him—and that was something I could hold on to.

Chapter Twenty-Four

For the next couple of weeks, Matthew kept his distance. I don't know how he did it but I didn't see much of him at all.

Just thinking about the last time we had spoken in the study made me touch my lips. They'd felt a little bruised but the intensity of the kiss had left my knees trembling afterward. He was different, and our physical reaction to each other had not been the same. It felt like somehow our roles had been reversed. I was the one with feelings and he was the one trying to fight it.

Pining for someone like I had for the last couple of weeks wasn't like me. I was about to bite my nails, but I stopped myself. Mark's constant reminders about my bad nail-biting habit had finally started to sink in. Or maybe it was that no one had tried to kill me in the last three weeks.

The longer it had gone without another attempt on my life, the safer I felt. Did I dare to hope Nick had given up trying to kill me? Mark was convinced he was biding his time, waiting for the right time and opportunity.

And trust me, there hadn't been any. I'd been holed up like a prisoner and being confined to the property was starting to drive me crazy. I wanted to be able to go out and walk in the crowds without being afraid. I wanted to go back to college. Being restricted wasn't my idea of fun and the absence of Matthew in my life only compounded the issue.

I would catch a glimpse of him talking to my father here and there, but he always ensured I never had the chance to corner him. It was frustrating and the hurt I was experiencing was only eased by the fact that I was convinced he still felt something for me despite his words.

Today I was determined to act like a normal girl my age. I couldn't leave the property, but there was stuff I could do around the house.

It had been warm and I decided to go for a swim. I went through some of my swimsuits and I smiled when I saw a racy red bikini I'd bought. It hadn't been bought for functionality, but for making a statement. I had no idea if Matthew was even around today; but if he saw me in this I knew it would be harder for him to resist. I was playing with fire and the thought of being burned only excited me.

I would take anything I could from him; the indifference was torture. I had tried to distance him from me to keep him safe but it hadn't worked. Being around him as nothing more than a person who needed to be protected was hurting me.

For his own safety I had been willing to give him up but he had been determined to stay in my life and there was nothing I could do to stop him. Having him around made it more and more impossible to stay away. He was the flame and I was the moth determined to get as close as possible no matter the pain that would result from it. I wanted him to hold me close, like he used to. That warm fuzzy feeling I would feel when he pressed a kiss to my forehead made me feel adored.

I slipped into the bikini, taking a quick survey of the tiny material that just barely covered the necessities in the mirror, and I knew it would be enough to attract Matthew's attention.

The house was quiet. My father had gone into the office and my mom was visiting one of the neighbors.

"Is that a bikini?" Mark asked, watching me descend the stairs.

"Yes," I said with a confident smile.

"You think that'll work?" he asked, raising an eyebrow as he surveyed me.

"Something has to," I said, not feeling as confident as I wanted to. I couldn't contemplate that he would have truly moved on from me already.

It didn't help that Mark wouldn't tell me much. They were best friends and that ensured his loyalty lay with Matthew.

"Did you tell him why I left him at the hospital?" I asked.

He shook his head. "He never asked."

It hurt but I refused to show it.

I walked out of the house and to the back yard. Inside the pool house I found a towel before I headed to the pool. The water was beautiful and I savored the smell of it as I stretched my arms above my head, breathing in the air.

The rays of the sun warmed my skin. I sat down by the side of the pool and put my feet in. The water was cool and soothing. I leaned back on my hands, tilting my head up to the cloudless sky.

"What the hell are you doing?" an angry voice cut in.

I opened one eye and saw Matthew standing beside me with his hands on his hips. Suits definitely looked good on him. Today he was wearing a dark navy one.

"I would have thought that was obvious." I inclined my head to the pool. "People call it swimming."

He was angry and he'd never looked sexier.

"Being outside isn't safe," he ground out. He turned his attention to the huge surrounding wall.

I drank him in while he continued to lecture me. "It's boring inside. I needed some vitamin D."

His eyes drifted back to mine. "Would you rather be dead?"

"Such a spoil sport." I shrugged before I got up.

He hadn't moved so I stood in front of him, our eyes meeting. His eyes broke from mine and drifted over me. He couldn't hide how his eyes flared as they took in the tiny ruby-red bikini. I smiled at him seductively as his gaze lifted to mine.

"You like what you see?" I asked him, teasing him lightly, my eyes sparkling with mischievous intent.

His features turned to stone but I could see the battle within him. His eyes didn't lie.

"I need sunscreen," I said, reaching for the bottle beside the chaise lounge. "Please?"

I swept my tongue across my bottom lip and his eyes followed the action.

"You need to go inside," he said through gritted teeth. His eyes were still fixed on my mouth.

He gravitated closer and I held my breath as I stayed still. I could feel the heat of his body as he leaned closer. The urge to surge forward to close the distance between us was tempting, but I kept fixed to the spot. I feared pushing him would push him away and that was the last thing I wanted.

Our lips were so close but I restrained myself, refusing to give an inch. He had to come to me. He stopped and I waited. Our eyes held.

"Go inside," he whispered. I refused by not following his command.

He swore softly under his breath and he sealed our lips together. His hands cupped my face while his lips moved against mine, taking me with force. I would have him any way I could. Even if it wasn't like he had been before. If that was lost I would make do with what remained.

I opened my mouth as I finally curled my arms around his neck. He took charge as his tongue swirled against mine. That familiar ache and need for him came alive, heating the blood in my veins.

His hands dropped to my waist, lifting me, and my legs instinctively wrapped around him. It was a need—not just a want. I felt like everything that had been happening in the last few weeks had led us to this point. His teeth grazed my lip and I groaned. He walked and the next thing I knew we were in the pool house. He kicked the door closed behind him.

I hung on to him as his mouth slid along my neck, nipping me with his teeth. He'd never been this in control and I reveled in handing it over to him.

He set me down. My legs felt unsteady. His mouth covered mine again as he backed me against the wall, his hands reaching the clasp of the bikini in front. The flimsy material slackened and it dropped to the floor.

With a hand on either side of me, caging me in, he kissed me again. It left my knees weak. He moved down and took a nipple into his mouth. While he sucked, I raked my hand through his hair as I closed my eyes, giving in to my body, which craved his.

When he straightened, I was hanging on by the thinnest thread, ready to break at any moment. My hands went to his trousers. I fumbled with his belt and then the top bottom. His lips dropped kisses along my collar bone.

I pushed his trousers down and then his boxers. My hand closed over his hardness. It was velvety and smooth. There were no words. He yanked down my bikini bottoms and I kicked them free. I needed him as much as he did me. He lifted me slightly and lined his body against mine. I sank down on him with a gasp.

It was unlike anything I had ever experienced with him. He fucked me up against the wall as I held his broad shoulders and gasped while my legs wrapped around his waist, angling our bodies as close as we could.

He set a fast pace and soon I felt the familiar tightening of my body as I came. He continued to thrust into me as I held on. His body tensed and he rested his head in the hollow of my neck as he released into me. I wrapped my arms around him and held him while we tried to catch our breath.

It had been wild and all-consuming. Every atom of my being was tuned to his and I didn't want it to end. I unwrapped my legs and Matthew disengaged. I leaned against the wall as he pulled away to get dressed.

There was no emotion in his features as I watched him. My chest was rising and falling quickly with each breath.

As the silence between us continued, it became more and more uncomfortable. I waited for him to say something but he didn't. He refused to look at me, turning his back while he tucked his shirt in and tied his belt.

Only when he was completely dressed did he turn his attention to me. I was still naked, having made no attempt to get dressed.

I stood with my arms at my sides, refusing to hide my nakedness from him. His eyes slid over me and I felt uneasy that he hadn't spoken a word. I had expected something, even if it was only in anger, but there was nothing.

Then without any forewarning he turned and I watched, stunned. He left the pool house and closed the door behind him.

The ache in my chest split open like a new wound and I swallowed hard. My throat burned as I felt the sting of tears. This time I didn't fight them. Something had been lost.

In all the time we'd been together he had never been this rough and I had loved every second of it, but the hollowness I felt at the way he had abruptly left without a word tainted it. I slid down until I rested my chin on my knees staring at the closed door Matthew had walked out of. I'd hoped once we'd been intimate again it would fix whatever I had broken but it hadn't. And I had no idea what to do next.

Lost was how I felt when I finally stood up and scooped my clothes up. I couldn't let Mark come looking for me and find me like this.

With shaking hands, I got dressed. I struggled slightly with the clasp of my bikini top. Once I was dressed I walked out of the pool house. Standing in front of the pool, watching the water glisten in the sunlight, I tried to figure out how it had all gone so wrong.

Remembering the way he had viewed my nakedness before he had left without a word made it harder to breathe and my eyes watered. A tear slid down my cheek as I continued to stare, unseeing, wrestling with the heartache I was experiencing.

The water beckoned to me, offering me a way to stop the pain. I fell into the pool. The shock of the freezing water wrapped around me, making me unable to feel anything but the shock of the cold. I let myself sink, allowing the coldness to ease the pain inside.

There was a sound of something crashing into the water, and a hand pulled me to the surface. I fought against it as it dragged me out of the pool.

"What the hell are you doing?" Mark said. His forehead was furrowed as he glared at me. He was soaked, his clothes matted his skin.

I pulled out of his grasp and waded over to the steps.

"Sarah." He wasn't going to let it go.

"It wasn't what you think," I threw over my shoulder.

He wiped his face as he followed behind me. "It looked like you were trying to drown yourself."

Remembering my reasons returned that awful feeling in the middle of my chest. The temporary numbness was already gone.

He stopped me just as I stepped out of the pool. My body was starting to tremble from the cold. Water dripped down my face and body.

"Why?" he asked. His eyes searched mine as if he could find the answer in them.

I closed my eyes briefly, trying to overcome the emotions I was feeling. "I just needed the pain to stop."

He frowned and began to look for injuries.

I pulled my arm out of his hold. "I'm not physically hurt."

Then realization filtered into his eyes. "What happened?"

I shrugged. I wasn't good at rejection or revealing it to someone.

"Does it matter?" It came out as a hoarse whisper and I felt like I was about to burst into tears. I gritted my teeth to stop myself, refusing to show how vulnerable I felt.

"What did he do?" he asked, still frowning.

"It's not his fault," I began to say and then I let out a deep emotional breath. "I did this. I broke us."

His features softened and he took the last step out of the pool to stand in front of me. His hand reached out and touched my arm.

"Everything you did was because you love him."

"It doesn't matter what my reasons were," I said bitterly. "The outcome is still the same." I swallowed hard, tying to keep my composure, but the softening in his features made it harder to keep it up.

"You want me to talk some sense into him?" he offered.

I didn't believe he could fix this. It would just probably cause issues between the two of them and I didn't want that.

"No. That would just make things worse."

I reached for the towel on the chaise and wrapped it around me, feeling a need to use it as a shield.

He gave me a slight nod, accepting my request before I walked back to the house, hoping I wouldn't run into Matthew again. I was feeling raw and vulnerable. There was no way I would be able to bottle up my emotions if I had to face him again.

From the pain in my chest I didn't know how long it would be before I would be able to see him again.

It was only upstairs in my bedroom after I closed my door that I felt I could release the tears. I sat down on my bed with the towel still wrapped around me. I could still feel Matthew's body imprinted against mine, the graze of his stubble against my cheek, while I cried for losing what we'd had.

Like I had told Mark, it didn't matter what my reasons had been. There was no guarantee that knowing why I had done it would wipe away his reasons for being angry with me.

And it was probably too late already. The hope I held before had disappeared and all I was left with was a nothingness. I wanted to remember what we had but I wasn't strong enough to endure it knowing it was already lost.

I didn't leave my room for the rest of the day. I tucked myself into my bed and hid from the world while I licked my wounds and tried to figure out how to carry on.

Chapter Twenty-Five

This time it was harder to pretend everything was fine. My heart had been battered and bruised, which only worsened when I caught a glimpse of the reason why. I'd seen him twice in the last couple of days and it had been enough to steal the breath from my lungs, making it harder to breathe.

Our eyes had met and the coldness in his eyes had stopped me in my tracks. He'd never looked at me like that. It felt like our brief encounter hadn't impacted him at all. It was like he'd shrugged off whatever happened between us and carried on like nothing had ever happened.

Not only had it damaged my confidence but it had only worsened my heartbreak. I had always been the one to walk away but this time I was the one being left behind.

It was just before lunch and I went downstairs to raid the fridge. I was craving some junk food. Dealing with a broken heart was making me crave sugar for some reason. I opened the fridge and leaned in, looking for something to fill the gap in my chest, but nothing piqued my interest. I closed the fridge.

I heard steps outside the kitchen and walked over to the doorway to see. I caught sight of the back of Matthew. It hit me square in the chest like a hammer, leaving me shaken. He was headed in the direction of my father's study. Did he have a meeting with my father? My father was working from home for the day.

I debated what to do for a few brief seconds before I decided to follow him quietly. He entered the study but didn't close the door. As I drew closer I could hear him talking to my father. For a moment I closed my eyes and listened to the sound of Matthew's voice. I missed it, and him. When I opened my eyes I released a quiet, emotional breath. I was about to turn and leave, scared I would be caught, when I heard what they were talking about.

"I'm not sure that's a good idea," I heard my father say.

Now I was curious. What did Matthew want to do? I pressed myself up against the wall and edged closer to ensure I heard Matthew's response.

"It's either that or we continue to wait," he said. "And we have no idea how much longer this will drag on for. We still haven't been able to link any of the crimes to Nick and the probability we'll be able to is lessening every day."

Matthew paused. "How long do you think Sarah will last?"

I was already feeling the effects of being imprisoned in my home. He knew me well.

"It's only a matter of time before she becomes impatient and pushes to carry on with her life. You can't keep her here forever."

"How sure are you?" I could hear the subdued thinking in my father's voice.

"There is no way to be sure," Matthew's voice sounded calm but tired.

What was he doing that was making him so tired? My mind was already racing forward with images of him and another girl, embracing and kissing. I tilted my head up to the ceiling to ride the anguish that washed over me, leaving me shaken and in more pain than before.

Stop it, I admonished myself. *Being tired doesn't necessarily mean he has found someone else.* Being overly emotional about Matthew was throwing my logic right out the window.

"Is it a risk you're willing to take?" My father's voice held its usual seriousness.

I frowned. I didn't like the sound of that one bit. What risk was Matthew taking?

I didn't hear Matthew respond. "Have you set up the meeting?" my father asked.

"Yes. It's tomorrow."

None of what they were saying made any sense. Who was Matthew meeting?

"Where?"

I leaned closer, feeling the information would be important. He rattled off an address. I repeated it in my mind a few times to ensure I didn't forget it. I didn't recognize the address so I would have to go onto the web and check where it was.

"It's going to be very dangerous," my father warned him. I felt the hairs on my arms stand up. A foreboding feeling stirred in my stomach.

"It's the only way." He sounded determined and I knew no one would dissuade him from what he set his mind to.

When I heard footsteps coming toward the door, I darted down the passage and slipped back into the kitchen. I put a hand to my pounding heart. Whatever Matthew was planning sounded dangerous.

I heard voices outside the kitchen. It was Matthew and Mark.

"I don't think it's a good idea," Mark said in a grave voice.

"I have to. It's the only way. If this goes the way I suspect I can have this whole situation resolved in a matter of days."

"It's a big gamble." Mark had always been the voice of reason.

I didn't like the sound of that at all.

"It has to be done." There was that determination I'd heard earlier. No matter what anyone said they would not be able to change his mind.

"What time?" Mark asked.

"Eleven tomorrow morning."

I wanted to stop him but I was fixed to the spot. The sound of the front door opening and then closing made me slump against the wall.

Mark strolled into the kitchen and I straightened up, trying to pretend I hadn't just been listening to them.

"You know it's rude to eavesdrop," Mark said, shaking his head at my visible attempt to regain my composure.

"What's he going to do?" I had asked the question I wasn't sure I was ready to hear the answer to.

He rubbed his chin as he watched me thoughtfully.

"If it has to do with me then I have a right to know what he is planning." I put my hands on my hips. From what I'd heard he was putting himself into a dangerous situation and I needed to know the details. My imagination was already leaps ahead with possibilities.

I'd nearly lost him once. I couldn't go through that again.

"The less you know the better," Mark decided.

"Why can't you tell me?" I asked, needing to know his

reasoning.

"Telling you will just worry you."

I frowned with my hands still firmly on my hips. "He is doing something really dangerous, isn't he?"

"I'm not going to tell you." He shrugged. I couldn't make him tell me.

I debated whether to ask my father but I decided against it. Maybe Mark was right—the less I knew the better.

"Will you at least let me know when it's over?" I bit my lip, feeling nervous.

He nodded. I made the move to leave the kitchen. My appetite was gone.

"Sarah." I turned back to look at Mark. "He knows what he's doing. He'll be fine."

"Then why did you tell him it wasn't a good idea?"

He shrugged. "It's a big risk."

That didn't make me feel any better.

I spent the rest of the day feeling restless. Nothing seemed to be able to keep my attention. And going outside wasn't an option.

Every time I caught a glimpse of the pool or the pool house, I was reminded of the last time I'd been there with Matthew, and the feeling of despair I'd experienced when he'd walked out on me haunted me.

That night I didn't sleep at all. I tossed and turned. For some time I stared up at the ceiling and thought about Matthew.

Being at the point where he couldn't stand the sight of me, I thought back to the very decision that had caused it. But no matter how much it hurt I knew if I could do it again I would make the same decision. Keeping him safe had trumped anything else.

But he is in danger again and you're in your bed, safe and sound. Finally resigning myself to the fact that I wasn't going to get any sleep, I swung my legs over the side of my bed and got up.

It was four in the morning and still dark outside. I went downstairs and made myself a cup of coffee. While I drank it I watched the sun rise. I couldn't shake the feeling that something bad was going to happen but there was nothing I could do about it. I was desperate enough to consider calling him to tell him not to go through with it. Besides, I couldn't figure out what he was going to do to sort this situation out.

I rinsed my coffee cup and put it next to the sink. I leaned against the counter and kept my eyes fixed on the time. Feeling tired and anxious I went upstairs to take a shower, hoping the task would help pass the time.

The house was quiet when I went back downstairs. I went to the living room and switched the TV on, needing it to distract me.

When Mark walked in later, I sat up.

"You going to be jumpy all day?" he asked, sitting down in the single seat beside the sofa.

"Yup," I said.

"Try and not think about it," he suggested.

"Easy for you to say. You know what he's going to do. You think not telling me is helping me, but trust me, my imagination is a lot worse."

Feeling like I was being twisted into a knot, I stood up and began to pace.

Then I remembered the address Matthew had rattled off to my father. I left Mark and went upstairs to check it. Inside my room, I opened up my laptop. I keyed the address in and hit enter.

It showed up on a map. The office building was only a half hour's drive from the house. I frowned as I stared at the street view of it, but there was no sign or name on the outside.

Frustrated, and with the worsening feeling that something bad was going to happen, I dropped my face into my hands. *Please let him be okay.*

It didn't matter if he didn't love me anymore and he left me. At least he would be okay.

I bit my nails, needing a way to deal with my rising stress. I watched the time. Seconds ticked by and minutes passed but it felt like the time was dragging by. By eleven I was pacing in the kitchen, constantly glancing at the clock.

"What has gotten into you today?" my mom said as she walked in with a bag of groceries that had been dropped off.

"Matthew is going for a meeting with someone at eleven."

My mom set the bag down on the counter.

"So?" she asked as she began to unpack the groceries. I knew when my mother was trying to keep something from me—she always refused to look me in the eye. My eyes narrowed as I studied her.

I walked over to her and sat down, facing her. "Do you know what it's about?"

"No," she said, looking intently at the breakfast box she had just taken out of the bag.

"Stop lying to me!" My anger sprang to life. It was one thing for Mark not to tell me what was going on, but it was a whole different story when it came to my mother. We'd always been so close and shared so much, more than most mothers and daughters.

She let out a deep sigh before meeting my gaze.

"He's going to speak to Nick," she said.

Horror filled me.

"Why?" I asked, disbelieving he would put himself right in the lion's den.

"I don't know all the details."

I stood up on shaking legs, feeling like my whole world

had shifted and I was trying to right everything. My mind went over all I'd overheard and the pieces finally began to fit together. What I still didn't know was the reason why he thought going to visit Nick would resolve the situation.

An image of Nick with his empty eyes appeared in my mind and I began to pace. *Oh, my God.* How could this be happening?

I put my hand to my forehead and shoved my hair out of my face.

"It'll be okay," my mother started to say as she put down the cereal box and walked over to me.

She tried to touch my arm with her hand, but I stepped out of her hold.

"None of this is okay!" I said, disbelief and anger filling me. "How could you let him do something so stupid?"

My eyes shot to the time. It was a quarter past eleven already. It was too late to stop him. I strode out of the kitchen in search of Mark. I found him checking the back yard.

He stilled when he caught sight of me walking to him.

"How could you?" I asked, feeling helpless.

"Do what?" he asked, cocking his head to the side.

"You knew he was going to meet with Nick and you let him." I had to take a deep breath.

"He is a grown man and he gets to make his own decisions." I hated how calm he sounded when I felt like my life was spinning out of control and there was nothing I could do to stop it.

"You're his friend," I said angrily. "You should have talked him out of it."

Would you have been able to? My anger evaporated and all I was left with was the realization there was nothing I could do. Even putting the blame on someone wouldn't change or stop what was happening.

"I can't stop him from doing what he thinks is right."

I put my hand to my head. All I could do now was hope nothing happened to him.

I'd paced so much there was a groove in the carpet beneath my feet. Every minute that passed felt like forever. By noon I was biting my nails again.

Mark walked into the living room and I looked at him expectantly. He shook his head. It had only been an hour, I reminded myself. I felt like I was going to go stir crazy.

But one hour became two, and then three.

When I saw Mark start to check the time, I had a sinking feeling in my stomach. While he had remained calm I had been able to hold on to the hope that things would be okay, but seeing him start to worry made me face the idea that something had gone wrong.

Mark started to make calls, but no one could reach Matthew.

I sat down, feeling stunned that my worst fears were becoming a reality. But it wasn't in me to just accept it. I loved him, irrespective of the events that had made me pull away from him. I'd only done whatever I could to save him.

Leaving the estate was out of the question; my parents wouldn't allow it and I couldn't sneak out with Mark around. I concentrated on finding a way to escape. I would need a way out without anyone realizing and I knew I couldn't do it alone. There was no way to know if Matthew was even still alive but I couldn't stay here and do nothing.

I began to formulate a plan to get out without anyone being able to stop me. First I would need a way of distracting Mark and then I would need a way out of the property without anyone noticing.

While everyone started to become more concerned about

finding Matthew, I went upstairs. In the privacy of my room where no one could overhear me, I made a phone call to a friend who lived nearby. I hadn't seen much of her since I'd left to go to college but I knew I could depend on her.

"Hi, stranger," Brandy answered in her usual drawl.

"I need your help."

"Sure. What do you need?" she asked.

I began to tell her.

"I can be there in thirty minutes." I felt relief that I could put the plan into action sooner than later. Every moment mattered.

Once I got off the phone with her, I did some research on the web. While everyone was still downstairs dealing with the whereabouts of Matthew, I was already starting to implement my plan.

Every time my emotions got hold of me and I wanted to give in to the fear, I pushed through it. I couldn't help him if I fell apart now. I had to be strong.

Chapter Twenty-Six

There was a flurry of activity. Everyone was trying to find Matthew. A cop car arrived soon after and two police officers entered the house, going directly to the study. Everyone was in the study when Brandy pulled up in front of the house. I wrung my hands as I waited for her.

"Geez, what's with the security?" she asked, looking more than a little annoyed. She opened the door to her car as I stood waiting for her. "I had to wait forever for them to let me in."

The security had been tightened up since I'd come home.

She gave a pointed look at the cop car beside hers. "What's going on?"

"It's a long story," I said. "Come in."

She followed me into the house and I led her to the kitchen, away from everyone else. I was thankful Mark was too preoccupied with Matthew to be aware of what I was planning.

"What's going on?" she whispered to me.

"Like I said, it's a long story."

"So give me the short version." She crossed her arms and looked at me expectantly.

I glanced around to ensure there was no one in the area outside the kitchen before I gave Brandy my attention. There was no way I could tell her everything. She wouldn't help me if I did.

"I need you to trust me," I said.

She frowned before she dropped her arms. "Okay."

"I need you to get me out of here."

"Why can't you just leave on your own?" she asked, looking a little baffled. "Am I missing something?"

"I don't want to go into the details but no one can see me leave."

She continued to frown as she considered my request.

"All I need you to do is drive me out of here. I'll hide in the trunk," I added.

"You know this sounds nuts." In her shoes I wasn't sure if I would trust as blindly as I was asking her to. "Why do you need to sneak out?"

"I can't tell you."

"You're asking me to help you without knowing anything about why."

"Please," I said, putting all my hope in my friend. I was afraid if I gave her too many details she would refuse.

She studied me for a moment before she said, "I don't like it but I'll do it."

Mark entered the kitchen and I felt like a five-year-old who had been caught stealing a cookie out of the cookie jar. My cheeks heated as his eyes fixed on me. It was difficult to read him.

"Everything okay?" he asked, looking from Brandy to me. His eyes were far too perceptive for my liking. He'd probably been informed of Brandy's unannounced visit.

"Yeah," I said, trying to calm my voice, otherwise he would know I was up to something. "I invited a friend for a visit."

He studied me for a moment. "I'll leave the two of you to it, then."

As he left I turned to Brandy and let out a nervous breath.

"Who is that?" my friend asked with obvious interest.

"It doesn't matter."

She nodded. "When do you want to leave?" she asked.

I bit my nails as I contemplated whether to leave straightaway or wait a little while. I decided the sooner the better. At the moment everyone was preoccupied in the study and not watching me. If I waited, my opportunity to slip out unnoticed would be gone.

"Now. Let's go."

Outside, she opened the trunk to her car and I did a quick check, knowing the angle of the video wouldn't allow the security watching the cameras to see me before I got in. Darkness surrounded me as she carefully shut the trunk.

I closed my eyes, trying to keep myself calm. Her car still smelled new. Brandy's father was super rich. He worked in finance and was apparently really good at it.

She started the car and my nervousness increased. I held my hands tightly together as I listened carefully when she came to a stop by the gate—my last hurdle. My body was rigid with nerves as I waited to see if my plan to escape unnoticed would succeed.

It was only a few seconds before the car moved forward and I felt relief—I'd made it out of the estate. But then again Matthew and Mark had put security in place to keep the danger out, they had probably never even considered I would try to leave. Why would I leave a secure place to put my life in danger? To save the one I loved, I was willing to risk it all.

After a few minutes of driving, Brandy pulled over and switched the car off. The trunk opened, blinding me slightly as I got out.

"What now?" Brandy asked, closing the trunk before she turned her attention to me.

"I need to use your car." It was asking a lot but I didn't have any other options. Time was running out.

What if you're already too late? I asked myself. I refused to even contemplate it. Matthew had to be fine; there was no other alternative.

"Where are we going?" she asked, but I shook my head. I couldn't drag her into this. Danger and even death lay in the path ahead of me.

"I can't take you with me," I told her. I dragged a hand through my hair as my agitation grew.

Her forehead creased as she watched me. And just when I thought she would refuse, she handed me her car keys with a defeated sigh.

"I have a really bad feeling about this," she said, holding my gaze. "But you're my friend."

It was a tough choice. In her shoes it would have been difficult for me to agree as well. Even without telling her more she could tell whatever I was going to do wasn't going to be easy. And at that moment I was so relieved she hadn't pushed me further for details. We'd been close friends in high school and even though we hadn't talked a lot since I'd left for college, we still shared a close bond.

She didn't ask me any more questions while we drove to a nearby shopping center, where I dropped her off. My mind was too wrapped up in what I had to do next. Would Matthew still be at the same address? The likelihood was slim. If something had happened to him, they had probably moved him. The thought shook me from the inside.

I was finding it more and more difficult to keep control over my spiraling emotions. Trying to shut off my mind, to think only about Matthew, was the only way I could cope. I had to believe he was okay, that he was alive. Any thoughts to the contrary had to be eliminated from my mind. And as long as I could keep thinking that, I could function enough to proceed with my plan.

I knew I was walking into this situation even though I had no idea how it would play out. There was a good chance I was doing this all for nothing.

"You going to be okay?" I asked as we stood beside her parked car.

"I'll be fine. I texted Daniel and he's on his way to pick me up."

Daniel was her boyfriend. I nodded, feeling too nervous and tied up in knots.

"I have to go," I told her, not wanting to waste a moment. Every second counted. A quick look at my watch told me it was three in the afternoon.

She hugged me tightly before she released me. "Call me later."

Even as she said the words I knew the chances I would be able to were slim, but I agreed anyway. I believed she needed to know that whatever I was getting myself into I would be able to get myself out of.

As she walked to the entrance of the shopping center, I got back into her car. I was about to start the engine when I thought about my phone. I had watched enough crime shows to know that with the latest technology it was possible to track my phone, so I switched it off. I put it back in my bag.

Feeling the rising panic overwhelm me, I took a couple of deep breaths and released them, trying to calm myself down. My hands shook and I tightened my hold on the steering wheel to ride out the wave of panic.

My car door opened unexpectedly, and I was confused when a bald guy pulled me out of the car. Horror filled me when I recognized the sunken eyes of the guy who had tried to shoot me. Then my instinct kicked in and tried to resist. He held me in a vise-like grip and I was unable to move. I felt a pin-pick before I felt my body go limp and the darkness took over.

I shifted slightly, feeling cold and uncomfortable. My head was sore. I reached up and touched my forehead slightly with my fingertips as I winced.

Slowly, as I began to recollect my last memories, and I opened my eyes.

Fear gripped me. I was lying on a thin, old gray mattress on a cold concrete floor in a dimly lit room. Beside me was a plastic bottle of what looked like water. I inhaled, and the room smelled damp. I tried to sit up too quickly and the room tilted. Putting out a hand, I steadied myself.

Where was I?

The last image I could remember was of the bald burly guy who had pulled me from Brandy's car. I pushed myself up against the wall and tilted my face up to the ceiling. My mind was still groggy and I was still trying to make sense of what had happened.

I remembered the slight prick before everything had gone dark. It had obviously been something to knock me out so he could take me without much resistance. Not that resisting would have worked. I had been no match against his strength.

Had I been followed? It was the only explanation. They had let me get far enough away from the house. I was thankful it hadn't happened earlier because then Brandy would be sitting with me. And it was bad enough I was in the situation; it would have been made even worse had Brandy been mixed up with it was well.

The feeling of being in over my head weighed heavily on me. My plan hadn't been perfect but I hadn't imagined it going this way. Would I have a chance to speak to Nick to find out if they had Matthew? That's if they hadn't killed him already.

No. I couldn't allow myself to think of the probability. I tried to focus my eyes on my watch and after a few blinks they focused enough for me to be able to read the time. It was five in the evening. I'd been out for two hours.

I stood up, still feeling a little unstable as I tested my weight on my legs. They held. Slowly I shuffled to the door. Fear like I never experienced before made me tug and twist to try and open the door to escape but it wouldn't budge. The door was locked.

Feeling weak, I rested my head against the wooden door. I turned around and leaned against it as I surveyed the small room I was in. The walls were gray and a small light hung from the ceiling, giving some light. There were no windows.

The realization hit that I was a prisoner. I shivered, and it had nothing to do with the coolness of the room. I shuffled back to the mattress and sat down, pulling my knees up to my chest. Now that they had me they would no longer require Matthew. They could let him go. But there was that niggling thought they wouldn't and he would meet with the same fate as I would.

Even with knowing how this had played out I couldn't regret my decision to try to save him. He would have done the same—had done the same. The fact that he was paid to do it didn't take anything away from it. The intensity of the emotions that filled me were hard to fight, and tears threatened. My throat burned as I thought about my last encounter with Matthew.

I burned every detail of his handsome face into my memory. That sexy smile of his that made my stomach dip and the way my knees weakened at the slight indent of his dimples. To keep the fear from taking over completely I allowed myself to think back to all the times I had shared with the sexy bodyguard who had stolen my heart before I'd even realized it was possible to love someone.

Love had never been a possibility for me, and now that I had experienced it I couldn't imagine my life without it—or Matthew.

I remembered him from our first moment in the cafeteria, to his deception. I remembered him saving my life when he'd put his body in the way of the bullet that had been meant for me. I remembered him even down to the last few memories I had of him, even though they were filled with anger at my actions.

The unknown scared me. I had no idea if he was still alive or not. There was now a very good chance I would never make it out of this room alive and that my actions had been in vain. All I had done was surrender to the ruthless men who were carrying out their boss's orders.

I felt weak. The determination and courage that had brought me this far had dispersed. Tears stung my eyes but I refused to allow them to escape. No—I wasn't one to give up that easily, even if there was no hope. I wouldn't allow it to be easy for them.

Anger sparked to life. I was angry at how things had turned out and how someone I had never met wanted me dead because of some sort of vendetta with my father. This whole situation was unfair.

I kept my ears alert, waiting for them to return.

I could just imagine how crazy my parents were going now that they had discovered I was missing. Mark would be pissed. The truth was it hadn't been his fault. I had taken advantage of a momentary lapse in concentration when he hadn't had his full attention on me.

Closing my eyes, I rested my forehead on my knees as I dealt with the reality that there would be no rescue. There would be no way for my parents, the cops, or Mark to track me. I hadn't told anyone where I'd been headed.

They would discover I was missing and even if they tracked my movements to Brandy's abandoned car in the shopping center's parking lot, there would be no way for them to track me to where I was being held as a prisoner.

For what felt like hours I watched and listened, straining my ears to hear any sound that would signal approaching danger. But other than the sound of distant footsteps, I didn't hear much.

My anger simmered beneath the surface as I waited to meet my captors.

I heard footsteps, but this time they drew closer. I could tell someone had stopped outside the door to the room I was being held in.

A key turned in the lock and the door handle squeaked as it opened. I remained sitting. Fear made me unable to move.

A guy I didn't recognize walked in. He looked at me with a cold smile. He was shorter than six feet and was a little heavier around the waist. His hair was neatly trimmed. There was no warmth in his dark brown eyes, which only reinforced my fear.

"Well, well," he said before coming to stand in front of me. I saw the big guy who had pulled me from Brandy's car standing behind him. He was even bigger than the fuzzy memory I had of him. He looked at me without emotion.

"I never imagined all our patient waiting would pay off, but...here you are," the guy with the slick brown hair said.

It confirmed they had been watching me.

"Matthew..." I whispered, my throat feeling dry.

He frowned as he stepped closer.

"I was looking for Matthew."

Here was my chance to find out what had happened to him.

"It doesn't really matter now. You're here."

"Where is he?" I asked, refusing to be brushed aside.

He held my gaze as he sauntered closer.

"Ahh, Matthew Weiss, the bodyguard."

The way he said it made me want to return a scathing remark but I bit my lip to keep myself quiet. Nothing good could come from riling him up.

"Where is he?" I asked, needing to know.

He studied me with a glee that amplified the sickening feeling in the pit of my stomach.

"He has been eliminated."

Chapter Twenty-Seven

Eliminated. The word echoed in my mind. He gave a curt nod to the burly bodyguard, and he walked over to me and pulled me to my feet roughly while I tried to make sense of what I'd just been told.

Matthew was dead.

My heartbeat echoed in my ears as my mouth opened slightly, trying to make sense of it. It couldn't be true. My eyes shot to the messenger who, by the satisfied expression on his face, was enjoying every moment of my reaction.

"You're lying," I whispered hoarsely, trying to find some evidence in his facial features that would tell me he wasn't being truthful. It had to be the only explanation. Matthew couldn't be gone. I wouldn't accept it. It was not possible.

"Why would I lie?" There was no way to tell if he was lying or not. It would explain why no one had been able to get ahold of him since his meeting that morning.

The man's hands dug into my arm and I winced. I tried

to pull free but his grip was unbreakable.

"He begged for his life," he continued to taunt me, enjoying my pain.

I couldn't imagine that. The Matthew I knew would never have given them the satisfaction.

"I don't believe it."

"That's irrelevant." He gave a dismissive shrug.

"So why me?" I asked. I already had a pretty good idea why they had targeted me but I wanted him to tell me.

He cocked his head to the side as he studied me. "Your father is to blame for the position you're in."

That wasn't news.

"He put a very good friend of mine in prison," he said, and despite the coldness of his voice I could tell he held some warmth for the person he was referring to. "This is revenge for that. It's quite simple. He caused a lot of grief for us and now I'm going to return the favor."

I looked from the muscled guy beside me back to him. I feared what they were going to do and I felt guilt for the responsibility my father would carry with him for my death.

"Marcus Cole," I murmured, knowing exactly who he was talking about.

"Yes." He smiled.

"So why isn't Nick here?" I asked.

"Do you think he would concern himself with something so inconsequential?"

"Then who are you?" I asked.

He paused for a moment as he considered my question. "Leo."

He said it flatly, which made him difficult to read—and more dangerous. Maybe it was a characteristic of a psychopath.

"If he hadn't broken the law he wouldn't have gone to jail." He frowned and I knew I had overstepped the line.

"We all break the rules, some more than others," he said intently, walking closer. I held still as he closed the space between us. "Putting my friend behind bars for a few crimes is a little unfair."

I couldn't stop myself from frowning. "A few crimes" was an understatement. He'd taken the life of another person —that was the ultimate crime.

"You think you know everything." He surveyed me with disgust. "You have no idea how the real world works. Not everything is black or white."

He studied me for a few moments. "Before you die you will learn some valuable lessons about what happens in the real world. I think it's time we give you a taste of it."

I tried to remain calm but there was no hiding my fear. They had been after me for months and now they had me in their clutches. This wasn't going to be a quick and painless death.

"Frank," he said to the guy who was still restraining me.

He nodded and released me. Instinctively my hand rubbed my injured arm.

The first blow to my face split my lip. Pain exploded in the side of my face as I tasted blood. He had hit me with an open hand. If he'd used his fist he would have done a lot more damage. My hand went up to deflect any further blows, but none came.

"That's enough," Leo instructed.

The pain throbbed through the side of my face as I faced him, unable to hide my fear.

"I wouldn't spend too much time thinking about Matthew. If I were you, I would think about what we're going to do to you. Your death will be slow and painful. I want your father to know how much you suffered."

With one last creepy, cold smile he left with Frank following closely behind.

My throat tightened and burned. The door shut and they locked it. I touched my hand to the aching part of my face as I slid my tongue over the cut on my lip. I hissed, feeling a sharp pain before I dropped my hand from my face.

I stumbled back and my back rested against the wall. This time knowing more about my situation made me feel afraid. The knowledge that I would soon meet my end was difficult to process.

Eliminated. The word kept repeating in my mind as I tried to catch my breath. I slid down the wall and sat down with my legs crossed.

The physical pain from the blow was nothing compared to the numbness inside. It crept through me, making me feel hollow and empty. It was as if the light inside me had been extinguished and now there was a darkness there that made me shiver.

I struggled to make sense of it. Images of Matthew smiling at me, kissing me slowly and hugging me, filled my mind. I remembered the feeling of being loved by him. It was like the tingle of the sun against my skin, warming my heart. He couldn't be gone.

I fisted my hands as my memories of him were tainted by images of him lying on the ground. Blood everywhere. I dug my nails into the palms of my hands, needing the physical pain to keep me together.

I inhaled sharply, trying to stop my emotions from suffocating me from the inside. The danger had brought him into my life and had taken him out of it.

I exhaled an emotional breath as a wrenching pain began to seep into me. Feeling the sting of tears, I put my fist to my mouth to stop myself, but I couldn't. They were powerful emotions needing to break free. One tear escaped down my face as I bowed my head, my hand still tight against my mouth to smother my crying.

I wouldn't be the only one to mourn his loss. An image of his family at the hospital appeared in my mind. My grief was made worse by how they would react to the death of their son and brother. It was the only consolation my own death would bring: I would not be alive to see them suffer.

I had tried to keep him safe by cutting him from my life but I had failed. Maybe I should have tried harder, but there was no use punishing myself over that. I couldn't go back and change things. What was done was done.

My parents would be devastated. I closed my eyes as more tears slid down my cheeks. It would be much harder for my mother because we'd been so close. She would miss me every day. My father would grieve but he wouldn't feel the same loss that my mother did. Or maybe his grief would be worse, knowing he was the reason why these guys had targeted me in the first place.

I still couldn't regret my decision to save Matthew. I could not have stayed at home and done nothing to find him.

Mark would be doing everything possible to track down his friend. He would take Matthew's death hard.

I bowed my head when I felt a wave of pain wash over me, leaving every part of me aching. Breathless and exhausted, I shifted slightly and lay down on the thin mattress, putting my hands beneath my head to pillow my uninjured side of my face.

I stared out into the darkness of the room as I wrestled with the fear of the pain and death that was to come and the loss of Matthew. While I lay there trying not to think about the threats from Leo and what was going to happen to me, I lost track of time.

Eventually, after what felt like hours, I drifted off to sleep.

I woke up with a start. Frank loomed over me. I pushed my hair out of my face and touched my bruised cheek. I winced. Despite having slept I still felt tired.

I was still disoriented when Frank pulled me up to my feet. Leo stood there, watching in an expensive suit. Crime clearly paid well.

I rubbed my neck, trying to get rid of the stiffness in my body. There was a wooden chair that hadn't been there before. The sight of the furniture did nothing to ease the growing fear I was feeling.

"Sit," Leo commanded. I refused. There was no incentive to cooperate. He had already made it clear I was going to die and it would be a slow, painful death, so there was no reason for me to go along with what he wanted.

Frank pulled me toward it and shoved me down. I glared at him, making it clear I wasn't happy with being shoved around, but he ignored me. My hand instinctively rubbed the area he had been holding. There would be bruises.

Leo paced a little in front of me. I had expected him to instruct Frank to beat me like he had before but this time he wouldn't tell him to stop. I was scared but I wasn't going to let them see that.

"I have a few questions for you." He stopped and turned to face me.

What on earth could I tell him? I remained tightlipped as I frowned, trying to figure out what he wanted to know.

"I need some information," he started. "If you cooperate, I'll ensure your death comes quickly."

Even without knowing what he wanted to know, I already knew I wouldn't tell him anything, no matter what he offered.

"I need to know the security setup at your parents' home."

My mind was already racing ahead with possibilities of

what he would do with the information, and none of it was good.

"I will also require a layout of the house."

Horror filled me. Was he planning on harming my parents even after my death? He let out a heavy sigh when he saw the resistance in my eyes.

"I won't tell you anything," I told him.

He studied me for a moment before he shook his head slightly, like he knew something I didn't.

"You think you can hold out, but let me assure you, you will break. It's just a matter of time." The deadliness in his voice scared me, but I refused to allow him to see my fear.

"No." I felt the stubbornness that my mother had always complained about when I was a child.

"Come on, sweetheart," he said, softening his voice as he cocked his head to the side. "Let's make this easy."

"Am I not enough for your revenge?" I asked him bitterly.

The smile he gave me made my skin crawl. He was evil. There was no doubt in my mind he had killed countless people without a moment of remorse.

"It seems a waste not to get all the information I can from you," he said, straightening up. "You never know what might be useful in the future."

He waited for me to say something, but I refused to say another word to him. He was crazy if he thought I would give him information that would endanger my parents.

"I think we need to give her an incentive to talk," he drawled to Frank.

This time the hit to my face was more painful than before.

"Ahh!" I screamed as my face was flung to the side from the impact of the hit. I groaned feebly as the pain throbbed. It felt like I had been hit with a sledgehammer.

"You ready to talk yet?" Leo asked.

All the anger at the situation I was in bubbled over and I flung myself at him, hoping to at least get a hit in—but Frank, despite his size, moved like lightning in front of him to block me from my target.

He shoved me and I stumbled back, knocking the chair over. He hit me in the stomach and I doubled over onto my knees. I felt winded as I tried to get up.

"You know there are other ways to make you more compliant," Leo said. I didn't like the tone of his voice.

"Frank," he said, turning slightly to him. "She's a pretty girl."

My heart tightened and my stomach turned.

"I wonder if her skin feels as soft as it looks." Leo's attention was back on me as the bodyguard looked at me with a hunger that frightened me. "I bet you she's a screamer."

I swallowed hard, not allowing my gaze to drop from his. I couldn't show my fear. The thought of Frank putting his hands on me made me sick to my stomach.

"What do you think, Frank?" Leo asked with a sly smile.

Frank smiled at me and I had to fight the urge to throw up, but I clenched my teeth together, not allowing them to intimidate me.

"I won't tell you anything," I vowed. They could do whatever they liked. I wouldn't allow myself to betray the people who had brought me into the world and who loved me.

From the frown on Leo's face I could tell my response had been unexpected. I expected a rain of blows in response —but then Leo's phone started to ring. He looked at Frank as he studied the ID of the caller on the screen. I squeezed my eyes closed as I fought against the pain in order to sit up.

"Yes," Leo answered. He nodded to Frank as he listened intently.

The smugness from before was gone; his features had become like stone. Something unsaid passed between Leo and Frank before they left the room without any explanation.

I winced and tears filled my eyes. My face throbbed and I gently touched my face to test the swelling. It throbbed painfully. Unable to stand, I managed to crawl back to the mattress slowly and lay down, facing up toward the ceiling.

Tears escaped down the sides of my face as I fought the pain. Every slight movement made me grit my teeth against the discomfort. My throat burned and the dryness needed to be quenched. I reached for the plastic bottle beside the mattress. My hands closed around the bottle and I opened it to take a few sips. I closed it and set it down beside me. I checked my watch—it was nine in the evening. I'd been missing for six hours.

And then the waiting game started. I expected Leo and Frank to return but they didn't. One hour became another. My stomach rumbled so I drank more water. I touched my face lightly to feel if anything was broken, but it was too sore. I hissed when I pushed too hard on the area.

Even more time passed, and I began to wonder if they had been called away for business. Or had it been Nick to get an update on my torture? Or was it just a ploy to drag it out, so I could spend more time thinking about what they had planned for me?

I tried to get as comfortable as I could to try and get some sleep but it was difficult because every slight movement reverberated through my body, making me gasp. I closed my eyes and tried to fight through the pain. It was unlike anything I had experienced before; but then again I had never been beaten before. My face felt like it was swelling up all over.

Then I heard the faint sound of footsteps. My heart started to race.

Leo and Frank were coming back, and my torture would begin again. I felt so tired, so sore, but I pushed myself up, refusing to allow myself to appear weak to them. I would fight them every step of the way.

As the footsteps came to a stop outside the door of my prison, I felt a shiver of fear about what Frank would do to me. For a brief moment I allowed myself to feel my fear before I pushed through it, determined to show them I wouldn't be broken.

Chapter Twenty-Eight

The door opened and Leo stepped in, followed by Frank.

"Get up," Leo commanded with a sweep of his hand. His voice was gruff and hurried.

It was the first time I had seen him looking anything but in cool control. I couldn't help but feel something unexpected had happened.

I frowned as I tried to get up. The pain in my stomach was agonizing and I gritted my teeth to stop myself from crying out. Tears of pain watered my vision.

"Get her up!" Leo instructed Frank.

The big burly guy walked over to me and pulled me up by a tight grip to my upper arm.

I groaned as a sharp, intense pain shot through me at the sudden movement.

"Shut up," Leo said angrily.

I breathed in sharply and released a breath slowly. It even hurt to breathe.

"Let's get out of here," Leo said to his right-hand man.

Why were they moving me? Why did they seem to be in a hurry to get me out of here? I put my hand to my stomach to ease the pain as I limped.

"Nick." The sound of the surprise in Leo's voice made me look up to see Nick Cole. He was dressed in black with a leather jacket. He looked the part of the mean gangster who ruthlessly ruled the members of his gang.

Leo took a step back. For the first time I saw a flicker of fear on his face. His reaction made no sense.

"You have some explaining to do," Nick told Leo with a cold voice. There was no mistaking the dangerous undertone.

Frank slackened his hold on my arm.

Nick entered the room. I'd never met him before but even I felt his commanding presence. My eyes followed him into the room.

"Sarah," a familiar voice said. My eyes shot back to the doorway to take in the unbelievable sight of Matthew. He looked just as surprised to see me before he rushed over to me.

His eyes darkened when he took in the bruises and marks on my face. My face was still slightly swollen from before. His eyes scanned my features as his hands cradled my face. His touch felt so good.

"Matthew," I said deliriously. I'd mourned him and here he was, alive. He put his arm around me.

"How did you get here?" he asked, looking bewildered.

"You didn't know I was here?"

He shook his head.

"I overhead you talking to my father about the meeting. And when no one could reach you, everyone was convinced something really bad had happened to you."

He narrowed his eyes. "That still doesn't explain how you got here."

"I snuck out of the house with a friend while everyone else was busy trying to find you."

"You put yourself in danger to try and find me?" he asked incredulously, our eyes locked together.

I nodded.

"Do you know how *stupid* that was?" he asked angrily, looking at me with disbelief.

"As stupid as you going to meet with the guy who wanted me dead?" I threw back, and then grimaced as my injury flared up.

Matthew frowned as he dropped his hands to the hem of my shirt and lifted it slightly.

"I'll kill them," he said, turning his attention to Leo and Frank, who were looking as guilty as hell.

"They will be taken care of," Nick said over his shoulder to Matthew as he took a menacing step toward my two torturers.

How was he going to take care of them? I had visions of them being killed and buried in cement. And after everything they had done to me, I didn't care.

Matthew's jaw tensed as he glared at Leo and Frank. He looked like he wanted to repay them with the same injuries I'd suffered. Then he swung his attention back to me.

"Can you sit down?" he asked when he saw me shift slightly and grimace when the pain shot through me.

"It hurts." I wasn't sure I could sit down.

He supported me as I sat down and I held my breath as I finally settled on the floor. The pain made me wince. He bent down beside me and pulled out his phone before dialing a number.

"I need an ambulance," he said after a few moments. He then gave an address I didn't recognize.

When he closed his phone he shoved it into his back pocket.

"Get them out of here," Nick commanded to the two other goons when they appeared in the room.

I watched as Leo and Frank were marched out of the room flanked by Nick's men. Nick remained and walked over to where I was sitting.

"How is she?" he asked, his gaze momentarily flickering to me.

None of what was happening made any sense. Why would he be concerned about me? Hadn't he been the one who'd wanted me dead?

"They beat her pretty good," Matthew answered. He lifted my shirt and inspected my stomach. "There is significant bruising."

Nick nodded. "They will pay dearly for this."

The sound of police sirens made Nick stiffen.

"Go," Matthew instructed. "I can deal with things from here."

Nick gave us one last sweep of his gaze before he left the room.

"I don't understand," I murmured, still fixated on the doorway he'd just exited.

"It's a long story," Matthew said. "We need to get you to the hospital to get you checked out."

I focused on Matthew and reached up with both arms to cup his face. The feel of his face against my hands was amazing, and my eyes watered. I brushed my thumbs across his skin.

"I thought you were dead." I swallowed hard, trying to rid myself of the lump in my throat.

"Who told you that?"

"They did," I answered hoarsely, still feeling the heartache and grief when I'd been told.

He tucked some stray hair behind my ear and touched my cheek. "I'm fine." Then he retracted his hand, like he remembered everything that had happened between us. I wanted to snatch his hand and keep it tightly in mine, but I stopped myself. I was feeling disoriented and was still trying to piece back together what had happened.

Then the cops arrived and a few minutes later so did the paramedics. They gave me something for the pain before they put me on a gurney and wheeled me out of the room with Matthew beside me.

There was a lot of activity when I arrived at the hospital. After being checked, I was moved into a room for observation. Despite Matthew never leaving my side, I felt he was distancing himself from me. And I wondered if all the stuff that had happened between us was still keeping us apart.

I loved him but I was scared to make the first move. I usually went for what I wanted without a thought to the consequences, but this time my heart was on the line. Before, he would have stood beside me holding my hand, but now he was standing a safe distance away at the foot of the bed.

"Are you going to tell me what happened?" I asked. "Wasn't Nick the one who wanted me dead?"

He shook his head. "It wasn't Nick who wanted revenge. It was a couple of the men who used to work for his father who did."

I pondered his answer. Leo had already lied about Matthew being dead, so it didn't surprise me he had lied about Nick being the one who had wanted me gone.

"Is that why you went to see him?" I asked.

He nodded. "Things just didn't seem to add up. It was a hunch."

I studied him. "So you put yourself in danger on a hunch?"

He didn't reveal any emotions as he held my gaze. "Mine was a careful plan with controlled risks. You did the same, but you went in blindly without any thought for your own safety."

My throat thickened. I knew exactly why I had made the decision to put myself in danger. It had been an attempt to save him.

"When no one could find you, I thought the worst. We all did."

"Nick doesn't trust easily. To meet with him I had to switch off my phone and leave it behind when he took me to another location."

It explained why no one could reach him.

"Why did you do it, Sarah? Why did you put yourself in so much danger?" he asked.

I swallowed. "The same reason why you went to meet Nick."

He pressed his lips in a tight line as our eyes held.

The door to my hospital room opened and my parents rushed over to me.

"Sarah," my mother cried as she put her hands on my face. She pressed a kiss to my cheek. I tried to hug her as she put her arms around me.

"Sarah," my father said hoarsely to me from the other side of the bed. My mom still refused to let go so I reached out a hand and my father held it.

I swallowed to stop myself from crying.

They were both so happy to see me but I knew I was in for a lecture later after I had recovered.

When I looked back to the foot of the bed, Matthew was gone. My heart felt heavy in my chest. I'd hoped he had just stepped out to give me privacy with my parents; but even later after my parents had left to get me some clothes and toiletries, he still didn't return.

The rawness in my heart was more painful than my injuries.

When Mark walked in to see me, it was late. The lights

in my room were dimmed so I could sleep and I shifted, trying to find a comfortable position.

"Mark," I murmured when he sat down beside me.

"Sleep," he said as he rubbed his chin.

The medication the nurses had given me made it harder to keep my eyes open, and I tried to fight the sleep that crept over me.

I woke up feeling stiff and sore. Mark was sleeping beside me in the chair. I tried to sit up and shift to ease the pain.

"Not so easy to sleep in a hospital bed," Mark murmured as he straightened up in the chair beside me.

"About as comfortable as sleeping on that chair looks," I said. He smiled briefly.

The seriousness I was so used to seeing on his face returned.

"You did a pretty stupid thing," he said as he sat forward slightly.

I nodded. "I couldn't do nothing."

"It was my job to keep you safe."

"You can't blame yourself," I assured him. "You were trying to keep the danger out. You had no idea I was going to try and expose myself to it."

He studied me for a moment. "Trust me, I want to yell at you and tell you how stupid it was to do what you did...but it's over."

"I'm sorry," I murmured.

"Knowing why you did it makes it easier to handle. That and the fact that you're safe now."

"Where's Matthew?"

"He isn't here." I had already guessed that much. Did he care so little that now that the threat was over he was gone?

Had I misjudged him before?

Were his reasons for meeting with Nick different from those I'd hoped they were? The only other reason I could think for prompting him into action would be to ensure there was no longer a threat to me, and he wouldn't be required to keep me safe. Was it his way of moving on?

I rubbed my forehead, not sure what to think anymore.

"I've never seen him look at a girl the way he looks at you." My eyes met his. I wanted to believe him, but I believed Matthew's actions now spoke volumes.

If he truly cared, he would have been here with me.

"I think I was just a job he is happy to be done with," I mumbled, letting out an emotional sigh.

"Give him a chance to deal. He'll be back," Mark said.

But he didn't come back the next day, not even when I got discharged from the hospital and was sent home.

And for the next few days there was no sign of him, either. Mark was still assigned as my bodyguard. It wasn't like there was a clear threat anymore, but my father wasn't taking any chances. I let it slide. After everything I had put my parents through, I owed them that much; so instead of kicking up a fuss or moaning about it, I shut up.

Although I was still physically recovering and hurting emotionally, the weight of life and death had been lifted from my shoulders. When Nick had told Matthew he would take care of Leo and Frank, I knew he had meant it. When a few days later a folder was left on my father's office desk with enough information to put Leo and Frank away for the rest of their lives, I wasn't surprised.

Brandy got her car back and a full rundown of what happened. Like everyone else she was just grateful I was safe.

My body began to mend but I couldn't say the same for my heart. I wanted to believe that after everything I had been through I would be able to go back to the life I had led before.

Once I'd healed enough I invited a few friends over to my parents' house. Mark had just raised an eyebrow when twenty of my friends arrived for the planned pool party. After being cooped up alone for so long, I needed company, and I believed a party would help me ease back into my old life.

I wasn't sure how the college thing would work out. I'd missed a lot of coursework, but I had been working hard to play catch-up.

There had still been no word from Matthew. More than a few times after experiencing a few moments of my strong emotions for him, I had resisted the urge to call him. He had walked out of my life without a backward glance, now leaving me convinced that my actions had dissolved any future for us.

That night I had even invited a cute guy from high school who I had found very attractive. His name was Liam. But when he'd arrived, my initial excitement had waned when I hadn't felt the same level of attraction to him.

Beside the pool, while my friends partied, I sat on the lounger sipping a soda, feeling more alone than I had before.

"You okay?" Mark's voice pulled me out of my pity party.

I plastered a smile on my face when I looked up at him. "Yeah."

I didn't want to admit my inner turmoil to him. I didn't want Matthew to know I was struggling to carry on.

"You're a bad liar," Mark told me when he sat down on the lounger beside me.

A girl yelled when someone pushed her into the pool and she resurfaced with a giggle.

"I'm trying," I murmured, fixing my eyes on my carefree friends who were have an awesome party while I wallowed in the emptiness of my feelings.

"Maybe this isn't the way to do it." He gave me a glance

and I took another sip of my soda.

He didn't try to give me more advice, and I spent the rest of the evening trying my hardest to fit back into the life I'd had.

I was exhausted by the time the party wrapped up and I closed the door on the last guest to leave. I said good night to Mark before I trudged upstairs to go to bed. I was feeling despondent and empty. Why couldn't I fit back into my old life? Before meeting Matthew, I would still have been attracted to Liam—but since Matthew had come into my life, everything had changed.

Was that it? I wouldn't be able to move on until I'd found closure with Matthew. Just the thought made my heart squeeze with pain. His distance from me hurt.

The hope I'd had that we would get back together had slowly disappeared with every day that passed without seeing him.

I'd never fallen in love before Matthew and I wasn't sure how to navigate my way through what I knew was inevitable: a confrontation with Matthew.

I needed him to tell me to my face that it was over between us for me to move on.

That night I lay awake thinking about it over and over again, trying to foresee how it would unfold. Even with all my chaotic thoughts, I finally managed to fall asleep at two in the morning knowing I had at least a plan of action.

Chapter Twenty-Nine

"We're going out today," I told Mark when I walked into the kitchen the next morning.

I had woken up feeling the familiar emptiness, but now I had started to feel angry and determined.

"Where are we going?" he asked, standing up.

"We're going to see Matthew." I stood with my hands on my hips with a determined look that even made Mark keep his mouth shut and nod.

I was done waiting. It was time to have it out. I couldn't go on like this wondering. This conversation was long overdue—eleven days overdue to be exact—and I had to know either way, good or bad.

"You sure about this?" he asked as we got into a car.

"Yes." There was no turning back now. This had to be my next move. Irrespective of the outcome, I had to know where I stood.

I started to bite my nails before I realized what I was

doing and gripped my hands in my lap to stop myself. I felt Mark's gaze but I refused to look at him. The tightened knot of anxiety I felt in my chest made me uncomfortable and I didn't want him to see how nervous I felt.

"We'll be at his place in about ten minutes," Mark told me, and I nodded.

His place. Was it a temporary place he'd held while he'd been assigned to me?

The apartment block Mark pulled up outside was nice and modern. I took in a deep breath as I looked up at the building. The closer I got to seeing Matthew the more nervous I got. My hands even shook a little as I undid my seatbelt.

Mark opened his door and I frowned as I got out of my seat.

"I want to do this alone."

He shook his head.

"After what happened the last time I let my guard down, I'm not taking any chances."

I put my hand on my hip and glared at him, but he was unfazed as he closed the door and walked around to wait in front of me.

My hands felt sweaty so I dried them off on my jeans. Not only was I unsure of what was going to happen with Matthew, but now I would have to do it with Mark around.

With each step I had the urge to turn around, but I was determined and focused on putting one step in front of the other as I followed Mark. We entered the building and decided to take the stairs instead of the elevator. I counted the apartments until Mark stopped outside the door marked "10."

You can do this, I told myself as I felt my mounting fear. There was so much on the line.

Mark looked back at me for a moment as if he was giving

me one last out, but I gave him a nod. I couldn't go on like this anymore. Good or bad, I had to know.

He knocked and stepped back. A few moments later I heard some activity inside and the door opened. And there he stood. Tall and handsome. I swear I felt my heart miss a beat. He still had that effect on me.

No hello, no smile. I swallowed.

He looked good dressed in jeans and a shirt, one that clung to his lean build—and despite my array of emotions I felt that familiar attraction to him.

"What are you doing here?" he asked Mark tersely before his eyes went to me. I frowned at his distant tone.

"We need to talk," I said, stepping forward.

When Matthew's gaze went back to Mark, he shrugged. Matthew studied me for a moment before he stepped aside and allowed me inside.

"I'll wait outside," Mark said.

The apartment was neat and only sparsely furnished. He closed the door and I wandered into the spacious living room. I didn't even think about sitting down on the inviting leather sofa.

The atmosphere was uncomfortable, and Matthew looked at me expectantly.

"What did you want to talk about?" he asked. His tone was unfriendly and stiff.

Had I been wrong to confront him? Should I have just accepted whatever we had shared was over? But here I was. There was no changing my mind now. Here it was. The moment everything was hanging on.

I gave him my attention as he stood on the opposite side of the room. He shoved his hands in his pockets. Was it so bad he had to stand that far away from me? I wet my lips as I struggled to put what I was feeling into words.

"Why are you avoiding me?" I asked, trying to suppress

the feeling of being abandoned by him.

I searched his eyes, looking for anything to see what he was thinking, but his features were void of any emotion. I shifted slightly when I didn't get a reply. The only reaction was his jaw tensing slightly.

"I need to understand what happened between us." Feeling more vulnerable, I linked my hands in front of me.

"You were there," he said tersely.

This wasn't going as well as I had hoped. I had the urge to leave before I made a bigger fool of myself.

"Don't make this harder than it needs to be," I said, frowning at him.

He pressed his lips together while his eyes were fixed on me. "You've never made it easy for me."

"I'm sorry," I said.

"Do you know what you're sorry for?"

I nodded. "I hurt you when I left you at the hospital."

"Yes, you did." The heaviness in his voice made me feel worse.

"I did it to protect you. When you got shot...the reality of my situation hit home. You could have died. I couldn't risk that happening again." For a moment I hesitated, fearful of how he had the power to hurt me, but I was willing to put everything on the line. "Leaving you was one of the hardest things I've ever had to do."

His eyes held mine. "You shut me out of your life. It was my job to protect you," he said. "What do you want? Do you want me to tell you I forgive you? Fine. I forgive you."

The anger that flared in his eyes made his words empty, but that wasn't what I had come for.

I shook my head. "I'm not here for forgiveness."

I wanted him—but I didn't know how to tell him that. I wasn't good at all this emotional stuff.

"I can't read your mind," he said when I remained quiet.

"You. I'm here for you," I finally said, having the courage to say it out loud. "I've tried going back to the girl I had been before I'd met you, but I can't. No matter what I try, I feel empty and lost."

I swallowed while he continued to watch me. "You changed me. With you I wanted more and now I can't go back. I need you." It was on the tip of my tongue to tell him I loved him—but I stopped myself.

He rubbed the back of his neck and I waited. The sinking feeling in my stomach grew.

"I want you." I shrugged, trying to lessen the rawness I was feeling. I had opened up completely and I had no idea where he stood. "I want what we had."

He shook his head slightly and I swear I felt my heart shatter. The pain was so intense it felt like a physical pain. My lungs constricted with shock.

"I don't want to go back to the way things were."

And there it was, his rejection. The pain was indescribable. I took a step back, feeling the need to run but he crossed the room and his hand caught my wrist.

"Where are you going?"

"You've made yourself clear," I answered tearfully as I tried to pull my wrist from his grasp. He refused to let go.

"We're not done."

He released me and I rubbed my wrist gently. His touch had left a tingle of awareness.

"You have no idea how devastating it was waking up and finding that you weren't there. Tracy told me you had left. I couldn't understand how someone who could love me would do that."

"I did it to keep you safe," I reinforced. Surely he had realized that?

"It doesn't make it hurt any less." He shrugged. "What you did was selfish."

Confused, I frowned. "Selfish? How is that selfish?"

He glared at me. "You cut me out of your life. You were only thinking of your own guilt and not how it would affect me. Yes, I was injured, but I knew I would be able to recover quickly because I was fit."

That hadn't occurred to me. Hearing his words gave me an insight into his struggle and made me feel guilty for making the difficult decision to do whatever I could to keep him safe. And even knowing that, faced with the same decision I knew I would do it again.

"It wasn't like that at all," I mumbled. "I just wanted to keep you safe."

"Like I wanted to keep you safe." And he had made his point.

For the first time I saw a softening in his gaze. That made me feel hopeful I was reaching the part of him that could still love me.

"Why didn't you come back after I was admitted to the hospital?" I asked.

He studied me for a moment.

"Do you know why I became a bodyguard?"

I shook my head. He'd never talked about it before.

"I've always felt naturally protective of people; maybe it was because I have two younger sisters. For every person I have protected, I have formed some sort of bond with them. Like with my friend Taylor. But you weren't like any of them."

He let out an emotional breath and I felt hope. It was better than indifference.

"The moment I first met you, I knew you were going to turn my world upside down." He'd never spoken so honestly about his feelings like this before. It was like I was getting a glimpse behind the curtain to see the true man behind it. "But even then I never could have foreseen how fast and hard

I would fall for you."

Our attraction and romance had been a whirlwind, taking us both by surprise.

"Protecting my clients is what I'm paid to do. But with you I was personally invested." He walked up to me and I stood there, transfixed, unsure of what was happening. He stood so close but he didn't touch me. "There was no doubt in my mind when I took the bullet for you. It didn't just come from a trained instinct. It was because I loved you. I put your safety above my own."

I felt the lump in my throat. He'd used the past tense.

"I was angry when you told your father you didn't want me as your bodyguard anymore. You were taking away my ability to keep you safe. I couldn't trust anyone else to protect you like I knew I could. It was why I went to see your father to ensure I still had full control over your protection detail. Every time I saw you I was reminded you had tried to keep me out of your life. It hurt."

"I'm sorry," I whispered.

"I wanted you to feel the same pain I was." It explained his distance and actions. Even the last time we'd been in the pool house. "But it didn't change how much I loved you."

And there it was again. Past tense.

"That's why you put yourself in danger and went to see Nick," I said.

He nodded. "The more I looked at everything, I began to realize that things didn't add up and the more convinced I was that Nick wasn't behind the threats. It was a hunch and I took a gamble. It was the only way I knew to ensure your safety."

"That was a very dangerous risk."

"Not as dangerous as what you did. You went in blind, and you're lucky we found you in time."

"There was no way I was going to do nothing when I

thought you were in danger." I wanted to reach out to him and close the distance between us. I was laying my heart out in front of him, still unsure of how he was going to respond. "You still haven't told me why you haven't been to see me since the hospital."

"Do you know how hard it is to see you injured when it was my responsibility to keep you from harm?" He raked a hand through his hair, his eyes briefly breaking from mine before I saw a glitter of emotion as they met mine again. "They beat you. I can't think about what would have happened if we hadn't arrived in time. And the worst thing was I didn't even know you were missing! I came so close to losing you it scared me...really scared me."

"But I'm fine. My bruises are nearly gone."

He reached out and gently touched my side. The slight touch of his hand, even through the thin fabric of my shirt, made me hold my breath.

"And I was angry with you and with your foolish actions." He dropped his hand from me and I took a breath.

"So where does that leave us now?" I asked. I still had no way of knowing what the outcome of this would be. What was done was done and there was no changing any of it. There was still a good chance he would walk away.

"My head tells me to get as far away from you as I can physically get."

I looked up at him, hoping this wasn't our end—but I felt winded by his words. Hurt.

"But my heart wants me to hold on to you and never let go."

My heart inflated and I looked up at him with some hope.

"Do you know what I want?" I asked. He'd been honest and now it was time for me to be the same.

He remained silent.

"I want you to hold me and never let me go."

His eyes held mine like he was trying to make a difficult choice.

"I need more than I think you can give me."

I frowned. I would give him everything I had. "What do you want from me?" I said. With him, everything felt so right.

"You. Forever."

That was what I wanted. My eyes teared up and I nodded. "I can give you that."

"With a ring and making it official?" He raised a questioning eyebrow.

When I realized what he was asking, a tear slid down my face as I nodded. "Yes." His finger caught it as it raced down my cheek.

His hand slid to the back of my neck and I tilted my head up to his when he kissed me. My hands slid against his shirt, bunching it up when his mouth coaxed mine open and his tongue caressed mine. I felt alive again. It wasn't just a physical reaction but a deeper one of love and affection that I held for this man.

When he broke the kiss he leaned his forehead against mine and took my hands into his.

"I love you, Sarah Reynolds."

"And I love you, Matthew Weiss."

His lips touched mine again. The feeling of secure love filled me.

"I have a request," I said, pulling away from him, nervous as to how he would respond, but it was something that was eating away at me.

"Anything," he assured me as he looked deep into my eyes.

"I know you love being a bodyguard, but I need you to be safe."

He nodded, understanding. "That's something I have already considered. The company is expanding and someone will need to take on a more managerial role. You were going to be my last assignment."

I was relieved to hear that.

My hands fell to rest against his chest as his arms wrapped around me. I leaned against him, breathing him in. It felt like I was finally home, where I belonged: with him.

His lips brushed against my forehead.

"It's been hell without you," I murmured, hugging him close.

"Same here." His hold tightened slightly. I looked up at him.

"If I hadn't come looking for you, we wouldn't have sorted everything out."

He shook his head. "There was no way I was ever going to let you go. If you hadn't come today I would have showed up at your house eventually, determined to show you we belonged together."

"Really?" I searched his eyes.

He nodded. His gaze dropped to my lips and I lifted myself up on my tiptoes to kiss him. My arms connected around his neck, bringing him closer. I wanted and needed more.

His mouth teased mine and my tongue slid tentatively against his. His hands tightened on my hips. My hand slid through his hair as he kissed me harder. My need for him pulsed through me and I wanted him so badly.

A need outweighing any reason took hold. There wasn't time to undress. In a frenzy of kisses, he backed me up against the wall. He bunched my skirt and ripped my panties off in frenzied passion.

I leaned back as he unzipped his jeans and pulled his boxers down.

In one swift motion he filled me and I gasped. I stopped myself from making any further noise, far too aware of Mark still waiting outside for me.

Slowly, he began to move, faster and faster. I clung to him. His mouth covered mine as I started to tremble. I closed my eyes tightly as my climax pulsed through me. His followed soon after.

Afterward my legs felt like jelly. He kissed my forehead before he got dressed and helped me back into my clothes. My torn panties I pocketed. I smoothed my skirt down.

"That wasn't enough," I said, walking up to him and pulling him closer for a kiss.

He smiled against my lips. "We have later."

Forever, I thought to myself.

Never had I truly believed in love—but now I did.

Chapter Thirty

Three months later

"Sarah!" Matthew called out from downstairs.

I smiled as I waited upstairs on our bed. That familiar flutter of awareness tingled through me as I waited for him to enter our bedroom.

The underwear I wore barely covered me and I knew I looked good in it. I lay on my side on top of the bed with my elbow bent and my head resting in my hand. I heard footsteps. I could imagine him dropping his jacket over the chair downstairs. Then he would be loosening his tie...

"Sarah!" he called out again, and this time there was a touch of worry in his voice.

"Upstairs!" I yelled, excited to see his reaction. I smiled smugly to myself, knowing the sight of me would elicit a reaction of want from him.

For three bliss-filled months we'd led a normal life. No threats to my life. Most of my time had been filled with assignments and it had been a boring office life for Matthew.

The sound of footsteps came closer to the bedroom and I smiled seductively in the direction of the door. Moments later, he filled the doorway.

His eyes darkened immediately when he took in my scantily clad body.

"If I knew I was coming home to this I would have come home earlier," he said, walking to me. I got that warm feeling in my stomach whenever he said the word "home." To me home wasn't a place made up of bricks or furniture—he was my home.

He reached for me and I allowed him to pull me up into his arms. His eyes swept over me, appreciating every inch that was displayed for his eyes only.

"You like?" I asked, watching his reaction.

"Yes," he murmured with his eyes fixed on me. He tugged me to him and I held the collar of his shirt as I pulled him closer and into a kiss.

His hands skimmed down my sides to rest on my hips. Our lips fused together and he explored the inside of my mouth with the gentle caress of his tongue against mine. I groaned and his arms tightened around me.

"The best part of lingerie," he began to say when he broke our kiss, "is taking it off."

My smile widened. I liked exactly where his mind was going.

"What's the time?" he then asked suddenly, pulling away.

I frowned. "I don't know. What does it matter?"

"We have dinner plans," he said, taking my hands into his.

"It's just dinner," I said, feeling a little annoyed when he took a step back. I put my hands on my hips.

"We can't cancel," he said.

I frowned at him. "I must be doing something wrong if you'd rather go to dinner than remove this sexy underwear I'm wearing."

He smirked at me and I felt my stomach flutter. "Trust me—if this wasn't important, you would be naked already."

"Fine," I said, feeling disappointed I would have to wait to have my wicked way with him.

I walked over to my closet. I pulled my little black dress out. I shimmied into it and Matthew came up behind me and zipped me up.

"I'll spend the rest of the evening thinking about what you have underneath your dress," he said, nuzzling my neck. I leaned back against him.

"Have I told you today how much I love you?" I said, feeling emotional.

His eyes met mine in the reflection of the mirror. "Yes, but tell me again."

"I love you."

He kissed my cheek as he turned me around to look up at him. "I love you," he said.

Instead of kissing me on the mouth, he brushed his lips against my forehead.

"We need to leave now," he said and I stepped away from him to fish a pair of high heels out of my closet. He was lucky I had put some makeup on already.

"Let's go."

He held his hand for mine. It was second nature to put my hand into his, and his fingers laced through mine.

On our way to the restaurant, we talked about his day. Since his meeting with Nick he had started to do some security for him. It was apparently all legit and above the table.

Over the past few months I had learned enough about Nick to change my opinion on him. If he hadn't helped

Matthew, they wouldn't have found me. I owed him my life.

I had learned later that Nick had been the one to take Courtney to the hospital when he had discovered she had been taken without his knowledge. He had punished the people responsible dearly for it. The three people who had been involved with Frank and Leo had also been jailed. He had also ensured she'd been watched to ensure her safety. It made me see a different side to the man I had first feared.

He and Matthew had even developed a friendship.

Courtney still didn't remember the kidnapping. The doctor said there was a chance she might never remember. Nature would take its course.

I gave Matthew a sideways glance when I saw him take the road to the college.

"I thought we were going to dinner?" I said.

"I just need to check on something," he said, sounding distracted.

A few minutes later he pulled up in front of the campus. It was the same place where he had been shot. He got out of the car and I slid from the passenger side just as he came around to help me out.

"What are we doing here?" I asked, looking around. There was no one else around.

I turned to face Matthew. Dressed in his suit, he looked so sexy—and the way he was looking at me made me feel all warm and fuzzy inside.

"You remember what happened here?"

I nodded. How could I forget? It was one of the most traumatic moments of my life.

"This was where you got shot."

"Yes, and it was here that I realized how much I truly loved you," he said. His words were pulling at my emotional side.

"Really?" He had never told me that before.

"When I took the bullet for you, there was no doubt in my mind and no hesitation." He took my hand into his. "That's why I wanted to bring you here."

I still wasn't sure where he was headed with all of this.

"Remember I once told you I needed more than I thought you could give me?"

It took only moments to remember that. I nodded.

"I think your exact words were, 'You forever.' And something about a ring and making it official," I said with a widening smile. "And my answer was yes."

Had he thought I had forgotten? That wasn't the type of moment to forget. He got down on one knee and produced a box. I knew what was coming.

"Here's the ring," he said, opening up the velvet box. The ring sparkled. It wasn't your typical solitary diamond— instead it was a sapphire stone, surrounded by many small diamonds. Beautiful.

"I want to slide this ring on your finger and know that you'll be my wife, and that you will share the rest of my life with me, making me the happiest man alive," he said. I felt overwhelming emotion that thickened my throat. I clasped my hands together as I felt the sting of tears and my eyes began to water.

"Yes," I managed to whisper. "My answer is still yes."

He stood up and slid the ring on my finger. "And now we're official." I clasped his cheeks and brought his mouth to mine.

I was breathless when he pulled away and looked down at me possessively.

"Forever?" he murmured.

I nodded. "Forever."

About the Author

Regan is a South African who is married to an IT specialist. She is also mom to a daughter and son. She discovered the joy of writing at the tender age of twelve. Her first two novels were teen fiction romance. She then got sidetracked into the world of computer programming and travelled extensively visiting twenty-seven countries.

A few years ago after her son's birth she stayed home and took another trip into the world of writing. After writing nine stories on a free writing website, winning an award and becoming a featured writer the next step was to publish her stories.

If she isn't writing her next novel you will find her reading soppy romance novels, shopping like an adrenaline junkie or watching too much television.

Connect with Regan Ure at www.reganure.com

73631324R00169

Made in the USA
Lexington, KY
18 December 2017